❧ MERE MORTALS ❧

MERE MORTALS

a novel

ERASTES

Lethe Press
Maple Shade, New Jersey

Published in 2011 by Lethe Press, Inc.
118 Heritage Avenue • Maple Shade, NJ 08052-3018
www.lethepressbooks.com • lethepress@aol.com
ISBN: 1-59021-043-3
ISBN-13: 978-1-59021-043-7

This is a work of fiction. Names, characters, places, and incidents
are products of the author's imagination or are used fictitiously.

Set in Caslon and Bodoni.
Cover and interior design: Alex Jeffers.
Cover art: Ben Baldwin.

LIBRARY OF CONGRESS CATALOGING-IN-PUBLICATION DATA

Erastes.
  Mere mortals : a novel / Erastes.
     p. cm.
  ISBN-13: 978-1-59021-043-7 (pbk. : alk. paper)
  ISBN-10: 1-59021-043-3 (pbk. : alk. paper)
  1. Gay men--England--Fiction. 2. Country homes--England--
Fiction. I. Title.
  PR6105.R37M47 2011
  823'.92--dc22

                           2011006968

Dedication:
To Chris Smith

Acknowledgements

To Tracey for unfailing support, to L,S & L for comfort when the words simply wouldn't come and to my Dad without whose assistance I would not be able to do the thing I love.

Thanks to Lethe Press, particularly Steve Berman, for believing in me and my writing.

Chapter One

Stifling a yawn, I attempted to stretch my legs a little. It was cramped in the coach and it had been an hour since Yarmouth. I had to desist in my fidgeting as the elderly man sitting opposite me glowered, his moustache fairly bristling with irritation. *It's not as if I am trying to claim some of his space*, I thought, trying to ease the pain in my calves by raising my heels up and down. The old gentleman had almost exactly the same expression as my headmaster's wife's terrier. I found myself on the verge of laughing as I noticed the comparison and had to bite the inside of my cheek to prevent myself from so doing. *It should be a grammar exercise*, I thought, still trying not to grin. *The dog of the wife of my headmaster has a face like the man sitting opposite to me.*

To bring myself down to earth, I stared out of the window for what seemed like the thousandth time. No doubt the landscape might be called picturesque in summer or spring, when the countryside was full of life and soft white clouds overhung the fields, but November really didn't do it justice. Looking at the bleak, flat grassland, I wondered if *anything* could do Norfolk justice.

From the first moment I'd heard my new home was to be on one of the Norfolk Broads, I'd been inquisitive as to what this corner of the world might look like. I had only read of their history very briefly, a few lines found in an old gazetteer. Other than knowing they were a system of lakes and rivers, I knew nothing more, and had cared little. Now I could understand the lack of detail in the book I'd read. There was nothing here to write about, or so it seemed. After so many years spent at school in the well-manicured quadrangle and playing fields of Barton Hall, this new landscape seemed empty, untidy and bleak. A light mist covered the land as far as the horizon, little more than a thin vapour, but it was enough to drain all colour from the scene passing by the carriage window. I gave a wry smile. *Colour that mainly consists of bleached dead reeds, brown ditches and brown muddy pools.*

Since leaving Yarmouth the coach had travelled slowly north, following the coast road, such as it was. The coachman had warned us passengers that the roads were bad at this time of the year and he wasn't wrong; more than once the three of us – for that's all there was, travelling in the filthy weather – had to alight, braving the vicious biting wind to assist the coach out of one of the larger ruts we encountered. Even inside the coach with the curtains drawn, the wind sliced its way through any small gaps in the woodwork.

I wrapped my greatcoat around me, as much good as it did. *Some welcome. If I'd seen the place in the summer, perhaps I'd not think it so grim.* It was, however, difficult to look at the drear, dun countryside and think of it as ever being green and full of sunlight and life.

"At least it's not raining." The man sitting next to me cheerfully addressed the terrier-faced gentleman, breaking the silence that had held within the coach since the onset of our journey. "With a rain following these Russian winds, you would feel it drive through to your very bones." He held out a hand to the terrier-faced gentleman. "I don't think you recognise me, sir, do you?" It was clear to me at least, if not to the speaker himself, that he was indeed not recognised, for the terrier expression deepened, and if he had indeed been a dog, the speaker would have been in danger of losing his fingers.

"I do not, sir," the bristly man growled.

"Barnabas Hurst, Dr Baynes, sir, at your service." The man paused, obviously waiting for some glimmer of recognition to appear on his companion's face. It did not materialise. "Hurst. From the living at Sea Palling. We met in Norwich last year." Hurst was displaying the patience of a saint. His face a picture of calm while he kept his hand held out for Dr Baynes to shake.

Forced to acknowledge the acquaintance, Doctor Baynes took the hand with some reluctance. I tried not to show an interest in the conversation, but it was difficult to do in the enclosed space.

"Hurst...Hurst," Baynes said, his face wrinkling even more as he concentrated. "Wait a moment – I think I remember. *You!*" Baynes suddenly looked apoplectic. "You were the man who could talk of nothing but railways."

Hurst looked a little abashed, but dropped his head in acknowledgement. "I admit I am a little enthusiastic on the subject."

"Dashed nonsense," Baynes settled himself further back in his seat as if to further distance himself from Hurst. "Railways branching throughout the country. It's errant bilge. What good will locomotives do here, sir? Can they travel over water, sir? Can they? Answer me that, sir!"

I was amused to see Hurst was completely unabashed by the doctor's irascible attitude but continued to speak as normally as if they were discussing the matter, relaxed and fraternal, over port and cigars instead of racketing around in a draughty, freezing coach.

"There are great plans to cross the Thames," he said.

"Bridges," snapped Baynes, in the same tone as he might have said 'the French.' "No good here, eh? More bridges than track. This your boy?" he said, suddenly, fixing his expression on me, making both myself and Hurst start.

"Dear me, no," Hurst exchanged a glance with me. I was amused to see the man had gone quite pink around the ears. "I haven't had the pleasure of... I mean. Nuptial bliss has so far eluded me..." He seemed so badly embarrassed, I took pity on him, sat up and joined the conversation.

"My name's Thorne, I'm travelling to Horsey Mere. Mr Philip Smallwood," I added, still not used to speaking the name aloud. "He's my guardian."

"Bittern's Reach?" Hurst turned in his seat and examined me more closely.

"Yes, sir." There was a moment of silence as both men seemed to be struggling for something to say. I glanced from one to the other, a little embarrassed. "Do you know him?"

"There's not many around here that don't know your guardian," Dr Baynes said. I couldn't help but notice that some of the gruffness had dropped away from his tone, that he too had coloured a little, and that his look of irritation had been replaced by a quizzical, curious expression. He offered me his hand. "I've known Smallwood since…well, for more years than I'd like to admit." He smiled, which was hardly a less frightening aspect than his ferociousness. "My house is not far from the Reach. As the crow flies, at least." That puzzled me a little, and I realised I was frowning as Baynes continued. "You've never been to Norfolk before, I take it?"

"No, sir."

"It's not far to walk from the Reach to my house, but you couldn't walk it. Marsh, rivers, and a broad in the way. It's a fair way by boat, but it's the only way to get there."

"I see," I said, as politely as I could, unable to think of much else to add.

"The boy will have to get himself a map," Hurst said. "I know of your guardian, of course. Never had the pleasure of meeting him."

"And unlikely to, if I know Smallwood," Baynes said.

"Yes…well…" Hurst trailed off, blushing again, and the three of us sank into silence once more, which would have become awkward had the carriage not lurched to a halt. One of the coachmen jumped down and opened the door. "Horsey, gentlemen. You'd best hurry. Tom don't like to be kept waitin' and who'd blame him in this chill."

I let Baynes descend from the coach first, then waited as my trunk was lowered to the ground. Hurst looked out of the window. "It was good to meet you, Mr Thorne," he said. "Perhaps we'll meet again." The coach rumbled off, leaving the two of us by the side of the road, next to a small track. A boy waited with a handcart and with my help, he lifted the trunk onto it, before trundling off, leaving Baynes and myself to follow in his wake, both of us still mired in uncomfortable silence.

❦ Chapter Two ❧

F
ull of questions I couldn't ask, I walked last in the small procession, my hands buried deep in my coat pockets, my collar turned up against the cold. Each side of the lane was edged with rotting reeds and tall, dead grasses, all rimed with frost, for there had been no sun to burn away the ice. After a short, muddy and slippery walk, the cart stopped. I looked up from taking care where I put my feet to see that we had arrived near to a small wooden jetty. Moored to it was the oddest craft I had ever seen, although, I had to admit, I didn't have a huge experience of boats in general. It was a long, low, boat with a black hull and one huge black sail. It looked stark and forbidding against the frost-laced landscape, and I shivered, not just from the cold.

You're being fanciful, I told myself, sternly. *It's a boat – a ship – whatever they call them here.* The boy had loaded the luggage, and he boarded the boat, holding his hand out to assist our removal from land to water. I did what I could to aid the elderly Baynes aboard, then made an undignified scramble across the gap, wishing I were as lithe and as confident as the boy appeared, and as at home on the water. I would have expected a rowboat, if I had expected any craft at all, a small craft like the penny ferry that had crossed the river near my school. I had not been in a sailboat before and felt my stomach lurch as the craft was pushed away from the jetty and into the river.

"Hold tight to the seat, lad," Baynes said, as the wind filled the flapping sail and the craft leaned worryingly to the side. "There's no danger, even in this stiff breeze. Old Tom knows the river better than he knows his own home but he doesn't want to be picking you up and putting you back on your bench because you aren't secure. Wind's in the right direction, at least."

"Are you going to Bittern's Reach too, sir?"

Baynes gave a short grunt. "No. I'm not. And you can tell your guardian… No, forget it. Tell him you saw me, though, if you will. You'll be pleased to see him again, I expect?" The old man looked at me with narrowed eyes, and with a most searching expression.

I felt myself colouring, and for a moment I turned my face away from the inquisitive face of my interrogator and watched the riverbanks drifting by as the boat increased in speed, the sail and ropes making the most alarming noises. "I'm afraid I've never had the honour, sir." I wished that I hadn't had to admit that – now I felt sure that more questions would be forthcoming, sure as night followed day.

"How long have you been Smallwood's ward?"

I'd expected something more personal, something impossible to answer, and the question took me by surprise. I answered him, relieved that I did not have to start my acquaintance with this man with a lie.

"I was told about it a year ago, sir." Not for worlds would I explain the circumstances of *that* discussion with a stranger. Just the memory – and shame – of my interview with the headmaster was enough to freeze the tongue in my mouth.

The headmaster had had his back to me, as if he couldn't bear to look at me, and from what he'd just called me, and the expression on his face as he'd listened to my side of the story; it was clear he was revolted.

"Normally you would be sent home…in…cases like this. Archeson has already been packed off and it will be up to his parents to deal with his…aberration."

I paled. I'd met George Archeson's father, as tall and dark and commanding as Archeson himself was blond and inhibited – they couldn't have been more different. I held my thumbs tightly, hoping against hope that Archeson wasn't suffering. Wondering if we'd ever meet again, and doubting it.

"Truly, sir, you shouldn't blame Arch."

The headmaster rounded on me. "I do not." The inference was clear, and I flinched under the fury of my headmaster's gaze. "As you don't have a home to go to, and your education is paid in full until you leave I have no alternative but to keep you, as much as I regret it." The man returned to his desk, pulling open a drawer and removing a sheet of paper. He handled with much distaste – as if I had written a description of what Archeson and I had been doing when caught, although in truth it was little enough. "I have a letter here from Mr Smallwood, who has asked for, and has been awarded your guardianship. He wishes you to remain here for the remainder of the year."

I felt as confused now as I had that day in the headmaster's study. Smallwood? Who was this man? Why had he decided to become my guardian? Was it he who had paid for my education? If so, why? I had asked the headmaster these questions but the man had nothing more to tell me, or had decided not to tell me anything, either for reasons of his own or from sheer bloody malice.

Baynes seemed to expect more from me, but didn't press for it when I failed to enlighten him, and I was glad to be left alone to study the landscape as it slid by. It was a different world entirely, here on the water; and considerably more quiet than the coach. The riverbank was edged with frosted and dead vegetation, as the road had been, but here huge, dark, overhanging trees crowded the banks as well, making it almost impossible to see what lay beyond. Strange birds, unlike anything I had seen before, swam busily about. Myriad familiar fowl and some most unfamiliar in their strange, brightly coloured plumage. I spotted small brightly coloured duck-like creatures with arched necks, black crests and sharp beaks. Swans flew overhead, and as the boat rounded a bend I saw two eerie, huge birds standing on the bank with their wings outstretched, for all the world like stage villains brandishing their cloaks. Windpumps stood like sentinels on every horizon, just as they had since we had left Yarmouth, but here, their great sails turning silently in the chill breeze, they seemed like unearthly dark giants, and I chided myself again for being too fanciful.

The boat turned, and the sail slid violently from one side to the other, making me duck my head – unnecessarily as it turned out, for I was seated too low to be harmed by the massive beam.

Baynes dug a sharp elbow in my ribs. "There, lad. On your right. There's your first sight of the Reach." I struggled to my feet as the boat slipped quietly towards a wooden jetty in the distance, and gradually a house emerged from the screen of bare willows. In the year since I'd been told about a guardian I'd never met, I had imagined many houses that the man might live in: everything from a smart, four-storey townhouse in Mayfair, to a sprawling moorland farm, isolated in some bleak rolling landscape. I had not expected a huge elegant red-brick mansion with curved ornamentation to the gables. As the boat neared the jetty it became clear that behind the house the river widened considerably into a large lake, or a *broad*, I realised I should call them.

"Do you sail, Mr Thorne?" Baynes asked The boat's captain shouted for us to sit down for the landing and we obeyed, my feet sliding on the wet deck.

"No, sir. That is, nothing much more than rowing. A little punting once or twice."

"Well, you'd best learn," Baynes said. "You can't see it from here, but the Reach is on its own island. Boats are the horse, the carriages and carts here. You'll find that out soon enough." Baynes held out his hand and I shook it, gladly. "Good luck, boy." He settled back down in his seat, leaving me no recourse but to say my farewells and to clamber ashore as gracefully as I could manage to watch the strange black boat slide away into the broad. No one waved to me from the boat, so I turned my attention to the present. My luggage was already on the jetty, such as it was, and I was about to drag it along with me when a shout sounded from the direction of the house.

"I say, leave that there, I'll have Witheridge send someone for it later." I turned to see a young man of a similar age to myself walking along the short path from the archway of the house. "Thorne?" The newcomer had a wide, friendly smile and as he neared the jetty he held out a hand, bare in spite of the cold, to be shaken. I did so, feeling some pleasure in at last seeing someone who seemed to be happy to see me. "Come in, you must be frozen." The young man took my arm as naturally as if we'd been friends forever and I, after recovering from the surprise of the warm welcome, felt absurdly pleased, if baffled. "We'd been looking out for you for the last hour," my new friend continued as he led me beneath the huge entranceway. "We had a wager as to when you'd arrive. I'm disgusted to say that you have lost me a bet."

"I am sorry about that."

"Not your fault, old chap. I underestimated the tenacity of the Yarmouth coach. Thought there'd be no way they'd risk it on a filthy day like today. For some reason I had it in my head you'd be held up a day at least." We had passed beneath the archway into a spacious courtyard. I could see the house was built not unlike my school, as the house boxed in the central grassed courtyard. The walls that edged each side were crenellated and odd structures that resembled small castles stood at two opposite corners of the quadrangle.

"It is a monstrosity, isn't it?" my companion said, leading the way to a nearby door. "The original house is buried somewhere in the western corner there, and they say that it is probably fifteenth century, that's the part with the twisted chimneys. Then some maniac with a castle obsession decided to improve matters in the seventeenth. There are books about it, should that sort of thing appeal to you, but as you've just come down, you'll probably need a rest from books and all that." He pushed open the heavy, ornamented door. "Oh, by the way, how remiss of me. I'm Middleton, Jude Dominic Middleton to be completely and *utterly* precise."

Opening my mouth to reply, for the young man had surprised me again, I was interrupted before I could speak by the clatter of footsteps running down the dark staircase at the far end of the hall. "Jude? What the blazes are you doing, hogging him all this time? Telling him all my bad points, damn you, I'm sure." The new arrival landed at the base of the stairs, pink cheeked and a little out of breath.

"Not at all, we chatted and sauntered, that's all."

"In this weather?"

"Thorne, allow me to introduce you to my impatient fellow in-mate, with whom I've been incarcerated in a lonely tower with no other company since my arrival more than a week ago. This ruddy-faced fellow is Myles Graham, Myles, Thorne. Crispin, isn't it?"

Graham's brown hair was flopped over his forehead with his ex-ertion and he pushed it back, saying, "So, that's all three of us, then. I vote we adjourn for tea now. We can show Thorne around later." As if upon Graham's invocation, a green-covered door opened and a grey-haired man, very obviously a butler, appeared, followed by another servant wearing a smart green and black striped waist-coat.

"Ah, Witheridge," Middleton said. "He's here at last."

"I am sorry to not have been at the jetty to meet you, Mr Crispin. I'll see to your luggage straight away." He gave a brief nod to the waistcoated servant who walked off. "Tea will be served in the Tudor family room as usual, so perhaps you will show Mr Crispin the way?"

"Thank you," I said, at a loss. I was confused and disorientated, tired but, I had to admit, extremely hungry. I longed for a damned good wash and some peace and quiet to think things over; that, and some answers to questions that were burning within me. However, I realised with an inward sigh as I was led away, arm in arm again with Middleton, and with Graham following in our wake, it seemed that this was an impossibility for the foreseeable future, so I allowed himself to be taken through the corridors of the house and seated in some resplendent splendour on a marvel-lous carved chair in an enormous sitting room.

"It's all right," Graham said, throwing himself leisurely onto a blood-red sofa opposite, "you can gawk at the house if you like."

"I…It's just that…"

"No, Myles is right. We might give the impression of pampered youths, attuned and regardless of the opulence of our surroundings, but nothing could be further than the truth. We neither of us had seen anything like Bittern's Reach before we got here. Even my school couldn't match it."

"Nor mine," Graham added.

"It's not dissimilar to mine, from the outside at least," I admitted, "but it was much plainer than this on the inside." The furniture, portraiture, suits of armour, and decoration were more lush than anything in my experience. Even Archeson's people's house, an imposing middle-class new-build in Surrey, came nowhere near the grandeur of Bittern's Reach.

I longed to ask the two young men how they came to be here, but at that moment the butler entered, followed by a maid pushing a trolley filled with sandwiches, cakes and pastries. After that nothing much was said for some time, and I was left to eat and to examine my new acquaintances without being bothered further.

Jude Middleton was a little more slight than Myles Graham, now I saw them still and sitting together on the sofa, and Graham's hair was a shade lighter brown than was Middleton's, but their height was similar, and both, like myself, had brown eyes.

Finally, Middleton stopped eating, wiped his mouth with an enormous napkin, and moved to a huge wingback settle where he stretched out, patting his belly appreciatively. "Well, that will keep me going until dinner," he said. "Much more of this and I'll need larger trousers."

Graham, who had done as much justice to the repast as either of us, raised an eyebrow, but said nothing, giving me a moment to finally ask a question. "How long have you been here, Graham?"

"Ten days," he said, emulating Middleton and stretching out, kicking his buckled shoes off. "A couple before Jude arrived."

"Are you both relatives of Mr Smallwood?"

Both boys looked at me, and Middleton sat up. "Oh, there's plenty of time to go into all that, don't you agree? As for this school name nonsense, Myles and I agreed that it would be easier to do away with the formality. We aren't at school, and…well, as I said, time enough to go into details. How about you call us Jude and Myles and we call you Crispin?"

"I suppose –"

"Then that's settled." Jude stood up. "Come on, we'll show you to your room, we are all together in the Gatehouse. It's wonderfully romantic, like princes in a fortress. It's where we saw you arriving; it's got tremendous views over the river and the Mere." With that he grabbed my hand and pulled me up from my seat and out of the library, leaving me little more enlightened than I had been when I'd set out from school.

Chapter Three

The house was easy to navigate, I was soon to discover. The boys led me what they called 'the long way around', up the stairs and left, away from the Gatehouse and in a large square along the stretching corridors that lay between the exterior walls of the courtyard. It was not the puzzling jigsaw puzzle that my school had been – where, as a gauche, nervous youngster I had been lost more than once and had encountered unfriendliness in areas which suddenly became dead ends, or in remote classrooms, far from help.

As we thundered through the seemingly deserted house – and I would have sworn it was, had it not been for the fact that the house was lit where needed, warmed where required and that I had already seen a butler, a maid and a footman – the boys called out the names of the rooms as we passed. "This entire row is kept for guests, Witheridge says. He let us poke around the first week, but they are mainly locked now. Nothing to see, I'm afraid." I felt an unwarranted pang of jealousy; I had to admit to myself that I would have liked to have been here when these two were exploring for the first time. They would have discovered everything worth finding out now, I was sure of it.

"The West Tower," Jude said as we came to the second corner of the house. "Comprising the King's Suite and the Queen's Favour."

"Favour?"

"It's above the King's Suite. There is only one entrance; directly from the King's Suite itself. One assumes," Jude continued, "that the favour was bestowed by the Queen when she felt it suitable."

"Or the King took it," Myles quipped with a leer.

"Did royalty ever stay here?" I asked.

Myles shrugged. "Who knows? Most of these big houses claim to have been visited by Henry the this or Charles the that. Robin Hood, Arthur… It's all just as unlikely."

"You have no romance in your soul, Myles," Jude reproached him. "No imagination."

Myles walked on without response. Jude was still staring up at the tower stair, curving up for two more storeys that could be seen, at least. "It would be nice to think so though, wouldn't it? Come on," he said, turning to me. "Let's get you to *our* tower. You look fagged out."

There was no denying that; the journey, the food and the whirl-wind tour had made me feel more weary than I'd felt in weeks, almost stretched as it were, and my legs hardly seemed as if they would carry me around the next corner. I smiled gratefully at Jude and followed him along the gallery, our shoes clattering on the deeply polished floorboards.

It seemed a long way back to the gatehouse stair; I was too tired now to look to either side, to take in the paintings and statuary. It would wait.

"Here we are," Jude said. Myles was nowhere to be seen. We had stopped at the front of the house. I could see, through the windows with their tiny diamond faceted panes, that we were to the left side of the gatehouse. I felt a little turned around, for I had lost my bearings. It disoriented me, for I thought I had been sure of our position. Jude pulled open a small, arched door and vanished inside. I followed, finding within a cramped and circular stone stair. I began to wonder, as the stairs wound, like a cool ser-pent around the inside of the gatehouse, if my legs would manage to make the top. But finally, my head emerged into a light and airy space, with whitewashed walls and two doors on either side.

"Witheridge said that this was the armoury at some point," Jude said. "Nothing left here now. It's all on show on the walls around the house."

I pulled myself fully from the stairwell and found that my head barely cleared the ceiling. "Seems that men were a good deal shorter in the fifteenth century."

Jude led me through one of the doors on the right; each door was set deep into the thick walls, and shaped like a shield. "You can have either of the courtyard facing rooms. Witheridge has put your belongings in here, but if you'd prefer the one across the landing, just say and I'll help you move." He looked a little abashed. "The view is better from lake-side, admittedly…but to be honest, we didn't even know of your existence until yesterday. We weren't to know. I would do the decent thing and offer my room up…"

"I wouldn't hear of it," I said. "Really. To be honest, I couldn't care in the slightest where I am put. It's good to just…stop." I sat heavily on the bed. It was soft, and the coverlet was of a soft gold satin. Suddenly, all of the questions I'd wanted to ask seemed like a mountain, stretching up impossibly into clouds of exhaustion. I'd waited a year, not knowing where my future was heading, what harm would a few more hours take? I could wait until dinner.

"Well, I'm next to you," Jude said, pointing to a connecting door, "and Myles is across from me." He moved to the door, and I noticed how fluid his movement was; he seemed to swim through the air, and was only anchored when he grasped the doorknob, or he'd float up to the ceiling. *Now I'm being fanciful again…* I thought, *it's just that I'm tired.* I untied my boots and leant back against the headboard. "Thank you…Jude," I murmured. "You will call me for dinner?" But if Jude replied I didn't hear him.

I woke slowly, and stretched luxuriously like a cat, flexing my back and my legs. I was warm and perfectly rested; with my eyes still closed I replayed the day in my mind – the journey, the landscape, the arrival, the greeting, before opening my eyes, wondering, as my stomach growled at me, what the time could be. It was quite dark outside, but candles had been lit in my room and a merry fire burned fiercely behind a sturdy fireguard. I had fallen asleep in my clothes, but some kind soul had covered with me a thick eiderdown quilt. The comforting weight of it added to my sense of peace and lassitude and I lay there lost in my thoughts for more than a quarter of an hour before I heard footsteps on the stone flags of the landing outside.

The door opened just as I was sliding to a sitting position and Jude entered, followed by the footman I had met earlier. Jude carried a bottle and glasses, whilst the footman held a tray. I marvelled briefly at his flexibility, that he had managed to bring such a laden tray up that corkscrew stair, but then the scent of meat and gravy reached me and I stopped caring about how the food was brought, just that it had arrived.

"I trust," Jude said, settling himself in one of the chairs, "that you will forgive that we let you sleep. Myles came to rouse you when the bell rang, but he tells me you were snoring so loudly that he could not make himself heard." The footman placed the tray on the bed in front of me, propped up on cunning little legs which dropped from some mechanism on the underside. I was delighted with the tray and wished that I was alone so I could examine the underside without seeming rude. However, the footman whipped the cover from one of the plates and for a while, I forgot about the tray entirely, and did justice to a very delicious pudding steeped in its own gravy.

Jude topped up my glass when it ran dry – the footman having melted away at some point after I began to eat. "What time is it?" I asked. With the dark evenings it was hard to tell.

"A little after ten," Jude replied. He looked perfectly at ease, his long legs stretched from his chair to the edge of my bed. "Myles is still downstairs, he wishes you well of the apple torte and regrets we left you none of the meringue."

"It is kind of you to keep me company," I said.

"Not at all. I've spent a week with Myles and am madly curious to know more about you. I wonder that you haven't already quizzed me to death. I know I wore Myles ragged by my questions. You, my dear boy, are a positive sphinx. More interested in the food then what your future holds. I think perhaps you are born to be a soldier."

I am ashamed to say that my mouth was full of suet crust and kidney at the moment and I took a little while to reply. Jude, exquisitely polite, waited for me to finish. His eyes were hooded, and he ran one slender finger around the rim of his glass as he stared at the liquid within the crystal as if he were seeking out the mysteries of the world. I watched his hands in short, almost guilty glances, for I hadn't seen their like. I was used to the large, able hands of my school friends, rough, ink stained, ruddy – not like these: so pale as to be almost blue. Had he lived his life wearing gloves like the rare few ladies that I'd seen visit the school? I swallowed the last of my pudding. I had delayed a little so I could observe his hands at their dreamy work, and he had not seemed impatient. "I *am* curious," I said at last. "It's just…well, it's hard to put into words, and I worry that I sound rather…"

"What?"

"Oh, I don't know. Fanciful. Idiotic. You can't understand, I suppose. I don't have parents, you see. I mean, I must have done," I found myself blushing, "but I don't even know who they were." Suddenly the words wanted to come pouring out, as if they were a sickness just poised on my lips waiting for their time to emerge and to heal. "I was the only boy in my school who…and, well –"

He met my eyes then, his expression even and almost serious, the most serious I'd seen him since meeting him at the pier. "As you didn't know who your parents were, you…how can I say… wished them to be something other than the parents of the boys around you? Is that it?"

I looked down, and removed the tray, placing it on the floor, ashamed that I'd said as much as I had. "I told you that it sounded idiotic."

He smiled again, and regained all of his friendliness and charm. "My dear boy, nothing could be further from the truth. I would imagine – and this, you understand, is only from my observation of Myles, your dear self, and my own experience – but every orphan seems to wish the very same thing."

It took me a second or two to gauge what he meant, but when I did I sat up, attentive, the apple torte forgotten. "You and Myles? Both of you?"

"Absolutely. Not a parent between us to rub together. What's more it appears that none of us knew who they were." His expression was a little challenging, as if he was inviting me to make more of the coincidence than was apparent.

I couldn't help but smile. "I know I should offer the proper condolences," I said, "and indeed I would, should any of us had lost a parent, but as we never knew them, or felt the loss…"

"Well, I shouldn't exactly say that," he said, his fingers once again stroking the edge of his glass. "But you are right, of course. The milk, being spilt, is not mourned."

I hardly knew what to say. I may have imagined what my parents were like, and had done so many times, but I could never truly say that I missed the lack of something I could not imagine. In my mind I imagined that my parents had been many things: sometimes an aristocratic young woman had an unfortunate tryst with a foreign prince, other times they were adventurous explorers who would not be separated from each other, leaving their baby at home with a wetnurse, never thinking that their ship would founder. It saddened me to think that my new friend felt the lack more keenly than I did. While I was still struggling for something to smooth over my apparent faux-pas, he changed the subject. "And you haven't asked about your host either, as yet. Really, your restraint impresses."

Stung, for I hadn't really been given much time to ask anything, I felt myself blushing. I bit my lip. "You must think me rather slow."

He raised his glass to me, "Not at all. I'm rather intrigued by you, Crispin Thorne. But seriously, do you not long to know about our mysterious benefactor? Have you not wondered the slightest thing about him? Or are you, like our dear Myles, simply grateful to have landed in this lap of luxury and don't look further than the next meal?"

"I am, indeed," I said, reaching down and grasping the dish with the torte.

"Perhaps you are a little of both," Jude said with a small laugh, as I bit through the pastry and covered myself with crumbs.

"I know nothing more about him than his name – and now where he lives. Do you know more? Have you learned more of him since being here?"

"Almost nothing at all," he said. "Myles has quizzed the staff, but no-one will say a thing. The only answer Witheridge allows – for I'm sure it is his iron hand that stops the staff from gossiping – is that the master will introduce himself when he arrives."

"You said 'almost nothing.'"

"Sharp sphinx you are. Yes. Almost nothing. We know what he looks like. Do you want to see?"

Chapter Four

For all that he called me uncaring, unquestioning, a sphinx, my curiosity bubbled to the surface once more. The lassitude in my limbs had faded and I sat on the edge of the bed, reaching for my boots. "Very much so," I said. "I don't even have 'almost nothing' to say about my knowledge. I've been in the dark for an entire year. Just because I haven't quizzed you yet, that does not indicate a lack of curiosity, believe me."

"Really. Look, don't worry about your shoes," Jude said, "come as you are." He grasped my wrist and pulled me up, then led the way back out to that exquisite stone stairwell. This time we went all the way to the ground, leaving me a little giddy from the speed at which we descended. I followed him as he turned right, moving towards what I remembered as being the room we had eaten in earlier, although its official name had quite escaped me. Instead of going in there again, though he passed it and opened the very next door. Then he paused. "There's no light. Hold on." He moved away muttering, "I should have thought." I was left in the dim hallway, itself only lit from one wall sconce nearby the door that Jude had opened. I stepped toward the open door and stopped at the threshold. The room beyond was huge; I could feel it stretching away from me, although I was sure that it was just the dark that emphasised the cavernous feel. I could see the moon glinting with fractured light through the mullioned panes, but it was not powerful enough to do more than to give a glimpse of the room, and none of its contents. I backed away from the door. I did not like the chill air, and I did not fancy stumbling around in the darkness.

"Here," Jude said, having arrived behind me without me having heard him. He was laden down with a single silver candlestick and a deeply ornate three-pronged candleabrum. "I found these in the kitchen. Witheridge probably had them in for cleaning. Let's hope I can get them back before he misses them or there'll be hell to pay." He moved past me and once again I was struck again by the grace of his movement; in the flickering candlelight he seemed to slide across the floor and his feet made almost no noise, even on the parquet of the room we entered. As the light diffused out into the darkness, it became clear that the massive room was a library, larger by at least twice than the library at my school, and stretching, from what I could estimate from my very slim acquaintance with the house so far, for at least most of the length of one side of the building.

I ventured in behind Jude, my head tipping back in awe at the shelves which reached to the ceiling, every single one filled with beautiful books. "Surely you are allowed to borrow the odd candlestick?"

"Oh, you'll learn. Things are run to Witheridge's tune here. He's particular – to make a vast understatement – about the house. Nothing should be moved, or changed. Here –" He took my arm and pulled me forward gently. His hand gripped my elbow with a surprising strength. "There." He lifted the candle up and I copied his action. "I think he looks better in candlelight, but Myles doesn't agree. He rarely does, I'm afraid. There. That's Philip Smallwood." As I stood there, looking up, Jude took my candle holder from me, and with his own, moved to the nearest sconces to light the lamps there.

The painting suited the room, for it was enormous; more than life sized. The frame was a plain, ungilded and beautifully carved wood, and I could sense, even in that dim light that anything more ostentatious would jar with its surroundings. I stepped back, and was immediately struck with the portrait; indeed I could not imagine anyone who had seen it would fail to be impressed, for it was wonderfully worked, and I wondered who the artist had been. My hitherto unknown guardian stared out of the picture, not eye-to-eye with his beholder, but staring beyond and behind me, his gaze set firmly on the distance. He was dressed in a distinctive embroidered coat, the like of which I'd never seen, gold and patterned with elaborate swirls in black and green, although, truth to tell, it was a little difficult to be sure of the exact colour without daylight. He held a cane in one hand, and the other rested on the head of a wooden bird, the carving of which was just as elaborate as the frame that held it. My eyes took this all in in seconds, sweeping up involuntarily to the man's face, eager as I was to see the visage of the man I had imagined for so long, who was shrouded in imagination and mystery. I found myself a little disappointed, I admit – for I had thought to find a Byron, a young Werther; some broad, glowering fellow with the tale of his life in his eyes, but nothing could have been further removed from the truth. Philip Smallwood was slender. His colouring was not quite fair, his complexion told of a life in the open, perhaps a keen yachtsman, I guessed – but his hair was tawny-brown, like the golden-brown of a owl's wing. It was difficult to ascertain his height, for there was nothing in the portrait – other than the large carved bird – to give any scale, but from his stance, and his slender frame, the elegant length of his legs, clad in dark blue trousers, I could guess with some certainty that he was tall, taller than I.

His face was rather square; it was the face that gave the air of a man who had no indecision in his life, had always known who he was, where he was from and where he was going. The mouth was set in a firm, patrician line, suiting the strength of the jaw. However, his eyes, which looked forever past the beholder, were filled with a merry light. I wondered what he was thinking, or what he was looking at, or whether it was just a trick of the artist to soften the otherwise rather formal aspect. That he was a determined man, I was left in no doubt, that he was handsome – or at least he had been when this portrait was done – I could not deny.

"Well?" Jude moved to stand beside me and joined me in looking up at the portrait. "There he is in all his glory."

"It's an impressive portrait," I said, rather loath to drag myself away. It was beginning to dawn on me this was my new home, and this man was the nearest thing I'd ever have to a father – this was my new family. It was sobering and exciting all at once. I did not want to discuss the man, so I sidestepped the opinion that I was sure Jude was waiting for. "The bird. It looks like a bigger version of something I saw swimming out on the river."

"It's a bittern," he said. "*The* bittern, I suppose. Witheridge showed it to me when I arrived, said the carving is somewhere in the house. It's a bird native to the area; enormous apparently and with…what did he say, exactly? Oh, yes. *With a cry that can still the blood in your veins.*" He laughed, "Witheridge is quite the clumsy poet underneath that dour exterior, I suspect. I would wager that he has a trunk somewhere, filled with writings of a gothic and ghastly over-sentimental nature." He gave a mock shudder and looked at me with a curious expression. "So, what do you think of Mr Smallwood?"

I still didn't really have an answer for him. It was hard to judge a man by how an artist had portrayed him. It was likely that the flesh and blood version of our guardian had been flattered in this portrait, or that it had been painted so long ago that the real man was grey and not so infused with life. "He seems…determined," is what I finally ended with. I was oddly reluctant to say that I found him handsome, imposing, *virile* – I was glad that the room was dimly lit, for I felt my face colour in the darkness as I thought the forbidden word.

I am sure that Jude must have been a little disappointed with my lack of enthusiasm. "Well, I suppose we'll find out for ourselves eventually," he said, gathering the candlesticks in both hands and leading the way back towards the hall. "Although God alone knows when. And Witheridge of course."

"Where's Myles?" I asked, curious as to the whereabouts of my other 'brother.'

"Probably prowling about. We ate together, that was the last I saw of him. He's a regular explorer, always poking his nose around the corridors and trying the doors that are locked, just on the off chance that one of them will be open."

"I thought you had explored together."

"Oh, well, we did for a while, but frankly it's dreadfully dull. Once you've tried a doorknob once, I find very little point in boring it with one's presence on a daily basis."

What's he like?"

"A direct question? The sphinx comes out of his valley. "I rather like him, although…"

"What?" Our voices seemed to echo in the dim, cavernous hall, and every footstep creaked as we mounted the stairs.

"He's a little too persistent," he said, but he said no more, as we reached the gallery and found Myles sitting on the top stair.

"You make me sound like some incurable snoop," he said a little sourly. My ears burned, and I felt ashamed that we had been discussing him and we had been overheard.

I think Jude must have felt the same because he said nothing else, but led the way up the winding stair. I said goodnight to them as we reached our landing, but neither of them replied.

Despite my weariness, I slept fitfully. I had never slept in a room on my own, not once in my life that I remembered. I was used to the rude health of young men and boys my own age, sleeping in ordered rows, and the noise and disturbance they make. For all that a prefect or housemaster may insist on silence after lights out, there are always noises. Boys will talk, no matter how rough the punishment for being caught, games are played, pranks undertaken and even when everyone has settled down and all is calm, there are…other noises. Noises that one gets used to, for one knows that the others have to be used to one's own noises of a similar ilk. So, without the constant interruptions, I didn't sleep well. When I awoke, disturbed from the light doze that I had finally dropped into, I found a young servant I had not met before drawing back the curtain. I felt that I hadn't slept at all, and lay there yawning and rubbing my eyes as the man moved competently about the room. There was a new fire already burning in the grate and the room was nicely warm.

"Good morning, sir," he said, noticing my movement. "There's a pot of tea there on the side table, and I've put some warm water in the ewer." He was dressed impeccably, in the same snug green and black uniform that the footman had been wearing the day before. I assumed it was the house's livery, although it struck me as rather incongruous for a house so remote, so cut-off, to have its servants in such finery, especially when the master was away. Perhaps the power of Witheridge was as formidable as Jude had hinted. "I've been assigned to your needs, sir," the young man went on.

I struggled up, propping myself up on the pillows, and reached gratefully for the tea, pouring it into the delicate china cup, so thin I feared the heat of the tea would shatter it. "I'm not sure that I need a valet."

"Valet-in-training, perhaps," he replied, "although I hope to be lucky enough to rise so eventually. My name is Albert, sir." He straightened up, wiping his hands on a small cloth. "Do you wish any help with your ablutions? Perhaps a shave?"

I touched my face. There was hardly anything to boast about but I was too untidy to go to breakfast with relative strangers. If I had been still at school I would have left it. "Er…I'm sure I can manage that."

"As you wish, sir," he said, "I'll be back to help you dress."

"No, really –"

"I won't be long, sir, and if you change your mind about the shave, simply pull the cord by the fireplace."

I gave up, his deference beating me down. I'd not been comfortable with a fag at school – although they were hardly what you would call deferential, particularly to a poor charity-case like myself. It looked as if I was going to have to bow to the inevitable and realise that maybe I might not be poor any longer, although still indubitably a charity-case. "Thank you, Albert," I said, sipping at my tea. He nodded, and left me alone.

I found that my clothes had been unpacked and neatly put away in the wardrobe, although when that had occurred I had no idea. My shoes were missing though, so I was stranded until Albert came back. I may have been padding around the house in my darned socks the night before, but I did not relish the thought of repeating the experience for breakfast. I washed hurriedly, wetting my hair and combing it back from my face before shaving what little manliness I had from my chin. I had just pulled the nightgown over my ears when the door opened. I found myself tangled in the sleeves and lunged for the bed, hoping to cover my embarrassment.

"Hold still, sir." Albert's voice calmed me a little although my face was flaming inside the nightshirt at my nakedness. "Let me get at the cuff buttons."

"No, really," I protested, struggling, but it was no good. He was there and close and determined to assist. I could feel his breath on my skin. If a person could die of shame, I would have done so. Luckily, embarrassment kept other urges at bay, urges which often sprang upon me when men came too close, which was something of a mercy.

"I've done it now, sir," he said and blessed relief as the constricting thing slid up and away, which left me worse off: completely naked in front of a stranger. "Sit down for a moment, sir, and catch your breath." I began to realise just what a perfect servant Albert might prove to be. His face showed not the slightest emotion and I recalled the very few other personal servants I'd met in my life – Archeson's family butler for one – he had that same demeanour, as if nothing could shock him, not the master's nakedness, or a tribe of natives bursting into the drawing room. However I sat with some enthusiasm and pulled the sheet over me a little as Albert rummaged in the wardrobe and chest of drawers.

I won't describe what it's like the first time a strange man puts on one's underclothes, suffice it to say that I bore the indignity well-enough, knowing that this was now to be part of my life and the sooner I got used to it the better. The one thing I will say that I wasn't in a talkative mood throughout the dressing process, as I dealt with all the new sensations. *They won't be new tomorrow*, I kept telling myself.

He dressed me swiftly with deft, expert movements and with as much care as if the clothes were something special and precious, rather than just my best clothes, and nothing special at all, some cast-offs from a moderately wealthy family. I imagined he would tut-tut over the shine on the jacket, or sigh over my appalling socks, but he did nothing of the kind; for that impassive control, I was supremely grateful and I felt myself warm to him. I couldn't help but wonder what he thought of me, what he thought of all of us.

Finally he had me placed in front of the long mirror in the corner and was adjusting my Windsor from behind me. I caught his eye in the glass and said, "Albert."

"Yes, sir, look up a moment, yes, that's right. Not too tight?"

"No, it's perfect, thank you. Albert. Have, has…" I realised I had completely forgotten the surnames of the other two. "Have the other gentlemen risen?"

"I couldn't be entirely sure, sir," he said, moving away and picking up my nightshirt.

"Oh, you haven't been in to see to them yet?"

"They have their own attendants, sir." By now he was pulling open the drawers and removing what little clothing I had in there. I flinched at the creased appearance of some of the more intimate garments he was now holding. "Mr Smallwood's specific request."

The extravagance shocked me. To have three valets – or valets-in-training, as Albert called them – for three young men who had been looking after themselves up to now to a great extent, seemed lavish beyond words. Even Archeson, he being my only link to civilised society out of school, had no valet of his own. His clothes were managed by the general staff, I surmised, and never had I seen anyone dress him when I had stayed at the house. If I hadn't been convinced of Smallwood's wealth by the house itself, the fact he had hired – and trained – three young men to look after three others was proof enough.

It was then in a contemplative mood that I descended the stairwell and reached the ground floor deep in thought. My whirlwind tour of the house had hardly impressed itself in my mind, and I stood in the hallway looking around me with some dismay, not knowing what to do, or where to go, cursing myself that I had not asked Albert before I'd left my room. I turned to the left and followed the corridor, for I could smell food and hoped that my nose would lead the way, but I blundered into a game larder, and a store-room and the kitchen itself – causing several busy servants to stare at me before I backed out, blushing. I had wandered almost the entire square of the house before I found Witheridge moving calmly along the passageway carrying a tray with covered dishes.

"If you'd like to follow me, sir," he said, anticipating me perfectly, "The breakfast room is this way."

Chapter Five

My new companions were already seated, but were not yet eating. Witheridge placed the tray on the sideboard, then left us alone, for which I was glad; I was not yet used to servants there for every little whim, and I wondered whether I ever would be. Myles stood as I neared the table and I followed him over to the sideboard where he pulled the covers off the many dishes there, revealing such an amount of food that my mouth began to water immediately. After years of schoolboy breakfasts, nourishing but dull and repetitive, this repast of kidneys, bacon, kedgeree, eggs of more types than I had names for and assorted breads stunned me with its opulence.

"Tuck in," Myles ordered, and I have to say that I did, following his suit and loading my dish up in a similar manner to his. Jude remained with his hot chocolate and toasted bread while we two ate, his thoughts obviously elsewhere. Sitting opposite to Myles I concentrated on him, as I had seen little of him the day before.

"Is there anyone else expected? Do you know?"

He stopped chewing for a moment, and waved his fork at me. "No. Just us three. Witheridge told me of both of your arrivals, on the day I got here. I'm certain he would have made it clear if there was to be another. Why do you ask?"

I hadn't really asked for any more reason than to make conversation, but a reason clicked into my head to save me. "Well, there are four bedrooms in the Gatehouse tower; it seemed likely."

"He has a point," Jude said, "and more of an enquiring mind than we gave him credit for." It was obvious then that they had been discussing me since my arrival. "But no, the fourth room is locked fast."

"Just us lucky three," Myles added. "This lucky breed, set in a silver sea –"

"Please," Jude interrupted, wincing, "if you are going to quote, don't *mangle*."

"So," Myles wiped his mouth with his napkin. "Tell us a little about yourself, although I think I could guess most of it."

"There's nothing much to tell of, or guess of," I said, uncomfortable with the avid attention of them both.

"Oh do let him try," Jude leant back. "He did the same for me, really – it's quite uncanny how much he can guess without being told. Really uncanny."

I looked between them both, a little nervously. I didn't want Myles to guess correctly. "No, I'm happy to tell you."

"I think I can guess, though," Myles said. Jude was leaning close to him, and both of them were staring at me. It was rather disconcerting. He continued before I had a chance to speak. "You're an orphan; you spent your life at school – not a first class establishment – definitely not Eton or Westminster, but somewhere deep in the country and well thought of. Am I right?"

I nodded but was unimpressed by his so-called guessing. I had admitted most of this to them already.

"Your schooling was paid for, but not extravagantly – you didn't have fencing lessons or own a horse – but your clothes, books, everything you needed was provided for, even a little pocket money from time to time."

"You are close to the mark," I admitted. I hadn't ever had any pocket money. I couldn't imagine what it would be like to go into any shop I wanted and buy anything.

Myles leaned forward and made a show of concentration, as if he were actually pulling my thoughts from my head. Nonsense and a pretence, of that there was no doubt, but he made a good show of it. "You were never told who your benefactor was, even though you asked..." He paused and looked deep into my eyes, his mouth quirked a little at one corner. "You had one good friend at school. Someone you cared for a great deal. A boy who took you under his wing, felt a little sorry for you."

"Hey," Jude said, "that's a bit –"

"One very *very* good friend..." Myles continued as if Jude hadn't spoken. "You studied together. Perhaps you even had a study together in your final year? Yes, you did. You visited his family...more than once...and they appeared to like you." His fingers drummed slowly on the tablecloth. "You were very close."

I felt my mouth drying. Guesswork, surely. He couldn't know. Or was this all some kind of trick? Perhaps the headmaster had told Smallwood and Myles had the story from him. No. I couldn't believe that, although I didn't really know what to believe.

"You were inseparable. Games, study, vacs. Others noticed your friendship. Perhaps they were jealous. Perhaps others said you two were...unnaturally close. Were you unnaturally close, Crispin? Or was it just nasty suspicious rumour?"

I could feel the colour draining from my face, and I pushed my chair away from the table. I knew that to react to what was possibly no more than the worst kind of teasing was to give myself away, but I thought this too late, after I'd reacted. How did he know, how *could he* know?

"Myles, stop it," Jude admonished, taking hold of Myles' arm. "It was different –" His face was anxious and drawn, looking from me back to Myles.

"I think he needs to know," Myles continued, mercilessly. "And then the rumours got too much, didn't they? You were questioned, perhaps? Or you were watched."

"I don't know what you are talking about," I muttered. "You filthy –" I stood up then, undecided whether to fly at him, fists at the ready, or to just get out of there.

"Then finally you were called into the Head's office – or perhaps you were caught... What were you doing, Crispin?"

Jude was standing now. "Myles, that's enough." He looked genuinely concerned; he attempted to pull Myles to his feet but still he sat there, his eyes fixed on mine.

"You'll shut up if you know what's good for you," I growled. There was no good running out, I needed to face this down, find out how much he knew, and how. What was going on here?

"What were you doing? Was it just an innocent kiss, languid and slow, shared over study books, or was it worse?" He exchanged a look with Jude, whose face was pinched and pale.

"You bastard, Myles," he muttered.

"Were you in a state of disarray? Hands caught places they shouldn't be? Hidden away in a dark corner, a cupboard, an empty schoolroom…"

"I said shut up!" My temper snapped in fear and I strode around the table and picked Myles up by his collar. "You're no gentleman – You hardly know me…you know nothing…"

"Enough, it seems," he murmured, slack in my grip. "Enough…"

"*Enough!*" A commanding voice cut through the air, a voice of such vigour and authority that we three – schoolboys that we were – obeyed instantly. I dropped Myles and we all stood almost to attention, spinning round to face the source of the voice. "What the devil is going on?" In the open doorway – with Witheridge standing impassively behind him – was the original of the portrait, our guardian Philip Smallwood, his face suffused with anger.

Chapter Six

It was unmistakably he, and I found myself comparing him with the painting, as I was sure my companions were doing at the same time. From the man in front of me, I could only surmise that the portrait had been done amazingly recently, for he resembled it almost completely. He wasn't as tall as I imagined, (but later on I realised that I myself was taller than I realised, being near to six feet than not, for he did not overtop me by as much as I had thought that he would), and he was thinner than the portrait had shown him. But he had that same impressive presence that the portrait had revealed; it had been proved by just one word. The man was used to command, it seemed certain, and he was used to being obeyed.

I found I was breathing heavily, as if I'd been running; I don't know how I managed to let myself get so distressed. Myles was straightening himself up, pulling his tie back into place and running his hands through his hair. Jude was simply staring at Philip as if he'd seen someone he knew.

"Thank you, Witheridge," Smallwood said, with just the smallest of nods to the butler behind him. "That will be all." The door closed and we were alone with our guardian. "Come here," he ordered.

For myself, there was no thought of disobeying. I was here, at this man's mercy – whoever he was, whatever reason he had taken us under his protection – and the best thing, the only thing I knew was to obey. It wasn't that I was frightened of *him*, exactly, but I was frightened at that moment, and I was ashamed of nearly causing a fight on the very first morning of his hospitality. *What if he decides that he'd made a mistake, not only with me, but with Myles and Jude?* Not that I knew them any more intimately than I did Smallwood himself, but to know that my stupid temper could endanger their futures as well as mine made me stare at the floor in dismay.

"This is not what I expecting," Smallwood said. His voice was deep and rich, but no longer held any anger within it. I lifted my gaze from the floor, and he looked straight in my eyes, holding my gaze with a stern, even look but that dark angry aspect had vanished as completely as if it was never there. "You," he said, nodding towards me, then pausing, his eyebrows drawing close together as he looked at me. "You must be…Middleton."

"Thorne, sir," I said, promptly. I glanced sideways to see if Jude, standing beside me, was going to speak up, but he showed no sign of it, staring straight ahead, his face blank. "This is Middleton, and —"

"That makes you Myles Graham," Smallwood said, transferring his gaze to Myles at the end.

"Yes, sir," Myles said quietly.

"Hmm. Follow me, all of you." He turned on his heel, leaving us no recourse but to follow in silence, although we exchanged nervous glances between us. Smallwood walked quickly through the house, stopping before a door on the northwest corner, unlocking it, then leading the way in. It was clearly his study, with a large, imposing desk by a stack of shelving and two antiquated globes flanking the desk itself. He sat down behind his desk and gestured to us to sit in the three chairs arranged in front of him. My heart was beating furiously, and I was sure that Jude, sitting next to me, his left hand gripping the arm of his chair so hard his knuckles were white, was feeling much the same as I.

"I, as you've probably surmised, am Philip Smallwood," he said. "I've lived in this house all of my life, and I hope that from today you will consider it to be your home. I know that none of you have had a home before," he paused a little, as if allowing us to nod, which we all did, "and may not be accustomed to such a house as this." He searched my face as he spoke, and this time I didn't drop my gaze, before his eyes moved on to inspect the other two. "I have been away from the Reach for a great deal in the last five years, but I plan to spend as much time here as I can from now on. Now that you are here."

The question *Why?* echoed through my head but I dared not speak. I had already shown myself in a poor light and did not wish to push myself forward.

"You will continue your studies," he said. "Just because you have left your preparatory schools does not entitle you to be men of leisure. There is very little society in this part of the world and I do not intend, for the immediate future, to move my establishment to London in order for you three to run wild. I must be…" he paused and for a second an odd expression fluttered across his face. It was gone almost as soon as it had arrived, leaving him to move his glance back to me. His face gathered a little darkness somehow, as if he was attempting to work out who and what I really was. When he spoke, I sensed a tightness in his voice, as if he were holding himself in check, although whether that was from disappointment with the violence of our introduction or for some other reason, I couldn't guess. "As well as book-study, you will learn other skills – some of which you may not have encountered before. Fencing, dancing, amongst others. If you yearn for Cambridge or Oxford, we will discuss that – but I think that it should be a year or so before you think of going up.

"There are few rules here. I expect merely that you behave as gentlemen, to myself, the staff – *and* each other. A locked room remains a locked room; I do not wish you in here, or any other of my private apartments, unless expressly invited. Your belongings are being moved from the gatehouse to more suitable accommo-dation. I will meet you next at dinner, where I can assess your table manners and conversation."

It seemed obvious that we had been dismissed; Smallwood leaned back in his chair and watched, with a curious blank expression, as we stood up, stammering our idiotic thanks, and made for the door.

"Thorne," he barked, as I was about to follow Myles out. "Wait here a moment, please." Myles, out of sight in the corridor, whispered, "Good luck, old man," and the door closed. I felt suddenly cut off, as if I'd gained a little family and had lost them within one day. My stomach churned in worry, but I walked back to the desk and stood before it. "Yes, sir."

He didn't ask me to sit, but looked up at me. "Well? What do you have to say to me?"

"I apologise," I said, "I am ashamed that I let my temper –"

He waved me silent. "As to your temper, that's something we can address at another time. I wish to know why you were manhandling young Graham in such a way. To my eyes, it looked that if I hadn't interrupted you, you might have done him harm. I cannot condone this."

I was caught in the eternal dilemma, to tell tales and to do myself no great service in anyone's eyes, or to dissemble. I paused, trying to meet his eyes but finding myself not up the task this time for his expression was so intense. If I told him the truth he'd know, not only that I was some ghastly squealer, but he'd demand to know why I was being teased and the details of it. That was something I was never going to admit to him.

"Speak up, Thorne; don't let my choice be wrong. I thought better of you."

I looked up, my mind made up, although his words had thrown me. He'd chosen me? He had expectations of me? Wild, boyish pride rose up in me at such a simple sentence. I was not going to let him down now, nor would I peach on Myles. "I'd rather not say, sir."

"And I would rather you did." His voice became more autocratic and masterful. "You'll tell me or I'll have you out of this house tonight! Well? What is it to be?"

It would have been so easy. All I had to do was to tell him what Myles had said – or maybe I could get away with just saying that Myles had been casting aspersions on me in another way, insulting my unknown parentage. That would work, and I nearly grasped that option with both hands. But I found I couldn't. If I did, perhaps Myles would be thrown out along with me, and I'd already done enough harm. "No, sir. I won't say. All I will say is that I'm sorry for it, and that I won't do it again."

He stood then, pulling his waistcoat straight and moving around the desk where he sat on the edge, in front of me. For what seemed like an eternity he said nothing. This at least, was something I knew of. Headmasters and masters had this similar tactic – and for a boy who had known nothing but school life, it was almost welcome. Familiar. I had the opportunity to examine him, whilst trying not to, probably making myself cross-eyed in the process.

He was broad across the shoulder, and the severe cut of his jacket suited his frame entirely. His clothes seemed, for all my inexperience, expensive and new. The kind of clothes that I would see on my school friends' fathers. His arms were folded, and he fixed me with the same penetrating gaze, as if waiting for me to say something further, to force me to change my mind and blame Myles entirely for the incident. But for all that, I saw nothing of the bully in him; nothing at all similar to Mr Snyder from Mathematics with his eager stinging ruler, which he carried at all times, or Mr Leach, much unloved tutor of History and Horace, who would shout and rage, belittling any boy that dared to be incorrect, either in his studies or his demeanour.

Smallwood seemed to be offering me a way to save myself; his eyes radiated some manner of curiosity as to what I might do, whilst still being stern enough to keep me silent. As for his face, it was as handsome as his portrait had hinted; the loss of weight he seemed to have suffered since the portrait was done suited him.

Finally, he pushed himself away from the edge of the desk and unfolded his arms, as if he'd decided my fate. I swallowed, as my stomach contracted in fear – not for any threat I felt from him, but from what he might say. I suddenly felt that to leave Bittern's Reach now, and be sent goodness knows where to make my own way in some poor manner, was the very last thing in the world I wanted.

"Very well," he said. "I will assume that the fault was yours, although I will ask young Graham for his version, you can be sure of that. You can go, and send Graham down to me." I gave a swift nod, and made for the door, expecting that at any moment he would call me back. As I pulled the door open I risked a look back, and found him watching me leave, but his face held the smallest of smiles.

The journey back up to the Gatehouse seemed to take forever; never had I noticed that there was so many stairs. I wanted to run, but servants seemed to proliferate like weeds on every landing so I kept my dignity and did not flee as if I was guilty of anything. Once back on the top floor I found all in chaos, and recalled what Smallwood had said: our belongings, such as there were, were being moved. My room, aside from the furniture, was entirely empty, the bed stripped, the wardrobe doors open, showing nothing but empty shelves. I met with Albert as he came out holding my second-best shoes.

"If you will follow me, sir." He stepped to one side to let me get behind him. "The master has allotted you rooms on the north side of the house."

"Wait. One moment," I said, and ducked into Myles' room, but it, like my own, was as sterile as an empty dormitory, with all traces of any personal occupancy erased. I had no choice then, but to follow Albert down the spiral stairs and around the vast quadrangle until we reached the north corridor, stretching between the King's Suite and the front of the house.

"You are in here, sir," Albert said, pushing open one of the doors.

"Which room is Mr Graham's?"

"The one after next," he said, disappearing into my new room.

I dashed down the corridor and found Myles at last, sitting on his bed, looking more worried that I thought he'd be. Another male servant, dressed as impeccably as Albert, moved silently around the room, packing things away. "Myles," I said, "you have to go back to the study –"

His face twisted a little as if he'd been sitting there waiting for that precise instruction. I'd seen the same look on boys waiting to be caned. "Of course I do," he sneered. "I'm sure you told him everything."

"You arse, of course I didn't."

"I suppose you expect me to do the same? Be all noble, too? I'm sure it gives you a smug satisfaction."

"Don't be such a bloody idiot all the time." I lost all patience with him. "Say what you want. It's not as if we were doing any-thing…like you were accusing me of, is it?"

"Nor ever will," he spat, and he left me feeling more annoyed than I had meant to be.

I had nothing else to do but to wander back to my room. I wasn't entirely surprised to find Jude sitting in one of my chairs and he waved expansively as if welcoming me to some gentleman's club. He looked entirely unconcerned by our recent interview, which rankled me not a little. I felt he could have been more out-wardly perturbed.

"Mine is almost identical to this, although sadly, no commu-nicating door, dear thing. This means that all my plans for secret midnight assignations have been entirely crimped."

It was a beautiful room, and unexpected for I had considered that the rooms in the Gatehouse would have been ours, and it was rather thrilling to be up in such a romantic hideaway, rather than here in the main body of the house. But I had to admit that the furnishings, the panelling, the rugs and the exquisitely carved fire-place, in which a merry fire warmed every inch of the room, made up for the change of location. and probable lack of privacy.

"Smallwood asked to see Myles," I said, sitting on the bed. The concern of our misdemeanour damped my enthusiasm more than a little. Perhaps I wouldn't have time to become accustomed to this elegant room.

"I'm not surprised," he said. "I dare say I'll be called down – summonsed to the King's study next. He's frightfully regal, don't you think? That aspect, that aristocratic brow. My dear, I could hardly keep myself from staring. I shall be crushed if I'm not interrogated."

I threw a pillow at him. "I wanted to ask him, about us. About why he chose us. I have so many questions."

"Of course you do, Sphinx," he said. "And you'll never get around to asking him."

"If I'm thrown out, you mean."

"No, because you are too well-behaved. I'll wager that Myles finds everything out before you pluck up the courage to ask Smallwood anything directly." He fairly bounced out of his chair, and flung himself face down onto the bed beside me. "Tell me, what did you really think of him?"

"I can't guess anything, not from that one interview. He seems…well, fair, I suppose. I thought he had reached his own conclusion, but…he gave me a chance to explain. It's more than most of my masters ever did."

"And mine." He rolled over with a grin. "I wonder what Myles is saying to him? Will he blame you? You were magnificent, if you don't mind me saying. I would never have thought you were quite so…physical. Let me tell you, there have been times when I'd wanted to do exactly that to Myles in the last week."

"You did warn me he was persistent."

Jude gave me a look which could only be described as pitying. "Not exactly what I meant, dear thing, but I'll let you find that out for yourself. Ah, here's the culprit himself." Jude propped himself up on the pillows as Myles came through the open door. "Do tell. Did he punish you? Omit no details."

"Jude, you have a nasty mind." Myles took the chair which Jude had vacated. "I've told you that before." He looked down at his feet for a moment before looking at me squarely. "Look, Crispin. You called me an arse, and, well, I'll take my medicine. Smallwood told me what you said."

I felt colour rising to my face, and I went to shut the door, hoping that Albert might stay away for a few minutes. "It's not as though I was likely to tell him what you were saying, is it?"

"No. And for what it's worth, I'm sorry."

Jude clapped delightedly. "Oh, you dear things, it's better than a play. Now I suppose you are going to shake hands and be all serious."

"I think we can leave things as they are," I said. "Did Smallwood say whether he intended to do anything about it?"

"He said that he would think, and let us know at dinner."

"Leaving us to worry ourselves for the rest of the day, that's unsurprising," I said. "But there's something I want to know, before we leave this alone, Myles."

The suspicious look returned to his face. "What?"

"How did you come up with your accusations?" I wasn't going to hint that he'd got them almost entirely right. "What made you say those things?"

Jude touched me gently on the elbow. "I rather think that's my fault," he said, quietly. "You see, I was sent down for those exact crimes. I suppose Myles assumed the worst of you, too."

Chapter Seven

There was a silence I found I couldn't fill. Both boys were looking at me, and after a sharp glance at each of them in turn, I turned away, gripped the overmantle with both hands and leaned in, biting my tongue, hiding my face from them, letting the heat of the fire conceal the fire in my cheeks. It was too much – Jude was unnatural? Inverted? That alone was a secret I didn't want, didn't need, but Myles held Jude's secret in his hands, as now did I. Just because he hadn't denounced me did not mean he wouldn't do the same for Jude. I didn't know Myles, didn't trust him – didn't know either of them well enough to trust them.

The coincidence stung me, and memories, which I'd forced myself to deny, surged back. The first time I'd heard that despicable, dirty, word.

"Inverted," he'd whispered, his hand brushing the side of my flannels. Imperceptible to the outside world, but a raw, warm secret for me as we sat to watch the second eleven make utter fools of themselves. "That's what they call us. What my pater calls…people like us."

I remembered the shock I felt at what he'd said. "Your father?"

Arch had laughed. "Oh, Thorne, don't panic. He doesn't know about us. To be honest, I rather think he suspects about me, I'm sure. He's not my real pater, of course…"

"I didn't know," I murmured. We had to stay watching the cricket, our attention focussed on the sport; it would never do to have anyone

see us looking at each other, not after I'd realised how much I cared for him.

"Mater married him the year I was sent here." His knuckles seemed to sear through the fabric of my cheap trousers. "He's interested in nothing but banking. When I announced that I would rather die for my country than follow his lead I thought I was rid of him for he had trouble breathing for a while afterwards."

"How did he, er, how did you suspect that he –"

"Suspected?"

"Yes – Oh well done, sir!" We applauded dutifully as Brentford hit a six and I returned my hand, casually, or so I thought, but a little further back, so my skin touched his.

"No, the idiot's fallen on the wicket," Arch said as cries of disappointment sounded from all sides. "Lord, Brentford is hopeless, really. I thought for certain he'd get replaced."

"Arch. Your father?"

"Oh, it was last Christmas," he said. "Remember I told you we were all dragged up to Yorkshire and imprisoned there in the snow? There was a cousin… Oh don't look like that," – he hit me rather too hard on the arm – "this was before…anyway."

It didn't stop me feeling sick with jealousy. "A cousin," I said, dully.

"And quite beautiful," he whispered, teasingly. "Lashes like a girl, and those exquisite blue-black shadows under his eyes, you know how attracted I am to the look the pale loitering knight, mildly consumptive. It's why I gravitated to you, after all."

"Arch –" I said, warningly, looking around. There was no one nearer to us than a group of third years who were in an impassioned argument about the play.

"Oh, Thorne, you'll really have to practise shielding your emotions. Everything shows in your face, it will get you into trouble one of these days. This cousin was not at all interested, and believe me I made it fairly clear; the only conclusion I could draw was that I don't think they have people like us in Yorkshire. I met with utter incomprehension. Pater found me in close conversation, that's all. That's all, I swear to you. I may have had his hand in mine, but I was being clever, or *so I thought, and was showing him the grip I use in tennis. We left Yorkshire the day after and I had an unpleasant interview with Pater in which he frankly accused me of inversion and I had to clear my name by spending the rest of the vac escorting some vapid girl to stodgy family gatherings."*

I felt a hand gripping my arm and I was pulled away from the fire. "You idiot," Myles said, "I could smell your trousers scorching." He was right, and now I had been moved to a cooler part of the room I could feel the sting the fire had left on my thighs. Pulling my arm from his grip, I looked over at Jude. He looked more miserable than I'd ever seen him, his legs tucked up around chin, his arms around his knees.

"Well, it appears I'll have to clear the air," Jude said, uncurling from the bed. "I went, as Myles guessed, to the same type of school he mentioned. I'm not going to go into details for Myles' pleasure," he threw a blank look at Myles who was standing on the other side of the fireplace, "but I was found in a certain state of *dishabille*, let us say."

"With another boy," Myles said.

"A person of my acquaintance," Jude said, looking away from both of us. "Hardly a boy."

Myles seemed to choke. "Oh come now, Jude, you aren't saying that it was a master?"

"I said that you'll get no details from me." He stood, moved next to me and touched me on the arm again. I had been staring into space, unable to meet his eyes, but I looked down as he touched me, noticing those beautiful, pale hands – priest's hands, an expression I'd heard a master say once. He drew his fingers back as I looked down, as though he had burned himself, and left me alone with Myles.

"What I want to know," I said to Myles, who was staring at the door, "is how you guessed his secret?"

He looked round at me with a sneer. "They had boys like him at my school. Elegant, always beautifully dressed. Ganymedes; peo-

ple who were going to be nothing but bachelors. We had prefects
who –"

"I would imagine that all schools have them," I said, angry at
Myles again, but for Jude this time, not for myself. "They don't all
look like Jude." *Some are square, and muscled, tall, and broad. Some
of them love to run and run. Their faces shine with sweat that tastes of
their secret sin.*

"I threw a lucky guess," he said, shrugging. "He admitted almost immediately that he'd been sent down – I said I had too, and
we played a game. We had three guesses each. He was laughing,
even after I got it right."

"And you," I said. "Why were you sent down?"

"Same game, Crispin? Three guesses?"

I glared at him. "No games, Myles. And for your information, I wasn't sent down, so you would be wasting your time." The
words were no sooner out of my mouth than I realised I could
have played the game with him and won. I watched him hesitate,
searching for words. He was obviously surprised at my admission,
and I don't think he entirely believed me, but what did it matter,
now, anyway? For one mad moment I bit down on the urge to
giggle, imagining that all three of us had been found 'in a state of
dishabille' with other students but cut the thought off as soon as
I made it. Even trying to imagine the prickly, angry Myles in that
position was impossible.

"I…" He swallowed and took a deep breath. "A small matter of
items I shouldn't have had. A misunderstanding. The boy had lent
them to me, and then denied it."

"Thank you, Myles. I'm sorry about it, all the same. You have
my confidence."

"For what good that is," he snapped. "Are you really that
thick?"

Apparently I was, for I did not know what he meant.

"Do you really think Smallwood doesn't know why we were
sent down? Jude and I? Of course he knows. Obviously it doesn't
seem to matter to him – who'd want two failures as wards? But I

admire him for that. He's obviously some kind of reformer. Wants to give us a chance we'd never have had. I don't think he ever meant to send us away. I think he's still sizing us up. Gauging our reactions."

It was something I hadn't considered, but with a sinking heart, I realised that Myles was right. Of course Smallwood would know. If he knew about Myles – and about Jude – he'd know about Arch. He'd know everything. Of course he would.

"He'll keep us worrying until dinner, of course. What did you think of him?"

Words failed me entirely in that regard, and I wondered how I could have been so stupid. "If you don't mind, Myles, I'd rather be alone for a while."

He patted me awkwardly on the shoulder. "You're all right, Crispin."

After he went, I threw myself on the bed, wondering how I could even look my guardian in the eye again, what he must think of me – and how long I could keep my secret from the others, when they'd been so open with theirs.

Logic – never my most exemplary subject at Barton Hall – told me that there really was no reason for me to continue to keep Archeson's secret. Funny how I still called it that.

"And after that?" I'd asked him. The cricket was over and we were 'studying' Aeschylus for the morning. This consisted of us together on our battered chaise, a castoff from Arch's mother, myself tucked into the fork of his arms and legs and both of us reading Agamemnon *in a half-hearted, half-heated manner. A chair was propped against the door, which gave us the confidence to kiss more often than our pauses for translation strictly allowed.*

"After what?" he murmured, his teeth nipping at my ear. The late evening sun poured through the wide bow windows, making us both drowsy. I remember feeling that I would like to live in that moment forever. Just the heat of the sun on my face and chest, and Arch's body warming me inside and out.

*"After your interview with your father, and the interminable squir-
ing of pudgy girls. Your father, how was he with you?"*

*"He said nothing afterwards, it was the only time he raised the mat-
ter. It wasn't a discussion, Thorne, it was an ultimatum. Either I was a
red-blooded man with a passion for women, or I was nothing to him.
That's why no-one can know."*

*"Well, obviously, you arse," I said, attempting to run my hand up the
inside of his thigh. I could feel his need for something more than kisses
as he clung tighter to me. "I'm not likely to spill, Arch. What did you
think, that I'd run to a prefect? Post your considerable attributes up on
the notice board next to the rota for cricket practice?"*

*"I mean, no-one. Not ever. Look, I know you, well, I know we've
never talked about it, but you have no expectations –"*

*"You always knew that," I said, still thinking it light-hearted. I put
on an affected common tone. "La, sir. Don't tell me you'll cast me off now
you know I'm worthless, with no dowry to me name?"*

*"Arse." Suddenly he was serious, more serious than I'd ever seen him.
He spun me around on the chaise, letting our battered Agamemnon
fall to the floor, and putting my legs either side of him. It seemed as if
he'd been holding something in. "All we have – all I have is this, don't
you see?"*

*"Arch, you have –" Parents I wanted to say, family. Mother. Aunts,
cousins. A beautiful house. A home. But his face stopped me from saying
any of that. He had me, and I understood that. Everything else was
make-believe.*

We never spoke of his family again, nor his expectations, nor
his father.

As if to drive the point home, Ellman Major, a day-boy who
had a loathing of inverts to rival any bile of Arch's pater, brought
a newspaper into Hall the next day. He and his cronies gathered
around it, laughing and sneering and from time to time. They
looked over at Simpson and Galling whom everyone 'knew' were
inseparable companions, with the occasional glance at me and
Arch. We took no notice, but as Ellman left, he dropped the newspaper onto Simpson's table, laughing out loud with his friends.

"He's going to get into a scrape, sooner or later," Arch growled, sotto voce. "I'll be pleased to rearrange his nose."

"You'll have to join a line, then," I said. Nearly everyone else had gone up to the their rooms, following Ellman's lead and I went over to where Simpson and Galling was reading. The article that Ellman had meant them to read was ringed in ink. Simpson pushed it across to me without a word, as if we were in a kind of silent confessional brotherhood. It was another Old Bailey account – for there seemed to be a mania for lurid detail of that sort – of a prosecution for 'unnatural' crimes. A well-respected magistrate had been regularly sodomising a seventeen-year old boy from the Telegraph office but the boy had turned him in, turned Queen's Evidence on him and the magistrate had been sentenced to life imprisonment.

As I lay on the bed at Bittern's Reach, I remembered the fury in Arch's eyes, as he'd read the news report. The desperation. I also remembered the fear. I wondered if I ever looked like that, if I ever would. I'd kept Arch's secret – our secret. I'd not given the Head a word of detail, even though after we were found out, he kept me under questioning for an hour or more. How could I ever explain what we meant to each other, when he was firmly on the side of the *Times*, and saw nothing but the 'unnatural' in what we did? His very intonation as he accused me of doing far worse to Arch than I ever did (although it wasn't as if I didn't dream of it) made it clear to me that he – and the world – thought it vile, filthy, reprehensible. Unforgivable.

I allowed myself to think of Arch, then, of the first time I'd seen him, dazzling in cricket whites with his hair blowing in a summer breeze – and the last time I'd seen him, being bundled into his family's coach, as I watched from our study window. I allowed myself, as I hadn't done for the year since that fateful night, to remember the hot fevered feel of his hands on my skin, and the way his tongue knew just where to tickle the crease where my leg met my arse. I remembered our first kiss, sudden and shocking as a summer storm as we returned the bats to the pavilion, and I closed my eyes, my cock swelling at the memory as I remembered our last kiss, interrupted by someone banging furiously on the door –

The knock on the door had frightened us to death, and my eyes flickered open, coming to my senses on my bed at Bittern's Reach when I realised that someone was knocking on my door too. The coincidence had my heart pounding like a drum. Pushing Arch to the back of my mind again, I slid off the bed and opened the door. It was Smallwood.

"Come in, sir," I said, stepping backwards, swiftly. "It wasn't locked."

He entered, his eyes raking around the room taking in every detail, like a housemaster looking for dirt and disorder. I wished I had thought to smooth the counterpane after leaving the bed, but then I realised, as he pushed aside the heavy lace curtains and examined the windows and the window seat that had I hadn't even seen was there, that he was inspecting the room, but not for any upheaval I may have made.

He turned to me at last. "We knock before entering rooms, Crispin." His face was altogether transformed. He looked warm, relaxed and handsome in his composure. "The family at least." I found myself beaming inwardly, for it was clear that Myles was right, he had had no intention of throwing us out. "It sends a measure of respect and privacy – which I know none of you will have experienced at school. The servants do not knock, and that is something that you will have to work out for yourself; the difference between why they don't and why you do. If you are indisposed, and wish for complete privacy you may simply lock the door and your wishes will be respected, although we may have to be reassured you are not ill, of course."

I nodded. "Thank you, sir."

"Philip," he said. "Sir – if you absolutely must when necessity takes you – but I am not your headmaster." He paused and seemed to taking a calming breath. "Sit down, Crispin." He took one of the fireside chairs and I sat opposite him. It was probably the most comfortable thing on which I had ever sat. "I wanted to talk to you all in turn alone – and indeed would have done after breakfast –"

"I'm sorry about that, sir…Philip."

"We'll start afresh." He smiled at me and I couldn't help but grin back. He was right, he wasn't at all as I imagined a father to be. More like the type of older brother who had inherited the responsibility of raising his younger siblings, or a stern but fair prefect who garnered respect and loyalty by the force of his personality. "I know that to move from school to here – your new home – must be a period of re-adjustment. For all of you, and me too, in a way. But I hope that you will soon settle in, get to know me – and each other."

"May I ask you something?" I was dismayed to find my voice quavering with emotion.

"Of course."

"You…aren't…are you my –"

He sat forward swiftly. "No, Crispin. I'm not your father. Nor do I know who he was. I've seen your birth certificate and…" he touched me gently on my arm, his eyes fixed earnestly on mine. "Forgive me if this distresses you; this is why I needed to see you alone. Your birth certificate gives no names. From what I can surmise your mother died in the workhouse where you were born, not telling the management who she was, nor where she was from." He paused, obviously able to tell how I was struggling with myself as the last of my hope dissipated like fog in sunshine. "I'm sorry, Crispin."

"Did you pay for my education, sir?"

"I did not, other than for your final year."

I found I was breathing deeply, but I retained what little composure I had.

"Then I thank for that. The others?"

"It is not my place to tell you their history, Crispin, you know that. Would you really like me to tell them of yours?" He looked into my eyes, and his expression was like a deep, deep well into which I could fall forever. He left me in no doubt as to what he meant.

I felt heat rise in my cheeks. "No. No. I wouldn't. Thank you, Philip."

He stood, and I followed suit. "You are pleased with your room?"

I think I was still reeling from the shock of being in a poor shabby study, high up in the stifling attics of my school one moment (I had been stripped of my shared study after my disgrace), and placed in this wonder of luxury the next. Even the masters' private rooms, rarely seen, had not these soft beds, these cushioned chairs. I had been here only for one night and yet I felt violently opposed to being torn away from it, from Jude and Myles; and from Philip. To say thank you again seemed trite, and over sycophantic, and when I examined his expression I had the feeling that he wasn't expecting thanks, but was genuinely concerned for my comfort. It warmed me more than the fire.

"Yes. It's like nothing I've ever had before."

He laughed then, taking me aback, suddenly seeming younger than he had appeared, and I wondered how old he was. Certainly over thirty, but how much? "Yes," he said, "I would imagine that it is." He held out his hand, an oddly formal gesture, but one, perhaps that he felt he should have made when he first met us all, instead of breaking up a fight. "Welcome, Crispin Thorne. I'll see you at dinner."

"Aren't you taking luncheon with us?" His hand was warm and firm and once again I was reminded of the prefect on whom I'd had the most enormous crush, Peters Major, head of the upper sixth and captain of the first eleven. He had held the passion of many in my year, prospective bachelors or not.

"No," he said. "I will see you at dinner. Albert will see to your dress." And then he was gone, leaving me panicking as to what he'd meant by that. I had no dinner clothes.

His very presence was as exhausting the second time as it had been the first; enough to leave me feeling as if I'd run a cross-country race against the wind. He dazzled the eye and the mind and then he was gone. I would imagine that at his own school he would have had a veritable gang of boys carrying heavy and well-lit torches.

Was he, as Myles seemed to think, a reformer? It seemed likely, and if he was the type to forgive one's past misdemeanours, as he had said he was, it gave me more hope for my future than I had ever had. Being raised, as I had, in a school – for I could not remember anything of the workhouse Philip had mentioned, I had rarely been outside the walls of Barton Hall. I knew always that I was an orphan with no-one to foster my development, and thus I had had little hope for my future. Other boys took great pleasure, Ellman amongst them, in pointing out that I would end in trade. Any employment was an anathema to most of my classmates. A position as a clerk was the best I could hope for; a clerk in a bank, or at the pinnacle of my hopes and dreams, perhaps an articled clerk, if I were lucky enough to find someone to give me the chance – and then by sheer hard work and luck to make it into the law. This heady dream, at least, might be a possibility. My future, once dark and with little promise, now seemed to branch with paths with perhaps enough illumination to guide my way. .

Chapter Eight

I explored my room while granted some privacy; it was light and airy, the huge mullioned window overlooked over the gardens which I hadn't really paid much attention to so far, and as I stared down at the elaborate knot garden and beautifully clipped triangular trees, I itched to get outside. A small door in the corner beside the bed led to a room I did not expect, set aside for ablutions with the normal pots and jugs and a magnificent shower bath, made of some dark wood and dominating the space. I wondered if I would ever have the courage to use it. Arch had said his father was thinking of having one installed, but I was rather put off by the fact that I would have to stand naked in the base while someone – most probably Albert – poured water over my head, and listened to me yelping. I thought I might stick to using the hip bath rather than suffer the indignity of a such a device.

My curiosity satisfied for my immediate surroundings, I set off downstairs, determined to explore the gardens and to take advantage of the weather, which was sunny, but no doubt as cold as the day I had arrived. At the foot of the stairs I was met by a footman who, upon hearing that I meant to go outside, bade me wait and he vanished behind the servant's door by the stairs. When he returned, he was carrying a dark blue coat, a soft dark grey hat and scarf – none of them mine. I let him bundle me up, lead me along the corridor and open one of the side doors to the outside. I admit being a little turned around and I half expected to come out in the central courtyard, but instead I found myself outside the outer walls, blinking in the bright, cold sunshine. I stood on a narrow path beside a high brick wall with the front of the house to my left, so I tucked my hands deep in my pockets and made my way down the gravel alleyway to the right.

Clearing the back of the house at last I was rewarded by the gardens, an intricate, old-fashioned network of low knotted hedges, heathers, and squat rounded bushes that it was impossible to identify, for I was no gardener, and in the winter dead shrubs look like dead shrubs. It seemed obvious to my uneducated eye that someone must tend the garden, even though there was no-one to be seen, for the gardens looked extremely well tended. No leaves lay underfoot, and there were no weeds anywhere. The entire garden, which stretched back some hundred feet or so from the back of the house to the wall which encircled it, seemed as frozen as the landscape itself and somewhat gloomy, as if awaiting the return of something more important than spring. I was a little disappointed that I couldn't see the water from the garden, so I didn't linger; there was no gate in the wall that might give me access to the riverbank, so I marched back around the other side of the house until I came out, finally, to the wide front of the house, and the jetty, which was overshadowed by the gatehouse.

I'd not had a chance to get a full feel of the broad when I had arrived, but now, standing on the jetty and looking out to where the boat that had brought me had sailed away, I could appreciate the raw, stark beauty of the place. The island that held the house sat just inside the mouth of the broad itself, and the mere widened out beyond the house and stretched into the distance. The water was almost glassily still, disturbed only by wild-fowl, and the chill wind. On the far side of the broad I saw a boat moving away from view, its sail dark against the horizon. And on every side the wind-pumps stood, like solid four-armed giants.

The path stretched a distance along the bank, and I walked slowly along it, unwilling to go back indoors, for to return to the house would mean I would have to start thinking about my place within it, and for now I was happy to push those concerns to one side, and deal with them when I had to. Around the bend of the path, almost obscured by massive overhanging willows, was a low wooden construction, built right into the water on wooden piers. A boathouse. The double doors which gave access to the broad were closed, and the entrance door was locked too, to my enormous disappointment. I was curious to see what kind of boat Philip owned, and wondered if he might teach us all to sail. He had mentioned lessons, after all, and sailing seemed far more interesting to me than yet more Greek and Latin, however much I might now need those dusty languages. As I turned away, I almost bumped into a man coming out from under the willows.

He looked up at me, and frowned, and his eyes and brows were all I could see of his expression, as a scarf was wrapped around the lower part of his face. "The boathouse is locked," he said. "And there is nothing there to see, even if it were not." His accent was similar to that of Albert, but rougher, sing-song in a way, and resembled the speech of the boatman old Tom so nearly it was clear it must be the local dialect.

"I wasn't…" I stopped, aware that I should now comport myself as the ward of the owner of the house and not some lurking culprit. I didn't need to excuse myself to anyone, save Philip. "I can see," I finished, coolly. "Is there a key?"

"I wouldn't know," he said without any effort at deference or further curiosity as to who I was, and walked off in the direction of the gate back into the garden. I was stung by his indifference, after the attentive manner of the staff within the house, and for a moment I considered chasing after him and demanding to know who he was, and what he was about, but as I stood there, dithering, I heard someone calling me from the gateway – and I turned to see Myles, coatless, his hands tucked under his arms for warmth. I ran to see what he wanted.

"You idiot, you'll freeze," I said.

"I didn't think it would take me this long to find you. What are you doing, wandering around?" He glowered past me as if to find what possibly could be entertaining me so.

We walked into the courtyard. "You've had a week to get to know the place," I said. "I was simply curious to see the island, that's all."

"It's an island, and not a big one," he said, keeping his hands tucked under his arms and letting me open the door. "Water on all sides."

"Myles," I said, leading the way in. "I think Jude is right, you have no romance in your soul. Don't you find it exciting?"

"Not really," he shrugged. A footman, and it could have been the same one although I couldn't tell, appeared as we made the main hall, and took my outside clothes from me. "I can't swim, don't fish, and I can't sail. Water doesn't excite me much. The lunch bell has gone, by the way, that's what I came to tell you."

"Thank you," I said to the footman, who, other than to disrobe me, took no more notice of me than if I'd been a hat stand. I followed Myles to yet another room I had not seen before, the formal dining room, in which Jude waited for us, looking as brittle and pale as china.

I retired to the library after lunch. I was learning my way around the house – or at least I was learning which edge of the square held which rooms, even if it meant I often began the walk towards a desired room and ended up traversing almost the entire courtyard before reaching my destination. In later days I was to learn that it was often quicker to cut across the courtyard than to trudge around three sides of the quadrangle. Needless to say, in this instance I took the long way around, but I enjoyed it. Being alone (other than passing those ever busy servants) I was free to stop and examine the portraits which lined almost every free inch of the walls of the house, even up the staircases. Two on that walk particularly struck me: a handsome, smiling, rogue of a man from the same era as Raleigh, by his ruff and considerable codpiece, and a grey haired man sitting in some kind of boat with Bittern's Reach behind him. The man looked kindly, and although the painting's plate gave a date of 1728, it was obviously an ancestor of Philip's, for he had an unmistakable look of my guardian about him.

Once in the library, I was struck again by the portrait of Philip. In the daylight it looked much more vibrant. The resemblance to the older man in the boat was not my imagination, and thought I would ask my guardian about him if I remembered that evening. The thought of the formal dinner, and the twin tests of manners and conversation struck a little chill inside me, for although at school we had been trained not to eat like savages, we were not served on gold-edged china, nor did we drink from cut-crystal glasses. We had had one – or at the most – two courses, so there was never any confusion regarding cutlery or wineglass. I had once been to a large family party at the Archesons', but all I could re-member of that night was trying not to make a fool of myself, and following Mrs Archeson's every move.

I gravitated towards the books with a sense of restless guilt. I wanted to pull the books from the shelves and to immerse my-self in them, but I had not asked permission and I didn't know if I needed to seek it. I satisfied myself with strolling around the room, examining the shelves closest to the floor (for they went all the way to the ceiling) and marvelling at the breadth of subjects covered: philosophy, astronomy, politics, history, engineering, the-ology... I felt sure that I could stay my entire life in this one room and never read them all. At last I came to a section of works in Greek and studies on Greek literature and my heart turned over a little to find *Agamemnon* sitting there just waiting to be read. I found myself looking around before I took the book out, before carrying it to one of the sofas to read. I found myself smiling at the thought that once I had to be forced to study when it was impor-tant, and now I read the words once more because to do so was to hear Arch's deep, warm voice in my ear and to feel his lips tickling the back of my neck. The daydream lifted me away and the words faded from my eyes.

I lost track of time and found, as I noticed the room dimming around me, that I'd not read past the first few pages of the book, and I was no longer alone. A maid was lighting the lamps. I jumped to my feet; I had not seen or even heard her enter. "No, it's all right," I said. "Please don't light them on my account. I won't be staying." She bobbed, put out the lamp she had lit and left without a word. I closed the book of Aeschylus, not allowing myself to look at its cream parchment again, and like an automaton returned the book to the shelf.

Somehow I made it up to my new room without encountering anyone, where I locked the door, threw myself onto the bed and allowed myself to cry, bitter wracking tears that I'd not permitted myself to shed for an entire year. It had taken me a long time to mourn Arch, and with a typical schoolboy stubbornness I had refused to acknowledge that I would never see him again, but now I had passed the point where I could fool myself any longer. If he had loved me, wanted me as much as I'd wanted him, he would have found some way to communicate with me in the year since he was sent away – but he hadn't, and I had continued to hope, like a child with a broken drum.

The sky outside my window was fully dark when I rose, roused by the door being rattled, followed by a soft knock. "Mr Crispin?" It was Albert, come, no doubt to dress me for dinner.

"Wait a moment, please," I said. I ducked into my bathroom, wiped my face before letting Albert in. I put my broken drum away. I gave up childish things, and was ready to move into my future.

He was carrying clothes over his arm, but he put them down on the bed. "Mr Smallwood says that he thinks the clothes may be suitable, although not perfect."

I lifted the jacket up and held it against me; it was a beautiful fabric, the shoulders cut with military precision. "Whose are they?" I asked. They were certainly not wide enough to be Philip's. "Maybe they were Mr Smallwood's when he was younger?"

"That might be, sir," Albert said, and began to undo my tie. In no time at all, he'd stripped me and encased me in the new outfit and apart from the wretched state of my hair, and the way my ears stuck out of it a little, I couldn't say I was displeased with what I saw in the glass. The jacket was a trifle loose, and the trousers were dependent on the braces, but the leg length was suitable. When he began to fuss with the tie I waved him away, it was something I felt I could manage myself, even thought he seemed to think I was incapable of coping with anything more complicated than a button.

"May I come in?" Jude said, from the door. He was similarly elegant in a black ensemble. "My," he said with a smile, "you look almost as delicious as…"

"You?" I was happy to see him looking so much better than he had at lunch.

"My dear boy, I could hardly be so arrogant. I stand before you in trousers that defy gravity and in a jacket which I doubt will stand the rigours of a dinner. I'm a scarecrow in comparison to you. But then of course you haven't seen Myles. Dear Lord above, if I were to believe in the old adage of clothes maketh the man…"

He rolled his eyes in pretended ecstasy and I laughed. In our short acquaintance I had found that Jude could always make me smile, although I was beginning to learn how much he swaddled himself in words. "Here, let me," he said, taking hold of the ends of my recalcitrant tie. He moved in front of me and busied himself at my neck.

I relinquished the task to him. It caught me a little unawares because I knew how to do it. Granted I was never perfect at the art. I had sat in Hall a hundred times glancing at the prefects' bows which never ever seemed to skew from the horizontal – but I hoped that I could do it decently. Jude however had the arcane art to it, for he undid the entire thing, pulled it from under my collar, straightened it out, before sliding it around my neck and starting from scratch.

The concentration needed made him silent and the sudden intimacy, the warmth of his breath against my cheek, startled me. I attempted to pull back a little, scared of my body's reaction as familiar, delicious warmth pooled into my loins, but he pulled me back towards him using the tie itself with a short reprimand, "Keep still, will you?" and I was trapped between his beautiful, pale hands, and trying not to look him in the eye.

He appeared, thankfully, blissfully unaware of my inappropriate reaction to his nearness and stepped back after a minute, his eyes appraising as he looked at his work. "Better than mine," he said, turning away, and letting me do the same as I fought for control. I knew it was only physical reaction, Jude couldn't be more different to Arch. Where Arch was broad, Jude was all litheness and angles; Arch had been bright, light, rude with health, whereas Jude himself would have drawn Arch's eye, for he was indeed a little like me in looks. But for a moment, I could have leaned toward him, over those inches that had separated us, and perhaps I would have been welcomed, too.

For something to do, I took the poker and roused the fire as my hardness abated, then turned to find Jude sitting on the bed with a pensive look. "So," I said with a brightness that belied my recent concern, "Myles fits his borrowed clothes better? Whose do you think they are?"

"I don't think they are any one person's," he said. "Perhaps Philip just borrowed them all in anticipation of our arrival. I hear we are to be measured for clothes tomorrow." He flung himself back onto my bed. "What utter bliss. I don't think I've ever had brand new clothes in my life. Is that entirely shallow of me?"

"Get up, you arse," I laughed. "Neither have I, but I don't think I'd go into paroxysms of delight about it." I'd had nothing new, not clothes or books. "Your clothes are a great deal better than mine."

"Oh. He got up, moving to the mirror to rearrange his hair. "We were both given those when we arrived. Were you not?"

"No."

"Ah, but you didn't arrive with nothing to your name but ghastly uniform, I recall. Thankfully I shall not be saddled with that particular burden again." He turned, stepped towards me and gave my tie a final light touch. "There. We are as good as we can be in our borrowed finery. Now let's go and get Myles. I doubt he can tear himself away from the looking glass without our help."

Disgustingly, Myles was, as Jude had predicted, admiring himself in the long glass in his room. Jude gave me a look before grabbing Myles by the arm and towing him out with us. Jude was right, though – whomever used to wear Myles' dinner suit had been his exact height and weight, for it fitted him as if it had been sewn on his body. I was appreciative of the quality of what I was wearing, and after all the displays of taste and wealth I'd seen since my arrival, that was hardly a surprise, but Myles showed me for the first time what money could do. He looked immaculate, his shoulders accentuated by the cut of the jacket and, walking behind him, I appreciated the way the tailoring clung to his hips. All in all, we were a smug little band that evening, and I began to look forward a little to the new clothes that Jude had mentioned, although I'd die before I'd admit it to him.

Witheridge himself met us at the bottom of the stairs and led us to the dining room, opened the door, and left us alone. Philip was there before us, and all thoughts of how well I looked, or indeed how well Myles looked, were wiped away by the sight of Philip in evening clothes. Jude pinched my arm hard and gave a sigh that I'm sure everyone heard, but it was well deserved. Thankfully, we didn't have the opportunity to stand and gawp, as Philip ushered us to our seats at one end of the table, waiting until we were seated before he took his own, at the head.

The table setting was every bit as intimidating as I had feared, far more so than anything I'd encountered at Arch's parents. Three wine glasses each, and knives and forks and spoons stretching out to infinity, or so it seemed, forcing us to sit a good few feet apart.

The dismay showed in my face, I'm sure, and as I looked up I could see that Myles was glaring at the silverware as if he wanted to swipe the entire conglomeration onto the floor. Jude, however, seemed as happy as if he sat down to a royal banquet every day of his life, and remained focused on Philip.

"It is generally polite," Philip said, "to greet your host as you enter a room. A handshake, even if you have seen him that afternoon shooting, or riding. Depending on his status you may need to bow; the depth of that courtesy is again, dependant on who he is, and how high up the social ladder he belongs."

I wondered at his words. Could he mean that we might one day be mixing with titles and royalty? I had assumed that Philip was shy of society, from what Doctor Baynes had said. "I hardly need to remind you that if ladies are present, one seats them first, not taking one's own seat until all of them are comfortable. Of course, as this is not a consideration here, you are forgiven." He grinned then, and I relaxed a little.

"If I remember anything of my schooldays," he continued, "and you must realise that being so much older, it is hard to recall times that long past, then mealtimes were mainly for eating. However, when we dine together – or indeed at any meal, although I won't impose myself on you terribly often – the conversation should take precedence. Myles, don't look so horrified, I'm sure that it's no more difficult than any lesson you've had to learn so far, and none of you are simpletons, particularly you."

Myles looked as though he was going to speak, but Jude threw him a glance, and he shut his mouth.

"As you are obviously aware, we are rather cut-off here, but supplies come from Yarmouth and Stalham regularly. I expect you all to read the newspapers every day and to keep yourselves apprised of current events. In this way, conversation will be easier, and even for the meals that I'm not with you, I expect you to practice this skill. Sometime soon I will be inviting various people from the neighbourhood – and yes, this is a neighbourhood, although a strange one to you all – to meet you. Yes, Crispin, you wish to say something?"

I felt myself colouring, but I spoke up. "Yes. It's just…I…"

"One thing to practice then," he said, but his voice was kind, "is to think clearly about what you wish to say, and have the sentence formulated in advance."

I had, of course, but when I'd opened my mouth it simply hadn't worked that way. "Also, this is not school, although you did not put up your hand, it was much the same thing, to interject into a conversation you need to find the right point."

"I'll try, si – Philip. On my way here, in the coach that is, I met with a Dr. Baynes and –"

Philip's attention froze on me; it wasn't that he stopped being pleasant, for the smile stayed on his face, but he almost stopped moving entirely and looked intently at me, for all the world resembling a pointer indicating a prospective kill. "I haven't seen the good Doctor for quite a while," he said, never taking his gaze from mine. "How was he?"

"I didn't speak to him for long, we only really became acquainted when the coach stopped at Horsey, but he told me to tell you that I'd met him. He seemed in good health, sir."

He was silent for a moment, then took a deep breath. "I will have to receive guests at some point, which is part of the point of this exercise." He returned to a more normal posture and the comparison between one state and other made it clear to me how tense he'd become when Baynes had been mentioned. I'd thought the old man's manner a little odd when we had spoken, but assumed it was from the surprise of learning who I was and my odd connection to a man he knew. Perhaps there was something more to it than that. As little as I knew Philip, I thought I could tell that Baynes wasn't his favourite person. "So you will be meeting certain people, and others that I consider to be friends."

"And others?" Myles said, interjecting into the conversation with more grace than I had managed.

"Well done, Myles," Philip said, making Myles look disgustingly smug. "Nicely noticed. Absolutely. When one is in a privileged position, as I am, and as now are you, one must entertain those whom one does not like. The trick is to fool the eye – and leave them guessing which is which."

Chapter Nine

We may have descended to the dining room as young men who thought we were poised and sophisticated, but we returned to our rooms like chattering schoolboys. Philip had inspired us with his elegant hospitality, his ideas, and his mercurial moods which shifted from serious to witty to acerbic like light shifting on the river.

"I wonder we haven't heard of him," Myles said, leading the way up the stairs, "he'd do brilliantly in Parliament, although who'd want to represent this load of marsh-crawlers? Are there even any constituents in Horsey?"

"I saw a few houses on the way in, it's impossible to know how many... We could ask Philip I suppose. He'd know." I paused outside my room. "Perhaps he just isn't interested in government."

"He had enough views on it, though," said Jude. "His ideas for reducing the potato famine sounded perfectly sound. But Myles is right."

Myles gave a mock bow and backed down the corridor towards his room, "Thank you, Mr Middleton, you honour me."

"Fool," Jude said smiling. We were all rather worse for wear, and would have praised a blood-stained Sikh if one had come charging up the stairs at that moment. In the process of the meal, we had been given other lessons. We were taught the names and history of the wines we were served. We had to describe their taste and commit to memory the best foods served with each. In this way,

I'd drunk more than I'd ever done in my life before, despite Philip's warnings that we should only sample each glass. Some were too delicious to leave alone. Myles crashed through his door, leaving us alone, and Jude wandered after me into my room. It seemed perfectly natural; for all that we'd known each other for such a short time, I felt closer to Jude than I did Myles, who was still for me such an unknown quantity. Albert was waiting inside and after he'd taken off my jacket, I waved his attentions away,.

"It's all right, Albert," I said, "I'll sit up for a while with Mr Jude."

"Ring if you need me, sir."

"I don't think I will, but thank you, Albert. Good night."

He left us alone and I turned to Jude. "Is your man so blessed attentive?"

Sitting on one of the fireside chairs and pushing off his shoes with a look of relief, Jude looked up at me a little blearily, proving he was almost as inebriated as I felt. "Oh, far worse, far far worse. He hovers, and he's almost completely silent. Ten times today he's nearly given me scared me to death with his silent creeping."

I laughed, and he went on, "You don't believe me? No, I can see you don't. At least your Albert has the decency to make noise when he walks. I swear Paul has glued green baize to the soles of his shoes. Look, I'll show you." He pulled me to my feet. "Stand here by the window, and gaze aesthetically and pensively out of it. Oh, do try and look artistic, and not just glazed, will you?" He draped his arms around my shoulders in an attempt to place me in what he considered to be a more artistic pose. All I could do was giggle. "All right, that'll do, although you look more like a drunken knife grinder than a poet. Now wait there. And don't look around."

It was easy to lean against the window, bracing my knees on the window seat, though I dare say I had none of the grace that Jude wanted me to portray.

"So, I hear the door open," he said, his voice a little unsteady as he made the other side of the room and I heard the door open and close, "and that's it. The next thing I know he's standing behind me. Like this."

Sadly he completely failed in his attempt to emulate the allegedly cat-like Paul, for I heard every footfall across the floor, despite the fact he was in his stockinged feet. But eventually he lurched behind me and said, "Is there anything you need, sir?" in an appalling impression of the local accent which had us both falling onto the window seat with laughter.

"All right," he said, leaning toward me, blasting me with the brandy on his breath, "perhaps it's not exactly like that, but –" He stopped talking and became very still, other than his breathing which was labouring under too much spirit. When he continued it was almost in a whisper, as though what he was saying was a secret, and he didn't take his eyes from mine. "He's a quiz, anyway. At least your Albert is all lantern-jawed and proper. Myles' man looks a knave who has strangled two wives before his twentieth birthday." I held my breath, unwilling to break the mood. "Crispin..."

"Yes?" My stomach was fluttering wildly and my buttocks were tingling with apprehension.

"You are very handsome."

"Yes, so are you," I said, with a small, breathy laugh.

"I'm going to kiss you, and you mustn't mind. It's just the alcohol, and you know how wicked I am."

"Yes."

"You won't mind?"

I leaned forward, tipping my head back a little and touching my lips to his, and closed my eyes. The brandy fumes wafted up between us and I wondered how he'd managed to drink so much of it. For a moment we paused, chastely, joined only in this way, then he shifted along the seat and slid his arms around my neck, opened his mouth and let me in. I'd loved to kiss Arch, but every kiss of ours had been tinged with fear, and never had I known the abandon and freedom that alcohol and privacy gave to a kiss. He clung to me, sliding his fingers around the nape of my neck and tickling me deliciously, and still I kissed him, tasting every wine we'd had, even a tang of cream from our dessert, and something else, something entirely Jude. Finally I had to surface for air and I pulled my head back. There was no retreating from what I'd done – I couldn't blame the intimacy of that kiss on the wine, and I couldn't now rail at him for being an unnatural cad. It was clear, too, that he felt the same, for as I opened my eyes I found him staring at me, his eyes almost black in the lamplight.

"Well," he said, exhaling. "You constantly surprise me, Sphinx." I leaned into him again but he matched my movement and leant towards me, his tongue coming out to lick his lips as if savouring the taste of me. "And I'm going to regret this…" His voice was husky and so quiet I hardly heard him, "But I'm going to bid you goodnight." I caught hold of his hand as he stood up, wanting to say something. He bent over in a courtly bow that would have pleased Philip or any crowned head of Europe and kissed my palm tenderly. "You dear, dear boy," he whispered. "Goodnight."

I slid back onto the seat in a warm daze, pulling my tie undone, my mind awhirl with the glamour of the evening, the heady mix of Philip, his topics of men, manners and methods – cigars, with which I was not familiar – topped with far too much wine. Was it a mistake to have kissed Jude? I wondered muzzily, pulling off my jacket. I knew I could blame it on the wine or I could, I reasoned, as I dropped my clothes into a messy pile on the floor and clambered naked into the huge bed, simply pretend I had no memory of the event at all in the morning. I burrowed under the heavy counterpane and felt deliciously decadent for being naked, and, for the first time in my life, having instigated a kiss, even though Jude had said he was going to do so. "I'm more wicked than you," I whispered, although I have to say, I didn't truly believe it.

My fingers traced the outline of my lips, attempting to recreate the soft, velvety feel of his mouth on mine, and I licked the tips of my fingers, gently rubbing the moisture around the skin that surrounded my lips, feeling it cool in the night air. In the utter dark, beneath the heavy weight of the quilt, I imagined the mattress beside me to shift as Jude changed his mind and slid in beside me. The pillow had to double for the phantom I raised in my mind, and I took it in my arms and pulled it on top of me, letting the pressure of the coversand the weight of the feathers do much of the pretence. But it wasn't enough; where there should have been warm, living skin, there was soft, yielding cotton and try as I might it could not convince. If only I had a connecting door, as we'd had in the tower room, perhaps he might have come back, perhaps I might have plucked up the courage to go to him. Frustrated, I turned over, letting my person, which was now fully roused and aching for release, rub against the sheets. It felt wonderful, more remote than my hand so, I opened my legs to gain the maximum leverage. I humped like the desperate schoolboy I truly was, gasping in pleasure and loving that no-one could hear me. I imagined that Jude, for all his restraint, was regretting his withdrawal and was lying on his bed, his member hard in his hand, thinking of me.

I hardly knew him, and yet I wanted to see that with my own eyes and not just the image in my head. The mattress proved to be an unsatisfactory lover, for the feathers retreated from my ardour and in the end I had to resort to manual manipulation, my fingers knowing the speed and pressure all too well. By the time I spent myself, sweating with the exertion, I was on my hands and knees, but still pumping away as if…as if I were buried deep in Jude's willowy body. My legs were trembling, hardly able to hold me, so I slid down, face first onto the slightly damp mattress, with myself still well in hand, seeking out every last sensation. With my face buried in the suffocating warmth of the pillow I murmured Jude's name over and over again before sliding into a self-satisfied sleep.

I awoke to find Albert picking up my clothes from the night before. The curtains were wide open to reveal a dark grey sky and heavy rain which spattered the tiny diamonds of the windows in percussive gusts. I found that I was wearing a smile a mile wide which I hid from Albert under the covers, peering out as I watched him moving around the room. I noticed that he had, oh so correctly, put a clean nightshirt on the edge of the bed and I grabbed it while he wasn't looking. Jude was right, Albert was rather nice-looking. It made me curious to see Paul, to see if he was the fright Jude had claimed him to be. When Albert disappeared into the bathroom, I quickly donned the nightshirt and struggled up to a sitting position, wincing as my member slid against the sheet. Despite my abuse of the night before I was hard again, and hoped that Albert would allow me some privacy before he insisted on helping me with my preparations.

"I'm sorry about the weather, sir," he said, as he came back into the room carrying a basket with linen in. "I'll fetch your breakfast immediately."

"We aren't eating downstairs?"

"It's not generally the custom when the master is in residence," he said. "Mr Smallwood generally stays in his apartments until at least noon. If you will excuse me, I'll be back with your tray, and your paper."

As soon as he left the room I dashed into the bathroom and relieved myself with a sigh of pleasure, letting my arousal abate, then scurried back to bed before the warmth in the sheets faded away. I felt entirely comfortable and relaxed; Philip, instead of being some ogre, abducting young men from the world, was an erudite, intelligent man who wanted nothing but the best for his new wards. I had a beautiful room, the promise of new clothes and two young men whom I already counted as friends. The thought of Jude and my fantasy of the night before brought a fresh interest to areas below my waist but I glared at the rain, imagining what it would be like to be caught out in it in just my nightshirt, and eventually the interest went away.

As luxurious as it was to be propped up in bed and having breakfast on a tray I found that I preferred eating with the others; it was probably a schoolboy habit for I had very rarely eaten alone there. It did not stop me doing justice to the meal, however, finding myself disgustingly hungry despite the five courses of the night before.

Albert helped me with my ablutions, avoiding my blushes with a stoic grace, and then dressed me with indifferent care. "You are engaged at ten, sir," he said, as he picked up my nightshirt. "Mr Smallwood has arranged several appointments for the young gentlemen in the morning-room."

I adjusted my tie, although it hardly needed it. "What appointments, Albert?"

"I am afraid I am unable to tell you, sir," he said, and he left me alone. It wasn't until I was wandering down the stairs looking for Witheridge that I realised the elegant ambiguity of his last remark.

Witheridge was nowhere to be found in the hall, so I went down to the morning-room myself to find it a hive of activity. The breakfast table had been moved to one side, and Myles and Jude were standing in the middle of the room. Around them gathered clusters of men with tape measures and pins. This, it seemed, was the promise of new clothes made real – although why Albert hadn't known about it, or had been so closed-mouthed about it baffled me a little. Myles waved and called me over. Jude, looking a little pale, smiled wanly, rolled his eyes but said nothing.

"We gave up waiting for you," Myles said. "What were you doing?"

I took a quick look around the room, but other than one footman and the busy tailors we were as alone as we could be, and there was no sign of Philip. "I was doing as we were instructed to do last night," I said with some dignity, "and doing as all gentlemen should do, especially after a debauched night. Taking a leisurely breakfast and catching up with the news of the day." I had the cheek to catch Jude's eye, as I said the word debauched, and a small expression of shock flickered over his handsome face.

Myles snorted. "More likely snoring your head off. My newspaper was a week old, so it was hardly of the day. Ouch!" He swatted at one of the tailors who was kneeling beside him. "That hurt."

I was scooped up by two of the men who left my friends and joined me and soon I was stripped down to my shirt and trousers and measured and prodded and as stuck with pins as a hedgehog. I didn't see Philip's arrival, as I was rather occupied with the process of being measured. It took a little getting used to. When I finally did notice him, he was conversing with the largest and fattest of the tailors, a man with a luxuriant moustache, fat as a leech and twice as shiny.

"They'll need two sets of evening clothes," Philip was saying. "Tweeds, morning coats, trousers – do you still have that grey-green…? Yes? Good, several pairs of those, you know the style. Shooting jackets of course, shirts for – well, you know better than I. Riding clothes. I'll have a list of –" he broke off and an odd expression crossed his face, as if he'd had an appointment and had forgotten to keep it. "I'll have a list brought down. Good work, Michelozzi."

"We will deliver in only four days," the man said. His accent was pure English which made me stare, and I only recovered my manners when I spotted Philip frowning at me.

"You have everything you need?"

"Si, signore, for no-one else would I move to such a damp town, however much they paid me. Yarmouth is full of fish and sailors – no style."

"I'm grateful, Michelozzi." He left without addressing any of us, and my attention at his leaving was disturbed when my attendants began to remove my trousers and shirt. "What the deuce…"

Michelozzi bustled over. "We must have the exact measurements, you understand. I will not trust the more delicate items to not fit, yes?" I found it amusing that the man spoke with an Italian cadence to his words with such an English accent. "Don't you worry, signore, we will not expose the whole person to the air, right?"

I could do nothing, the man had his instructions and there was nothing I, not Myles or Jude could do about it and in seconds we were all stripped down to our smallclothes and socks. We were measured again, delicately and rather too intimately. I tried not to look at my friends, but it was hard not to. For one thing I was facing both of them, and they I, and it was at least easier to catch their eyes when tape measures were put in places that such things really didn't belong, than to look at the tailors or, heaven forbid, the impassive statue of the footman.

Myles was, as his clothes had hinted, of a broader build than Jude; his shoulders were not that much wider, but he was solid in the chest and hips, his legs thicker and covered liberally with brown hair. Jude was a little taller, his skin more pale where it showed at neck and shoulder. He kept his eyes cast downwards for most of the procedure, only meeting my glance once or twice, and then looking away with no more than a small smile, or a sideways glance at Myles. I had been warmly happy about our stolen kiss, but to see him so obviously uneasy about something – and I could hardly imagine what else it could be – worried me not a little. Did he think I would tell anyone? Or perhaps he himself had told Myles…my stomach churned at this new thought…and was worried himself at the broken confidence. I could not imagine what disturbed him, and each thought was worse than the next so I decided to ask him outright about it when I next had the opportunity.

Chapter Ten

That ambition was not so easily realised. For a start Jude was released before me, as I was last in, and when I went to seek him out I couldn't find him. I wandered around for a while, from the library to the empty dining room to the morning-room and even poking my nose into one or two rooms, but I found no sign of him, and spent the time till lunch alone in the library.

At lunch we were without Philip and there was no opportunity to speak privately, due to the constant presence of the staff. Philip was clearly used to talking freely in front of them, and he no doubt had years of practice but we three were accustomed to Hall tables with a hundred or so eager ears. It would take us a little longer to be so urbane. So we talked a little of the tailors – expressing our embarrassment at being so manhandled – before lapsing into an awkward silence. I was now convinced that Jude had said something to Myles; and if he had, I was a little ashamed that I had hidden my past, when the other two had been so trusting and so open with me. What would they think of me? I thought back suddenly to that moment in my bedroom when Jude had moved as to touch my elbow and then had moved away in such a hurry. I had thought little of it then, but his pinched, worried face, despite his usual airy manner, and the look he had given me after that kiss… *my dear, dear boy*…what did he think? That I'd done it for a joke? That it was pity? That I thought it was what he wanted, or perhaps was too drunk to know what I was doing? I'd had my chance to admit the truth, and it was going to be harder to mention it now.

But there was no time for discussion afterwards; we were taken up to our bedrooms and a man measured our feet with a most peculiar device before providing us with a selection of boots and shoes which delighted me, as I'd rarely had more than one pair before in my life. When I exclaimed how I liked them, the man – Mr Pillar, pockmarked, and his fingers stained yellow – from his trade no doubt – made a face. "This are just poor things, provided in various sizes as requested. Your replacements will be with you in a week or so, after which time you can burn these embarrassing and quite poorly made monstrosities." I tried to argue with him, turning the highly polished evening shoes over in my hands, for never had I seen a shine on shoes as these had,, but he would not be placated. It seemed that there were fit for nothing and to hand them over to such gentlemen's sons was an insult to his craft. He was the most depressed man I think I had ever met.

Left alone with Albert, who was putting the new shoes away, I made for the door.

"I'd wait a while, sir," Albert said, from the depths of the wardrobe, "that is, if you were intending to visit Mr Myles or Mr Jude."

I was faintly nettled, but intrigued. "Why is that?"

"Well, they will be having the same attention given to them, that is Mr Pillar will be visiting them both, and then Mr Smallwood will be attending you."

"All of us, individually?"

"That is what I was advised, sir," he said.

There was nothing else for me to do but wait, and I wished for the time to run down to get a book. I was unused to sitting and having nothing to occupy my mind. I sat and watched the rain-soaked Mere for a while, but in such filthy weather there was nothing much out there to draw the eye; even the ducks were keeping out of the cold, and I could not blame them. In the end I let my thoughts run on to how I would broach the subject of my leaving school, whom to mention it to first, and what excuses I could make for not telling the whole truth. As both Myles and Jude had told me their stories, I couldn't see that Philip would object to my being honest with them.

As to Jude…I had to admit to myself, for there was little doubt, that I found myself attracted to him. I don't know how long it might have been before we should have found this out, but the alcohol had certainly hurried things along. It was strange to me, because with Arch everything in our friendship had been set in place first. Neither of us had known of each other's habits when we first met. I had had a small encounter or two before, once with an older boy and once with a younger, but they were nothing more than the sort of thing that many do, whether they would marry later in life or not. When Arch moved into my study we hit it off immediately, liking sport and the same kind of adventure books. I had more than a healthy crush on him, but had given up all hope of it ever being reciprocated for although my tastes were known – no-one keeps secrets in Hall for long, except from the masters – Arch was new and no-one had anything to say about it. I had long carried my torch in secret, happy with our friendship, and so I have to admit to being completely surprised when one evening I saw him looking at me curiously across our shared desk. I asked him what he was thinking and he'd said, "What you'd do if I did this," and he took my hand.

I didn't know Jude, other than he was funny and perhaps a little nervy and his mouth was soft and sweet. I didn't know what I wanted other than to kiss him again.

I heard the door close, and thinking it was Albert leaving, I didn't move, warm and comfortable on the window seat, but was roused when a deep and thankfully amused voice said, "Don't get up, Crispin." It was Philip, and I was lolling around in my stockinged feet, half asleep.

"I do apologise, sir," I said, leaping up. "I didn't –"

"It's all right, Crispin, sit down. I broke my own rules and didn't knock, but the door was open and Albert said you were waiting."

"He said you would be coming."

"I won't disturb you long; I wanted to give you these." He handed me a small sheaf of paper, a notebook and a box. "The papers outline your lessons, the notebook, well that should be self-explanatory. Don't worry about the other until I've gone." He smiled disarmingly. "I'm not good with thanks. I'm going to be away for a few days, but should be back within a week at the most. Your clothes and shoes should arrive by then, so –" he touched the shiny fabric of my jacket with a wry expression, "Albert can make some dusters with this. You'll be pleased to see the last of it, I'm sure."

"I can't disagree," I replied.

"I've already spoken to the others, and so I'll say the same to you. Stay away from the water. It's bitterly cold, as you can imagine, so I don't suppose any of you will be interested in swimming…"

I laughed, "Certainly not in this weather –"

"Not in *any* weather," he said, and his face darkened, his elegant brows drawing together. "The Broads aren't subject to the tides, they are nothing more than stagnant pools and they are filled with chills and treacherous weeds even at the very best of times. They are not safe. You must promise me, Crispin. I've exacted the same promise from the others, and they have given me their word." I wondered at his passion, he looked almost angry, but not with me, it was quite disconcerting. "You must give me yours, as a gentleman." He held out his hand, "Crispin? Your word, sir."

I took his hand. "Certainly, sir…Philip. I didn't know how treacherous they were. Although you are right, no-one would want to swim in the winter." He was still frowning. "You know this place better than we. I give you my word."

He exhaled, his smile replacing the clouds. "Thank you. I promise you that I only want the best for you… The Mere is not a place to take lightly." He shook my hand, bade me goodbye, and left me to examine what he'd left me.

The little box was made of a shining ebony and had my initials – my new initials, *CDT* – picked out in a white wood on the top. Within, a beautiful watch lay in a moulded bed of velvet, complete with a matching silver chain. The case of the watch was engraved with a tiny and faithful representation of the front of Bittern's Reach, and the back had a picture of a peculiar fat little bird – was that a bittern? I opened it, finding my hands shaking a little for never had I owned anything so beautiful. On the inside of the case was inscribed: *"A welcome gift for a welcome arrival, Philip."*

The warmth, the excitement of the day seemed to overwhelm me and I felt tears pricking at my eyelids. This was my home, and although I had been aware of it for a year, I had not truly registered that it was true. All the fantasies I'd held, those stupid nursery-tale imaginings about my real parents – my fantastic lineage that would one day be revealed to me – all that fell away from me like cobwebs being blown away in the wind. This was real; this watch, now warm and solid in my hand. This was a pledge from the man who had not been responsible for my existence, but who had *chosen* me – for surely there were a hundred, a thousand boys with no prospects in schools and orphanages around the country. Out of anyone he could have taken on as ward, to share in his life, his wealth, he had chosen *me*. I clutched the watch with both hands and held it close to me. I would never part with it, never. Hardly able to see through my blurry, tear-filled eyes, I fumbled for the chain, and attached it to my waistcoat. It was a substantial and unaccustomed weight and I liked the way it felt – it was unlikely I could ever ignore its presence, and just to have it there would remind me of Philip's faith and trust in me. I had let him down once before, I would not do so again.

It was difficult to walk into Myles' open door with a straight face, wanting to pull back my coat and show off my new acquisition and wondering what Philip had bought for the others. The two of them were playing draughts, lying flat on the floor like children and not grown men. At my appearance Myles sat up, his face full of nothing but smiles and welcome. *Perhaps*, I thought, *Jude hasn't told him – or he doesn't care.*

"You'll have to adjudicate," he said, indicating the board. "Jude cheats abominably. I think that it's best we know this sort of thing early on in our lives, don't you? If one of us is destined for ruin, at least we know who it is."

Jude's face was a picture of innocence and the pair of them made me laugh so hard I forgot my dignity and threw myself onto the floor with them, all thoughts of responsibility and showing off my watch and chain forgotten. "Don't worry, Jude," I said, settling myself comfortably with a cushion that Jude had given me, "if you end up in the Fleet, we'll send you parcels."

"The Fleet?" Myles said, "Newgate and a public scandal for Jude and nothing less."

Jude looked artificially haughty. "I should *hope* so. If I am to go down – or go down any further in my nefarious life, I hope it will be an enormous scandal – all the newspapers in the land reporting my every *bon mot*. I can see it now," he looked theatrically into some distance, a hand to his throat. "Secrets discovered in my palatial house in Mayfair, State Secrets that could only have come from the Home Office. Letters found, bound in lavender ribbon – the government falls as one of its worthies is broken, his words of love for a handsome Russian spy printed for all to see."

"At least they won't hang you," I laughed. His idiocy was infectiously funny.

"They might not hang him for the buggery," Myles said making Jude blink at the coarseness, "but if that's what really happens, Jude, they'll hang you for treason."

"Ah, good point, dear boy," he said. "Perhaps I'll burn the letters."

We spent an hour or more playing; Myles beat both of us regularly until we surrendered to him unconditionally. Then we lay by the fire, and talked at first of Philip, and then of each other.

"He was a master, yes," Jude said, at Myles' question.

"Perhaps Crispin doesn't want to hear your sordid past, although I do."

Jude moved his head, resting on his arms, and looked at me. "Crispin?"

"Oh…yes – of course."

"There were certain prefects who...would ask for certain boys to fag for them."

"Don't tell me," Myles growled, his eyes firmly on the fire. "And it wasn't a good idea to refuse."

"Social – as it were – suicide, in fact," Jude said delicately. "And if the masters didn't seem to know about it, then it was a fair clue that they did, if you see what I mean."

I nodded. It had been much the same at my school, although I had been spared, obviously not appealing to the boys at the top at the time. You didn't say no, if asked. It meant a hundred ways for them to make your life more awkward at school, and for most boys, it was awkward enough, trying to wade through each term without disaster.

"Mr Armitage seemed to know immediately; he took over my House when Old Frobisher died of an apoplexy watching the football, and screaming abuse at the opposition." He shook his head, "It wasn't terribly polite. And the game had to be stopped." Myles hit him on the arm. "All right, all right, I'm getting to the gory details. He put a stop the...arrangements within a few weeks of taking over and it caused a fair bit of revolution. The Upper Sixth were all for a strike, but someone with more sense talked them out of it, saying that fagging would still continue. It did, but things changed. Doors had to be left open, and fags went in teams of two. I'm not saying it stopped entirely, of course..."

"No, they always find a way," Myles said. His face was red, although he was sitting closer to the fire than I. "Go on, Jude. So, this Armitage, was he the one?"

"I don't think he was the *one*," Jude said with something approaching his usual veneer, "but he was rather delicious. Tall and dark and...wide. Large hands. A fiery temper. Not handsome, no. But..." He waved his hands around. "Sweeping. Clutching. Passionate."

"Rather ironic that he stopped the special fagging duties and then..." I broke off, not really knowing how to express it.

"I don't think he would have, but I didn't really give him much choice." He gave me a small grin, unseen by Myles who was still staring at the fire. "I can be quite irresistible when I put my mind to it. I don't think you could say he took advantage of his position."

"There's no need to sound so smug about it," Myles said. "If you were sent down, what do you think happened to him? You landed on your feet."

Jude went silent then for a moment, his eyes half hooded. "I know. We were careless. I'd taken some papers down to mark – no-one was fooled, not the boys who knew about that sort of thing, but I don't believe, still don't believe that anyone of the faculty knew. It was the first time after the summer vac and…well…we'd been apart. We were impetuous, and careless. We didn't check the door. It was one mistake, just one."

"Someone would have found out, sooner or later," I said. "Or you'd simply have left school and that would be that. But it's a shame for him, all the same. Do you know what happened to him?"

"No. I didn't get the opportunity to leave a message with anyone. I was kept in isolation for three days, then bundled into a coach and brought here. I have his address, or where he was lodging, at least. Perhaps I should write. I'd hate to think that anything awful happened to him."

"Two years to life is pretty awful," Myles said. "Well worth a fumble in your drawers."

"Myles, stop it," I said. "You can't blame Jude alone, the man knew what he was doing. Jude, as much as he likes to play it, isn't Salome."

"It's all right when it's mutual," Myles said. He sat up and turned away, hugging his knees. "Your Armitage sounds like a decent cove, for a master, even if he did find Jude *irresistible*."

"Can you blame him?" Jude said.

"Shut up, Jude," I said, looking daggers at him. "Myles?"

"That's all," Myles said. "Just that. All those fags who didn't get 'saved.' At your school, at mine. At Jude's. All over the country. It's wrong."

"That's a bit harsh," I said. "It's tradition…and…" I fought for the words. Everyone knew it was how things were. Making boys into men. "It's always gone on, and it's not always about…that, you know it."

"Yes, but you can't say no," Myles said. Jude and I exchanged glances. "Not if you want to pass exams which the Sixth are marking. Not if you want to get on the teams that matter – that you *know* you deserve to be on." He was talking quietly now, all the anger gone from his voice, as if he was talking to himself. "How would you like it if your House blamed you for being at the bottom of the tables, and it's all your fault because to get on the team, all you had to do… All you had to do, is…something you'd have done anyway. All you wanted was a choice."

My jaw had literally dropped open, but Jude gave me a meaningful look and mouthed, "Go. Let me speak to him." I didn't want to, but Jude gestured towards the door and I beat a retreat. Closing the door as quietly as I could, I leaned against it for a moment to catch my thoughts; the afternoon had changed so suddenly to one of quiet companionship to something much darker. My stomach clenched in sympathy as I relived Myles words and I realised that I'd never given much thought to boys in his position. One simply fagged. If you were lucky, that simply meant endless chores, fetching water, running to the shop, doing errands, running messages, making tea, being yelled at. Beaten when cheeky. But some older boys wanted more, and Myles was right – to say no was stupid, so everyone said yes. Even Myles.

Chapter Eleven

I sat on my bed for a while, feeling a little shut out. I knew that Jude and Myles had had a few more days' companionship so it made sense that Jude perhaps would find it easier to talk to him alone, but still, I couldn't help but feel excluded, and I hadn't quite got over my concern that Jude would tell Myles about our kiss.

The weight of my secret seemed heavier than ever with Myles' admission, and after ten minutes or so of pacing around, I went back to Myles' room and knocked.

Myles opened it himself, and stood aside to let me in. "Jude's gone," he said. His eyes were a little pink but I knew that it would be vile of me to comment on it.

"It's not Jude I wanted to see," I said. "Myles…I… I haven't been entirely honest with either you or Jude. I wasn't sent down."

"You already told me that."

"Yes, but that's it; I wasn't being honest. I wasn't sent down, but…well…" I fixed him with an imploring look, "my friend was, you see?"

"Oh." Myles sat down with a thump. "I do see. Unless your friend was the Old Man's wife."

"Don't be an ass." I sat down opposite to him. I'd decided to tell him that, and no more. The kiss with Jude was nothing to do with anything, and matters were complicated enough.

He was frowning, deep in thought, then said, "You know what this means?"

"I don't see that it means anything."

"Philip knew about all of us."

"But you…you said it was theft."

"I lied – or rather, only said half of it. I was accused of theft – and…the other thing. When I arrived, and they told me there were going to be three of us, of course I thought I was going to be the unnatural one. Then Jude turned up, and –"

"You had your suspicions about him?" I risked a smile.

He responded to that, smiling back, broadly. "He doesn't make much of a secret of it, though, does he? So I thought I'd test him out, gave him a few opening salvos, as it were, but he didn't seem to know what I meant."

"I rather think he did," I said, remembering Jude's hints of Myles' 'persistence.' "But with both of your stories, I'm not surprised he didn't seem to. You must have startled him."

"I hadn't thought of that. Ring for some tea, will you?" He pointed to the bell pull by the fireplace. "I'll find Jude in a while. So what's your story?"

I rang the bell as directed. "Much the same as both of you, except that for some reason they didn't send me down and kept me there for another year until after my exams."

"Both of you?"

"No, my friend left immediately, he had family to take him away. I don't know why Philip kept me there for a year."

"So this happened a year ago?" I nodded. "Well, it proves it, doesn't it?" he said, as a servant, obviously his valet (and looking quite as forbidding as Jude had described, dark and swarthy with hollowed looking cheekbones) arrived. We had to pause while Myles ordered tea and when we were alone again, Myles jumped up. "What I mean is – it proves I was right about Philip – not only does he want to give us a second chance, but he picked us! After being sent down we'd have had little enough chance as it was, but with that added scandal on top of it all? Did you have anywhere

Mere Mortals

else to go? Anyone who would have taken you in? Anyone you knew who would have given you a career?"

"No." Archeson had, of course, promised that I would always have a place in his family's business, but that hope had been torn from me after we'd been caught.

"Me either, and I'll wager a shilling, if I had one, that Jude didn't either. No – it would have been the workhouse or the streets for us. Left to do as well as we could – and that's all we could have looked forward to. Philip saved us, more surely than Jude's Armitage saved those fags."

"You're right," I said, "And it's not something we'll ever be able to thank him for."

Myles grinned. "No, that's probably true. I'll go and find our Salome, shall I? We can celebrate our good fortune by stuffing ourselves with pastries."

I laughed as he fairly ran out of the door; it seemed food was Myles' solution to all life's peaks and troughs.

Tea arrived carried by a parlour maid, and Michael, which I now knew to be the name of Myles' valet. When they finished setting it up, Myles and Jude reappeared and from their smiling faces I could see that the status quo had been restored. With the door safely locked, and enough crumpets and cakes to satisfy even Myles' constitution, Myles encouraged me to tell my story to Jude. He had the good grace to look suitably surprised, for which I felt grateful.

Feeling warm and full, I undid my jacket, and Myles looked over at me. "New watch, Crispin?" He pulled open his own jacket and showed me a similar timepiece. "Jude too. I like the way he treats us all entirely the same, even down to the inscription, if yours is the same as mine?" He unscrewed the chain and handed me the watch, with the case open.

I smiled. "Yes, exactly the same. But then, wouldn't be right for him to have favourites."

Myles reached down beside the fireplace and pulled up a sheaf of papers, "I'm assuming you all received these too? Have you looked at them?"

We both admitted that we hadn't, and both for the same reasons, we'd opened our presents first and then had forgotten the less interesting pull of schoolwork. Jude and I exchanged guilty glances at that. "So tell us, then," I said, "as you are clearly dying to, and we are ignorant of the toil we are going to be undergoing."

"It's not what I was expecting," he said. He handed me the first page which had been neatly written in a meticulous sloping hand. "Languages of course, because we'll need those if we plan to go up to university but nothing else in a scholarly vein."

Jude leaned over and read over my shoulder. "Fencing, politics, dancing...dancing? Music, literature, riding." He looked over at Myles. "That's an odd mix. Unless there's a dungeon below the house flowing with fresh water and green grass, where the blazes are we supposed to be learning to ride?"

"It's all to polish us, I suppose," Myles said. "Philip didn't exactly make a secret of the fact that he considered us a little unsophisticated."

"That's hardly anything to be surprised about, though, is it?" Jude said, "We didn't have the advantages of mixing with the cream of English youth." I looked at him sharply, but he appeared for once to be serious and not attempting wit. "Perhaps the best schools have a lesser selection of orphans."

"That's probably exactly it," I said. "Our educations were paid for by someone – our natural fathers, perhaps."

The other two nodded, and Myles took over. "Men, who out of duty felt beholden to provide some sort of education, but, as no-one will ever know that they *are* the father, other than their legal representative – who of course will keep their secrets for as long as they are paying – there would no need to spend too much on a secret son."

We were silent for a long while after that, then Myles said, "But with Philip, do you think that's the reason he's done this?"

"It would make sense," I said, nodding. "Perhaps he failed a natural son, didn't provide an education for him."

"Or," mused Jude, "he never found him. He knew that he'd fathered a child, but the mother disappeared without trace."

"Another thing we can never ask him," I said.

"He might trust us enough to tell us one day."

"Or the servants might tell us," Myles said.

"Myles!" Jude said, sounding shocked, "you wouldn't indulge in servant's gossip?"

"Can't see why not," he said. "They know everything, you know that, or you should, if your school was anything like mine."

"No, but…it simply isn't done."

"He's right, Myles," I said. "You can't. And Philip – we've got to earn his trust."

"Oh you two, listen to yourselves! I'm not suggesting going downstairs and befriending the scullery maids. I'm just saying that servants tend to talk, to themselves and to their charges. We've each got a valet, so if they say anything, remember it and let the other two know. I want to know more about Philip, and I won't believe for one minute that you both aren't burning with as much curiosity as I am."

"Well, yes…" Jude admitted, "but…"

"I won't ask you to dent your sensibilities, Jude, I'm simply suggesting a way to find out about our mysterious benefactor that doesn't include snooping in his study or asking questions that Witheridge is likely to report back."

I felt uncomfortable at Myles' suggestion, even though I realised it was likely the only way that we'd find anything out about Philip at all. There was no-one here to ask, and now I was here, cut off with no-one but my new friends and the staff to call upon, I wish that I had been bold enough to ask Dr Baynes more about my guardian, and had not been mired in self-conscious shyness and shame.

"Has no-one called here since you arrived?" I asked them.

"No-one," Jude said. "I can't say I'm surprised. The weather being as foul as it has been, and of course Philip wasn't at home and that would be known, locally, wouldn't it? Why do you ask?"

"I met someone on the way here. We shared the coach and the boat."

"Wherry," said Myles. "You came in Old Tom's wherry. So did we. My valet told me the name for it. Who was it?"

"A doctor. Dr Baynes."

"You mentioned him at dinner."

"Yes… He said he lived nearby as the crow flies, but a fair way by boat, which was the only way you could get there. Didn't you see Philip's reaction when I mentioned him?"

"No, I didn't. Did you, Jude?"

"Not really," Jude said. "Or, not at all, to be perfectly frank. Why, what did Philip do?"

"Nothing, of course," Myles said. "Crispin's making it up. He was perfectly normal all the way through the meal."

"No, seriously, Crispin," Jude repeated. "What did he do?"

"Well…" I regretted saying anything. Myles had gone back to scowling. "Not anything startling, but he just stopped speaking." It sounded unreal and stupid, even to my own ears.

"He stopped speaking while you were," Myles said, dryly. "How terrible."

I gave up and gave a laugh, but the feeling of curiosity didn't die away. Despite their scepticism, I still felt there was something between Baynes and Philip, and although it was none of my business, I couldn't help but wonder what it was, even if the other two didn't.

Over the next few days we revelled in what little leisure we knew we had left. We assumed, although no-one had specifically advised us, that we wouldn't be embarking on our schedule until we had the clothes for the various activities involved, and as no-one gave us any instructions it seemed that our guess had been right.

However, on the fourth day after Philip's departure, and just as expected, for I'd been looking for it since finishing breakfast, I saw Old Tom's wherry coming into sight around the bend of the river. I couldn't see who was in the boat with him, but the wherry tacked across from the far side toward the jetty and I raced along the corridor, calling out the news to the other two.

We hung over the stairs, like Arch had once told me had done at one of his parents' parties, children to our core, expecting presents. It was mildly disappointing, as no-one called us down, and our valets did not appear with armfuls of packages. We eventually made the trip downstairs en masse to seek information. It has to be said that in the main, and apart from lunch and dinner, we had stayed upstairs while Philip was away because there was something so glacially polite about Witheridge that we all, I'm sure we felt the same way, felt intimidated. Although I was becoming accustomed to asking Albert to do my bidding, and gradually was learning to give him orders, the thought of facing Witheridge in the same way would take more courage than I currently possessed.

There was no-one around in the hallway. Jude looked down the gallery and shook his head. "Perhaps we could go into the morning-room and ring?"

"And ask what? Who arrived?" I said.

"Why not? We are, although it takes some getting used to, the heads of the household in Philip's absence. Who's oldest?"

We swapped birthdates and found that Jude was the eldest, by a month, and that I was the youngest, by six.

"Well, it was your idea," Myles said with a smile, "and as you are now in loco parentis, go to it, sir. Although, don't try bossing us around."

We followed Jude into the morning-room and stood grinning while he stood by the bellrope as if summoning up some courage, before pulling it sharply. Myles and I threw ourselves into the chairs around the fire, affecting what we hoped were natural poses. In less than a minute – and every tick of the clock of that minute was as loud as any I'd heard – the door opened and Witheridge himself sailed in. I know that I was hoping that a footman would be considered good enough for the young gentlemen, and I could see by Jude's face that perhaps he felt the same.

"Yes, sirs?" Witheridge said.

"Thank you, Witheridge," Jude said. "We noticed Tom's wherry pulling at the jetty earlier. We wondered if anything was wrong."

"Nothing wrong, sir," Witheridge gave the smallest of nods, his sang-froid entirely in place. "Merely the usual delivery of provisions. He calls here on a regular basis, brings what is ordered, and takes the post."

"And he didn't bring anything for us."

"No, sir. Were you expecting something in the post? The master did not acquaint me –"

"No, it's all right, Witheridge," Jude said, handling himself far better than I could have done, magnificently managing the butler with not even a stammer to betray any insecurity. He might have been giving orders to servants all his life.

"Was there anything else, sir?"

"No, thank you."

Once Witheridge had gone, Jude sank onto a chair, a feeling of relief on his face. "Phew," he said. "I suppose one will get used to doing that."

"You did well," I said. Myles was chortling.

"It was a little like summoning the Head to one's own room. And it didn't achieve anything. I was so hoping it was our pretty new clothes."

"Why didn't you ask him that, then?" Myles asked.

"Oh, I don't know," Jude said, "it didn't seem to be the sort of thing one asks. However," he said with a smile, "I hadn't thought about post. I think I'll take your advice and write to my friend. Just to see if he is all right."

"And what do you think you could do if he's not?" Myles said with a sneer. "Are you sure you'd want to know if he'd been arrested? More to the point, wouldn't you be concerned that he might turn Queen's evidence like that sod did over the telegraph case?"

"I read about that," I said. "Myles is right –"

"Thanks, Crispy!"

"God, Myles, don't ever call me Crispy again. But no, Jude, Myles is right, you do need to be careful. You can't guarantee that Philip would support you publicly, it's quite likely he wouldn't."

"And it's not just you, either," Myles said, hotly. "You've got to think of the rest of us. If your past gets dragged up, then they might start digging into all of our pasts and then how would it look?"

I looked aghast at Myles. "Surely you can't mean –"

"You know what the newspapers can be like, same as I do," he said. "I think you should ask Philip before you write, Jude."

"At least wait until he comes back," I advised. "Then think about it."

Jude sat looking at us for a moment, his face serious, and a muscle twitching in his cheek. "I know," he said finally. "I know. You are right, of course. One forgets that one isn't really safe, even now."

With a repeat performance of the day before, the clothes arrived the very next day and they fulfilled all of our expectations, even Jude who was shameless in his adoration. Myles refused to join in the unpacking at all, closeting himself in the library as the valets deposited box after box in our rooms. I left Albert to it, and found Jude who was giving Paul difficulties by insisting on examining every single article that came out.

"Look!" he said, upon my appearance. "Three sets of evening clothes. Three! I asked Paul if perhaps yours and Myles' had been packed with mine but it appears not. And look at the shine on these shoes! Riding is certainly on the agenda..." He leaned forward and grabbed some riding breeches, half buried under embroidered waistcoats and delightfully coloured ascots and held them up for my inspection. His enthusiasm was impossible to ignore and we went through every item which I was expected to admire thoroughly. It wasn't hard to do. After an hour pandering to Jude's happiness I felt exhausted but now more excited to see what treasures lay in my own room. Finding Albert gone, I pulled open the top drawer of my clothes chest, almost with a sense of an explorer finding a secret cave.

It was hard not to be impressed with the luxury and largesse of Philip's gifts to us, but his extravagance was understandable. We were now under his protection, and as such, we must appear as well-bred, and as well-dressed as he was himself, particularly once we began to meet his friends and neighbours, as he had promised that we soon would. But as I worked my way through the drawers and opened the wardrobe to see the wonders hanging there, I noticed something familiar in the styles and patterns. Pulling out one of the brocade waistcoats, gold satin with a pattern of black flowers, I held it up to the light, scrutinising the exquisite stitching. It definitely looked familiar. Taking it with me, I took it through into Jude's room. He was still there, wallowing in the clothes on his bed.

"What is it?" he said, noticing the waistcoat.

"Haven't you got one like this? I'm sure I saw something like it."

"I'm not sure. Maybe it's already been put away, Paul, check the waistcoats for Crispin, will you?"

I handed the thing to Paul and left him to search Jude's wardrobe. After a moment he handed me back the waistcoat and another one, identical in all respects save for the placement of the flowers stitched upon it. He left us alone after that.

"Well, that's a mercy you spotted that," Jude said. "How galling it would be to be wearing them both at the same time."

"May I have a look through your chest of drawers, Jude?" I said, suddenly inspired by an idea.

"My drawers are at your convenience."

I pulled open drawer after drawer and was soon convinced of my theory. It seemed sensible, I suppose, surely it was easier to buy three sets of the same clothes in differing sizes, than to ask a tailor, at short measure, to provide so many different items.

"It looks like we've got identical wardrobes," I confirmed, finally. "I'll wager that Myles has too." I expounded my theory of convenience, and Jude nodded.

"Well, I am pleased you noticed," he said. "And it explains why we have three sets of evening clothes, at least. I don't think it will present much of problem, with the amount we've been given. We will just have to communicate with each other so we don't end up in the same ensemble. Of course I will outshine you all, even if that were to happen."

Laughing, I pushed him over onto the bed, and he sprawled, loose-limbed among the waistcoats and cravats. His eyes were dark with wickedness and when I kissed him they closed, but the wickedness remained. "Lock the door," he said. It was the only coherent thing he said for a long while.

Chapter Twelve

It was almost decadence to get dressed that evening. Taking Jude's suggestion we agreed (although it took a little arguing and not a few coin tosses) who was to wear which evening suit. Albert took extraordinary pains with my toilette, and insisted that I use the dreaded showerbath at last. "The master stressed that it must be used," he said, his voice brooking no objection.

"I swear," I grumbled, stepping tentatively into the apparatus, "you are as much a tough as any boy at my school. Are you sure that water isn't too hot?"

"I have tested it sir, and it gets cooler at every moment." He sounded a little reproachful and I shut my mouth, which indeed I had to do as the water cascaded down over me. It was quite a singular experience, but not entirely unpleasant. However, all in all, I thought that I preferred a normal bath; at least I was left alone, and had time to think. I scrubbed dutifully until he was quite certain he'd soaked me enough then dried my eyes, stinging from the soap, with the cloth Albert passed me. I stepped out at last, into a robe held out for me, and wallowed luxuriously in the feel of the padded satin against my skin.

"Sit down please, sir," Albert said, indicating the dressing table. I did as I was instructed, while Albert wrapped my shoulders in snowy white cloths.

I frowned. "You aren't going to shave me again?" I complained. "It will take me a month just to grow the skin back from last time."

"Not at all, sir." He picked up a bottle from the table. There were a dozen there, and they all looked the same. None of them were labelled, but it seemed Albert knew which was which. "My father worked at the late king's Shampoo House, and I learned the tricks of the trade, so if you'll allow me?" He poured some of the liquid onto his hands and then worked it into my hair. It was cold but I didn't complain, I thought I'd been enough of a baby for one day.

"What is that stuff, Albert?"

"It's simply a preparation to invigorate the scalp, sir," he said, rubbing briskly. He was certainly good at it. No-one had done anything like it to me before, you certainly couldn't count the very few times I'd been scoured by attendants at school when found with parasites of one type or other. His fingers were strong and soothing and before long I'd closed my eyes and let myself relax my head dropping back, supported only by his hands. I may have even dropped off, because it seemed only a moment before he was saying, "I'll have to wash off the lotion now, sir. I have had some more warm water brought up."

Feeling beautifully refreshed, I let him lead me back through into the bathroom and let him rinse the lotion into a bowl. "The water looks dark," I said.

"You might find that the Broads water reacts on your hair, sir," he said, as he rubbed my hair dry again. "It's a peculiarity of the region, I believe. Something to do with the excretion of the sap in the reeds, I've been told. However you should become acclimatised in time."

"What sort of reaction?"

"Your hair may darken a little," he said. "Mine did, when I first moved here."

His hair was not too dissimilar in shade, so it seemed he was right. I peered in the mirror. It was impossible to tell if there was any difference, with my hair still damp, but perhaps a change had already begun, I didn't make a habit of gazing at myself endlessly and my hair colour changed anyway, with the seasons, so it didn't bother me much.

So eventually I was primped and preened and dressed in clothes that seemed suitable for a crown prince. Even Albert looked a little pleased as he regarded me over my shoulder in the looking glass. He gave an almost paternal nod, as if admiring his own work.

We admired each other in our sartorial glory during dinner. It didn't bother Myles in the slightest that we all had the same clothes, and I rather expected it would not. "Let's face it," he said, stifling a yawn, "we've never had anything like them unless they were hand-me-downs from older boys with no brothers."

We both nodded, although I hadn't even had as good as that. My clothes were generally what I could scramble from a pile of discarded uniforms at the end or beginning of each term. Sometimes the trousers were scratchy, and brought my legs out in red spots, and sometimes (or to be honest just once,) they were 'inherited' from the son of an Earl and were as smooth and cool as a silk glove against my skin.

"Why are you so tired, anyway?" Jude asked Myles. "I've had to walk around the house ten times today just to relieve some of the tension." I jumped as he rubbed his lower leg against mine, but I don't think Myles saw.

"My man had me trying on every blasted outfit in every permutation possible," Myles said, grimacing. "It was hell, and it felt as though it took a week."

"I can imagine," I laughed, grateful that Albert had spared me that.

"You didn't think –" Myles said, looking from me to Jude, as if realising how ungrateful he sounded.

"Don't mistake us, Jude," I said. "We are not ungrateful. We are just unused to it. I myself think I'm never going to be a silk purse, although you are already more than halfway there, and I think Myles could pretend to be so."

"Well, thank you," Myles said with a gracious nod. "But he's right. I'm more than a little concerned that all the lessons and clothes in the world won't make my edges smooth." He yawned again and pushed his glass of port away. "I'm going to bed. Early start tomorrow."

"What?" The wine had made my wits a little dull, and I smiled, recalling Myles words. Rough edges.

"The schedule, timetable, whatever you call it," he said, pushing his chair away. "No, it's all right, Evans," he said to the footman who was still attending us, making me wonder at his ability to have learned the servant's name. I hadn't managed to name more than the valets and the butler. He stood up. "The schedule, it starts tomorrow. We have music at ten. And as I have heard Jude's impression of Tormequada on the piano, and you, luckily, have not, I intend to have an early night so at least I can sit there with a smile on my face and not nursing a headache."

We bade him goodnight and after settling down in a corner of the withdrawing room, a bottle of brandy between us, Jude dismissed the footman, Evans. Jude gave a heavy sigh when the door closed and I looked over at him, with a questioning expression. "So, you find them a trifle…over attentive, too, do you?"

"I do, dear thing, although I am trying to fit into the mould that seems to be so readily there for us." He sat back, his brandy untouched by his side. "It's simply that one hasn't been used to it. Oh, I know we *think* we know what is expected, I'm sure that like me, you learned most of it from simply being there, from being the smallest one at the table, learning how to pass the salt and finally graduating to the port after years of an education of watching, listening, observing. Never really fitting in, because to be – to have, no, *to be* nothing, was somehow not done. And how dare you be nothing in their school, in their presence?" He gave a small, tired laugh. "It was almost a relief when I found out that I was different, because I'd felt like an outsider all my life and suddenly I had a good reason for it."

"I know how you feel," I said.

"Of course you do," he said gently. "And Myles too. I think he's taking it hardest, although there's no need for any of us to struggle." I looked up at him and found him looking straight back at me. "Don't you think? We are all flies, trapped in beautiful amber."

"I…" He confused me.

"I mean, you sweet old thing, that Myles is right. We only need to accept…all this. We are gentlemen enough to put on a brave face, and the servants here are like something from a play, or a palace. I think that if we ran naked, painted bright green with weed from the river, that they would do nothing more than wait silently with warm towels. It appears they were well prepared for us," he finished, "even if we were not."

"They are a little daunting."

"Of course they are, They serve," he waved an eloquent hand around, "all *this*. They have reason to be proud. You could put them into powdered wigs and knee breeches and us into fashions of two-hundred years since and nothing would have changed, not below stairs, I'll warrant it."

"Nor much above it," I said, with a glance around at the portraits and displays of china. "I suppose the big houses are like that."

We sat in silence for a while longer, but neither of us said much else. I was wondering what 'music' meant in the morning, for I had no experience of lessons in the subject. I also wanted to kiss Jude, for watching him staring into the fire, lost in thought, he looked as if he needed me to. But the moment passed and we stood up as the clock struck eleven.

"I'll say goodnight here," he said, at the door. "I'll leave the ubiquitous Albert to tuck you in. I want to find a book."

"Goodnight, Jude," I said. "I look forward to hearing you torture Philip's piano. Although how hands like yours could be anything but artistic, I can't imagine."

"How kind of you, dear Crispin," he said, brushing a finger down my cheek, his airy flirtatious tone having returned at last.

"Goodnight, Jude," I said again, but I was stayed by his hand catching mine, stopping me from opening the door. I turned to him, and found his face quite serious, his eyes large as if asking a question I'd already answered, days before. In a heartbeat he was close, then closer still and there was nothing but Jude, his scent, the butterfly whisper of his hair against my cheek as he buried his mouth against my neck. Tingles ran down my spine, delicious shivers that I remember from when Arch used to whisper wickedness into my ear. I laughed softly, tipping my head to one side to give his mouth more space, for there was not much, with my cravat as it was. He pressed his body harder against mine, his arousal obvious and meeting mine with firm determination. I wrapped my arms around his waist, and let them slide down, seeking the curve of his lower back, that subtle curve some men possessed, and which always drew my attention, especially in the fashions of the day.

He groaned as my hands slid beneath his coat tails and he raised his head, his lips damp in the candlelight. His lips opened even as I bent towards him and the kiss was sweeter than the one I remembered. There was something beautifully yielding about him, and it was new, so new to me, for Arch had been all heat and muscle. With Jude I had time to taste, to feel and to explore as he waited, patiently, for me to find him out.

"Jude," I said, pulling back.

"No," he said. "Not yet." His hands fumbled with my trouser buttons, and there was nothing I could do to stop him, nor did I want to. "Not yet."

I claimed his mouth again, as he opened my buttons and took me into his hand. The fear of our situation melted as all thoughts of where or even who I was vanished for the moment. I found myself making noises I'd never made before, small desperate cries of pleasure, which only spurred Jude on, I could feel him smiling against my mouth, and when he broke away himself, he whispered my name, sounding like *yes*, and *now* and *thank you* all at the same time. After a year of being untouched, there was no way I was going to last long and I knew it, as warmth and pressure built and burst almost before I had time to really enjoy it. I felt a cool cloth against the sensitive top of my member, the thoughtful man had anticipated my emission (although, really, he hardly needed to have any mind reading abilities).

I huffed through my nose in an embarrassed fashion, and looked away. "I'm sorry…"

In response he kissed my cheek. "Don't be absurd, dear, that was rather the point, was it not? And after all, this is a new suit of clothes. The kerchief I can wash out, or at the very least Paul will think nothing of a cloth in this state. But I would not want to leave a stain on this lovely suit that would need to sponged out. Questions might be asked below stairs, if so." He stepped back, letting me button myself up. "I think it's best to avoid that, don't you?"

I moved to pull him towards me, but he skipped to one side. "Goodnight, Crispin. Think of me, won't you?" And he slid out of the door leaving me rather weak in the knees. It took me a few moments to pull myself together before I left the room and went to bed, and I lay awake for a long time reliving the feel of his hands on my cock and the feeling of his breath on my skin. The night crawled past. I watched the moon arc slowly across the sky, cut into little pieces by the tiny diamond window panes, as I tried over and over again to sleep. In the end I rose, lit some candles and sat in the window seat, wrapped in my counterpane, while I tried to read. Something was nagging at my brain, and as much as I tried to recall what it was, I couldn't recall it. It was like attempting to remember a dream; the more you try to hold on to it, the further and faster it slips away. In the end I made do with my book, letting my mind loose in adventure and mountains and ladies in peril.

The moon had vanished completely by the time I was tired enough to try to sleep again; I was just pulling the heavy covers over me, wishing I had the gall to ring for a new warming bottle when the missing memory slid back into my mind, like piece of a puzzle that had never been away. *Music.* Myles had said music, but that wasn't right, was it? I clambered across the bed, pulling open the drawer on the far bedside table, where I'd put Philip's notes after a cursory glance. The papers spilled onto the bed, and I searched through them hurriedly. Yes – there it was. The next day, clearly delineated in a neat list. Morning: Latin. Afternoon: Greek. There was no music on it. . I frowned, then realised that there was nothing I could do about it now. Myles would realise he'd been wrong in the morning and we could tease him about it, that was all.

❧ Chapter Thirteen ❧

It was with a very thick head that I faced the world the next day. Albert woke me after what appeared to me to be moments after my finally managing to sleep; I did not thank him for it. He brought me coffee and eggs but it didn't help to refresh me for my lack of sleep; I wished myself back a day, so I could curl back into bed with no duty. This was impossible, of course, for Albert stood, patient as one of the windpumps on the horizon and just as immovable, waiting to ready me for the work to come.

The other two were nowhere to be seen as I was led into the morning-room, in which a table had been laid out with pens, ink and paper, and an easel-style chalkboard at a short distance from the door. I sat at the table and waited, for it was yet two or three minutes from the hour. The textbooks were familiar to me, which reassured me. Latin was, at least, one subject I felt comfortable about. I was less confident of my Greek, for although I had taken end of school exams, and my ongoing studies would not be as vital as would Myles' and Jude's, I felt that a general polish of Greek would do me no harm at all.

I stood as the door opened, realising for the first time that who-ever would be teaching us – unless Witheridge was hiding a talent for tutoring – would be a stranger, and indeed he was. The man that entered was the epitome of how I imagined Philip would look when I saw him in my mind's eye, except not so tall. Stocky, with broad shoulders, black, curling hair with matching sideburns.

He was dressed, (surprisingly, for I was used now to everyone in Philip's employ to be dressed beautifully), in rusty black, shiny around the lapels. As he reached my table, he dropped a book, knelt down to retrieve them, then raised his eyes to meet mine. With the lower part of his face obscured by the table. I stiffened in surprise; it was unmistakably the unmannerly man I'd met by the boathouse, the one I'd assumed to be some kind of gardener. With the same dark, suspicious glance, it was impossible not to know his face and I couldn't help but wonder what he was doing there, and why he had been so rude.

His name at least was soon to be no mystery. "I am your tutor for today, Mr Thorne. My name is Heriment. If you will pick up your Cicero, we will begin." Other than the wary glance he'd given me, he showed no sign that he'd seen me before.

"Good morning," I said, forcing him to glare further at me as I underlined his unmannerly behaviour "Is there any reason why we are not being tutored together?"

"My schedule tells me that for Classics I tutor Mr Thorne on Tuesday, Mr Middleton on Wednesday and Mr Graham on Friday. More than that I neither know, nor need to know."

Although he gave the impression that he was speaking with the same implacable response as did Witheridge and the valets, I could sense that it was not the unruffled sang-froid the other servants displayed. He was an interesting man, this new tutor; I was looking forward to swapping notes with the others, as well as anticipating as to what the others would say the music tutor was like.

I could get nothing more from Heriment for the remainder of the morning; we went back to what he probably considered to be basics, and he tested me thoroughly on grammar, as well as making me copy out sections of Virgil in précis to see whether I was legible and could understand the concepts. He did not let me know one way or the other within the lesson, and gave no indication – his mien being disgruntled throughout – as to my merits or failure. At precisely thirty minutes past midday he closed his book, and left the room without even a word of farewell, leaving me feeling as if I'd been quizzed by the most ardent scholar, and much in need of sustenance perhaps accompanied by a very large glass of hock.

Myles was in situ at the table, ahead of me in the wine by at least one drink, as there was only a drop at the bottom of his glass. I threw myself into the place set opposite him. The footman poured for me, and set the table-napkin in my lap.

"You have ink on your nose," Myles said. "What a schoolboy you are."

"I don't care. I could be covered in ink for all I care. I had the worst Latin lesson I've had in my life. The tutor is unbearable." I took a large mouthful of wine, then another before setting my glass down and taking a deep breath. I could feel the wine sliding into my limbs and calming me down. "Where's Jude?"

"I have no idea."

"Was his playing so awful that he's retired to kill himself?"

"He wasn't with me. I assumed he was with you."

"No, I wish he had – I wish you both had been, it would have been far less of an ordeal if you have been there. Oh. That confirms my suspicions then – we are all doing different things at different times." I finished my wine as a plate of sole was placed in front of me. "It seems very practical."

"Typical Philip, in fact," Myles said, raising his refilled glass as if to toast the man. "Or what we've seen of him so far."

I nodded and turned to the footman. I didn't have the faintest idea whether it was the same one that Myles had mentioned before and I reminded myself to speak to Witheridge; we needed to learn people's names. "Is Mr Middleton to join us?"

"No, sir," he said, without looking at me. "Mr Middleton will be lunching elsewhere."

"In the house?"

"No, sir."

"Where, then?"

"I'm sorry sir, that's not something I can say." Again, answers which meant nothing. He didn't say he didn't know, just that he couldn't say. As correct as Philip's servants were, they were infuriating at times.

"Is Mr Middleton expected for dinner?"

"He is, sir. Should I let you know when he comes in? I could arrange for Albert to inform you."

Nettled, I snapped, "Yes. Thank you. If you'd be so kind."

"Very good, sir." He left the room with the empty decanter and I applied myself to the sole with some irritation.

I looked up to see Myles smiling at me.

"Well, Crispy. You are a surprising mix. I can see what Jude means. One moment a purring cat, the next spitting venom. You could have been raised to privilege."

"Well, I wasn't. I wish I had been, if it meant I knew how to deal with these footmen. I think I'll pay more attention when Philip returns and see how he does it. And don't call me Crispy."

"I would suspect that he doesn't need to try. He has breeding and privilege running through every vein. His family is ancient. I doubt there's ever been any time when the Smallwoods haven't expected to be obeyed."

I finished my sole and looked across at him. "What do you know about Philip's family?"

He smiled, a new smile as if I'd said something to make him happy. It suited him. "There's a library, remember? Filled to the brim with books, and unsurprisingly there are quite a few books on the Smallwoods. It's funny, isn't it? There's us three with no lineage, empty words in empty spaces. And he has books on the subject."

"When you say ancient, how ancient?"

"The only ancient that matters. His great-great goodness knows how many greats-grandfather came over with William the Conqueror, of course. Moinsbois they were called then. It seems the Moinsbois displeased the court at some point, and settled in Norfolk."

"Not here. The house isn't that old."

"Of course not. This place came a lot later but the family re-mained Catholic. Which is interesting."

I perked up at that, every schoolboy knew about Henry the Eighth and his removing himself from Rome. "That couldn't have been easy."

"I bow to thee, master of understatement," Myles gave a short laugh.

"And still Catholic today?" To me, coming from a diet of unre-lenting Church of England hymns and prayers, all I knew of the Catholic faith was what I had learned in books. Shadowy figures, enemies of the crown, massacres and persecution. A faith that had split the country more than once. Catholics had converted to the Church of England or pretended to, or they'd fled the persecu-tions. Even in these times where it was once more a matter of little note, I found it fascinating. I wondered where he worshipped, and wondered why, if he was a Catholic, it hadn't been mentioned. I couldn't see any of us refusing to convert. After all, he'd request-ed other things from us before we'd met him, I'd agreed to take Dominic as an additional name, for one.

"As far as I can tell, it's not something I've asked our new guard-ian. What denomination was the priest you met on the coach?" Myles asked.

I admitted I hadn't the slightest notion and at that point the footman returned with the beef, which we devoured in compan-ionable silence, or if we did speak, it was in generalities. I asked him about his music lesson and he was a little reticent, which sur-prised me, Myles usually being anything but.

"I have dancing later," he said suddenly. "Bally stupid idea if you ask me. Who am I supposed to be dancing with, that old fossil who took me for music?"

"Old fossil?"

"Oh, completely. Claims to have studied under Beethoven, but anyone could say that. Perhaps he had a few lessons with the man when he was too young to learn anything. Perhaps he met him once. Who knows? He's useless. His hands can no longer span the octave and he beats his cane out of time with the bally metronome. He didn't know what Jude was up to, and I've given up asking. Serves me right for being nosy about the wrong things. What about you? What do you have this afternoon?" he asked, looking up at the clockface.

I made a face, "More of the same, I'm afraid. Although Greek torture, not Latin."

"Greek, eh?" He gave such a wicked grin that I choked on my wine, then coughing, I stood up, knowing I was blushing and waved away the proffered apple tartlet. On my way out I grabbed a couple of slightly soft apples from the bowl and made my way back to the morning-room. I was fairly sure that my tutor of the morning would be the same and I wasn't disappointed in that respect and knowing well that my Latin far eclipsed my Greek, all I could do was to be grateful that we were going back to basics and that I didn't have to dazzle anyone with my recitation. He was no easier on me than he had that morning and by four in the afternoon, when he left me feeling trampled, with a headache rising behind my eyes, I was glad to see the back of him.

I went to my room instead of seeking the others out and rang for Albert. It wasn't until after I'd rung the bell that I realised how comfortable I was becoming with some of the customs of the house, ringing for servants, waving aside food that once I would have been grateful to receive. I was flat on the bed when Albert spoke from beside the bed. "Yes, sir?"

I struggled up, my fringe falling into my eyes. I pushed it back and peered at Albert, and my head throbbed at the effort of my movement. "Albert, do you have anything to ease a pain in my head and my eye? I'm afraid that the first day's study didn't agree with me at all."

"Of course, sir. If you wish I'll douse the lights nearest to you?"

"Thank you, Albert," I said gratefully, and slumped back onto the pillows and waited. When he returned with something in a glass, I swallowed the bitter liquid without caring or questioning what it was and lay in the blessed dark as the headache overwhelmed me. I'd had these headaches before, but rarely in the winter and it had been months since last I'd felt as bad as this. The potion made me sleepy, but the pain didn't recede. It came and went in waves, pumping in time with my heartbeat and finally creating a feeling of sea-sickness which led inevitably to me losing what little lunch I had managed to eat. After that I just lay miserably, listening to the quarter hours chime interminably and wanting to die – and dreading that I wouldn't.

The first time Arch had seen me like this, he'd been shocked – like so many bluff sportsmen, he was rarely ill himself, and when he was it was usually with something physical like a sprained wrist or a torn muscle. I think that he didn't believe, not truly, in my headaches, that he couldn't believe that a "mere headache" could completely poleaxe anyone. The fact that it often coincided with a spat between us, or when prepping for exams, added to his derision. He'd tell me to "buck up" and "not to be an ass," more often than not.

I must have fallen asleep, perhaps aided by Albert's magic liquid and when I woke I opened my eyes slowly, gradually realising with the elation that always followed such a bout of pain, that the throbbing nausea had gone. My left eye and temple could still feel the after-effects but it was almost gone. I pushed myself up, to find both Myles and Jude sitting in the gloom by my fire. Jude appeared to be asleep, his head resting on the wing of the chair, but Myles was awake and he turned, hearing me shift in the bed.

"I have to say, Crispin, this tutor of yours has made Jude and I a little nervous. If he can enchant you into insensibility after just one day."

"Shut up," I said. I felt embarrassed. "I'm starving. Did I miss dinner?"

"You can't be that ill, then. Yes, you missed it but your Albert said to ring when you woke up, and he would bring you up a tray. He knew almost exactly to the quarter hour what time you would wake, too, so we thought we would sit and wait." He looked over at Jude, who was snoring gently. "At least I managed to keep my eyes open."

I slid off the bed and moved closer to the fire. Someone had removed my boots, cravat and jacket while I had slept and I hadn't even noticed. "Ring the bell, then," I said. "Where was Jude today?"

"Outdoor pursuits." Myles face cracked into a grin a mile wide, as he pulled the bellpull. "You should have seen him when he returned. Ruffled would not be describing it. He could hardly walk."

"Riding?" I looked at Jude. Dressed impeccably as he was right now, it was hard to imagine him even slightly ruffled.

"And carriage driving. Not exactly what any of us are used to. Have you done much riding?"

"None at all," I admitted. "You?"

He shook his head. "However, we know it can be done, at least. If Jude can manage it, I mean." He chuckled. "Covered in mud, he was. I think he was hoping to make his room before anyone saw him, but the noise he made climbing the stairs attracted the attention of the house. Apart from you, of course." He kicked Jude on the side of his leg. "Jude. Jude! Wake up. You are drooling."

"You lie," Jude said, coming to himself with a start. "I was merely resting my eyes. How's our patient?"

"Awake and hungry."

"My dear Crispin, if a little Latin and Greek can fell you like a mighty oak – particularly after you passed out from your school and we poor fools have not – I live in hope that my appalling performance in the equine arts does not rate as the most amusing of the three of us." He yawned. "Philip is back, by the way."

"What?" Myles said, leaning forward, "and you chose not to tell me earlier? How do you know?"

"I chose not to tell you earlier, because I wanted to tell you both at once, and this is the first opportunity I have had. As to how I know, it was Philip himself who attended me at my lessons." He looked at his hands. "I have sympathetic hands, apparently, but a seat like a bag of excrement."

"You ride like a sack of shit, in other words."

Jude looked pained. "If you insist, yes. I disappoint even myself."

"How many times did you fall off?"

"I think that question should be banned from polite society in same way one never asks one for one's age."

"You can't remember," Myles said, roaring with laughter.

"I refuse to answer the question," Jude said haughtily. "I admit that Philip had to assist me on the odd occasion."

"I bet Philip wondered what on earth he'd taken on."

"My driving was better," he said. "We'll see how you get on tomorrow, then, shall we?"

That meant I had music and dancing. I breathed a sigh of relief, as Albert brought in a plate of sandwiches and slices of pork pie, enough for us all. I was pleased to have a further day in the house, and one with a less demanding tutor, by the sound of it; I wasn't particularly looking forward to the rigours of being thrown from a horse for the first time, as I was sure would happen.

⚡ Chapter Fourteen ⚡

O n my way to the larger drawing room the next morning,
I caught sight of Jude making his way down the stairs. I
stood a moment to watch him, a little concerned at how
awkwardly he walked, obviously unaware that he was observed.

Last night he had told us of his first foray into equitation, and
in doing so had not instilled any great confidence in me, for one.

"The horse, I mean, the thing from hell," he'd said, once he'd
awoken sufficiently, had sympathies heaped upon him for his
aches and pains and had been encouraged to tell all. "Surely it
would be better to put us up on something smaller, less than head-
height, at least," he'd grumbled. "I was hoping for something like
our headmaster's wife's trap pony. Small. Grey. Fluffy."

"And it wasn't?" I laughed at the image of Jude, his long legs
almost to the ground on some small grey pony.

"No. It was about twelve feet tall, red as a harlot's knees and as
hard as sin."

"Hard as virtue in your case," snorted Myles.

"And Philip was there? Where was this?"

"He met me there. Paul woke me at some God-awful hour,
helped me to dress, then I was whisked off in a rowing boat be-
longing to a man from the village. The lesson took place on Horsey
beach. No-one told me Philip would be there, so it was a pleasant
surprise. I was frozen, even with the two wool vests I'd insisted on
wearing. God alone knows where the horse from hell came from, I

asked Philip directly and he said he didn't own any horses himself these days."

"He did at some point, then?" I said, interested.

"Apparently so. It seems unlikely but even in this peculiar lake-land but there are hunts. Although I hope," he said, with an exaggerated shudder, "that Philip is not expecting me to mount that…thing…and to go chasing a fox, or anything else at any pace faster than a walk."

He went on to tell us how Philip had told him that he once he had kept his horses at livery at the hunt stables, a fair distance away in Holt, but the horses he was using for lessons were hired from a more local source.

"So how did you fall off?" Myles said.

"It was more a case of how didn't I," Jude said, stretching an arm and nursing his elbow. "You would think that sand would be soft too. The horse didn't like me. I think it sensed I didn't have any authority. All it wanted to do was to eat, and every time it did, I was pulled over its shoulder."

We had roared with laughter at this, thinking that Jude had been thrown while gallantly cantering beside Philip, not standing still and being pitched repeatedly over the horse's head.

Looking at him that morning, as he gingerly made his way down the stairs, it certainly looked as though he'd taken his falls whilst hunting. I assumed he would be grateful to at least sit still for the day, and silently I hoped that he would achieve a more cordial association with Heriment than I had done.

I had more than half an hour to fill before I had to be in my lesson, and after my experience with Heriment (and Myles' description of Drummond, the music "fossil") I wasn't in any mind to be earlier than I needed to be. My musical talent, as far as I knew, was negligible, having never been tested, and I'd never danced in my life. So I wandered off around the house, letting my feet take me the long way around, stopping to look at portraits I hadn't examined before. As I approached Philip's office, the man himself came out, dressed normally, not in riding attire as I imagined he would be. He smiled, seeing me, and I felt that instant warmth of his personality – the way he could make me feel that I was the most important person right now, just because he had turned his attention to me was always a little overwhelming.

"Crispin."

"Good morning, Philip," I said, wishing I had something more intelligent to say than that.

"Come in for a second." He pushed his study door open and let me pass before following me through. "I'd forgotten something, and I'd like a moment with you." He passed through the room, telling me to sit down, which I did, and he disappeared into another door between his bookcases, leaving me alone. I'd been there for a minute or two when the hallway door opened and a footman bought a pile of letters in on a salver and put them on the desk without a word. Philip had not returned and the temptation to take a peek at the top letter was almost irresistible.

Something shiny glittered in the reflective shine of the tray and I leaned around to see what it might be. Almost covered by the pile of correspondence was a watch, and it seemed to be the twin of mine own, the beautiful and precious timepiece that Philip had given me as a welcome gift. In almost a reflex action, my fingers moved to my waistcoat, knowing, before they even reached the chain, that my own watch was in place, familiar to me now by its weight in its designated pocket. I felt myself pale a little – Myles – or more likely Jude, in his tumbles from his hell-horse yesterday, must have misplaced the watch and whichever of them it was, they hadn't noticed. Without a second thought, I reached forward and snatched the watch from the tray. It was cool and heavy in my hand. I felt like a thief, but I wasn't. Not really. I was only returning something to someone who was a little careless – and if the footman didn't mention it to Philip later, which I hoped that he would not – there was no reason why Philip needed to know how negligently his gift had been treated. It should at the very least shame Myles or Jude into looking after the gift in future. Plus, I thought, pocketing the watch furtively, just as Philip came back into the room holding fencing masks and gloves, it wouldn't do my standing with either of the two other boys any harm either.

Philip sat on the edge of the desk and waved me down as I moved as to stand. He looked at me appraisingly. "How are you?"

"I am quite well, thank you. All the better for having some sunshine," I said, glancing out at the watery winter sunlight.

"It helps," he said. "But Witheridge apprised me of your condition last night."

"It was only a headache, sir," I said. "I'm quite well, I assure you."

"Hmm," he said, frowning, and obviously unconvinced. "Pain in the head. In the eye too?"

I nodded, surprised.

"Nausea?"

"Not always, sir, but yes. I am forced to admit it."

"No need. Be assured that I am well informed on what goes on and you are under my protection. How often are you afflicted in this way?"

"Not regularly." I felt ashamed, as if I were less than he had wanted. A sickly ward, an expense he was not expecting. It surprised me that he seemed not to know of my affliction, whatever else he had learned about me, my headaches were obviously not known to him. "The last one I had…" I thought back; I remembered being stricken after Arch had left, but there had been at least a couple of others since. "…was in July, or August. After the rest of the chaps had gone down."

"And you are quite recovered?"

"Absolutely, sir. Ready to sing, or dance, whatever might be the order of the day." I dared not say I suspected it was the weight of the lessons with Heriment that had caused it, for I was not secure in my place to criticise anything that Philip had in place.

He smiled again at that, and I risked a small one in return. "Good. But you must ring for Albert immediately in future, and that's a rule specifically for you. I will not have you ill alone and no-one attending to you. Albert should have…"

"Oh, don't blame him," I said, hurriedly. "He didn't know. I should have rung."

"He should have been on hand when you left your lessons." Philip's voice made it clear that Albert was in disgrace and I felt for my valet. He had done nothing wrong in my eyes, but I didn't know the breadth of Philip's instructions regarding our care. "But it has passed now. Just promise me you will let him know hereafter. In the meantime I will have a physician attend you."

"Really, sir. It's not necess –"

"Please." He raised a hand, his voice as commanding as the word. Then he continued, his tone a little mellowed. "As I am clearly not allowed to blame my staff for their inattention, kindly allow me to decide on whether I wish to summon medical care?" He was smiling, and my nervousness subsided. "That's good. Now, pick up those," he said, pointing to the masks, "and follow me."

He led me into the library where a footman waited. All the furniture had been moved to the sides of the room, leaving the gleaming honey-coloured parquet clear. The footman approached me, waited for me to unbutton my jacket and slid it off my arms, then handed me a pair of canvas shoes and took my day shoes from me. The watch I had taken from the study clinked against its chain as the jacket swung loose but Philip, inspecting a rack of fencing swords, did not look round. The footman held a fencing jacket of some sort in his hands but Philip strode over, took the jacket from him, and turned to me.

"Take off your waistcoat," he said, brusquely. I did so and he dressed me in the padded garment, ordering me to turn around and about as he saw to the fit. "We'll have to get you all your own," he said, as he buckled me in. "I'll send to Michelozzi to organise it. This is hardly ideal – an ill fitting jacket could be lethal – but I'll be gentle with you." He gave me a lop-sided grin. "How do you feel?"

"Awkward."

"Swing your arm, no, just the right. He adjusted the fit some-how. "Better?"

"A little, I still feel…padded."

"It's necessary, I assure you. This is a beginner's jacket, and is too small." He stepped away and put on his own. To my ignorant eye, it fitted him perfectly, and wasn't as bulky as the one I was in. Stripped down, without his outer clothing, I could quietly admire his physique; his legs were beautifully long, and the trousers he wore emphasised that. As he turned away to pick up the several swords he'd chosen, the trousers hugged his behind like a second skin. I looked away, hurriedly, feeling heat rising through my neck and face. I was shocked at my own reaction. Philip was the nearest thing to family I would ever have. My guardian. It was one thing to let one's eyes linger on Jude's rear end or that of a prefect, but to allow myself such familiarity with Philip… Luckily he didn't seem to notice and handed me a sword, grabbing hold of my hand and feeding my fingers through the grip. "No, there, that's right. Now, extend your arm, like this. How does it feel?"

Like any boy, I'd played swordfights with my friends before. Tearing whippy branches from the poor abused trees in and around the schoolgrounds, and playing the fool, taking our fights from such books as *The Three Musketeers*. I'd never held a real fencing sword in my life, and the weight surprised me. "I'm not sure," I said, finally, waving my arm a little and feeling rather dashing.

"It's well balanced, and should suit you, but we'll see." He passed me a mask which the footman helped me with. The swords were protected at the ends with little metal knobs but I was aware that even so, to be caught in the eye would not be desirable. Philip knew what he was doing, obviously, and I followed his lead. I admit that, behind the safety of my mask (for I could not see Philip's face, once masked, and I was sure he could not see mine), I gawped at his catlike grace as he moved around the floor testing each sword. Finally, when he'd picked one he was pleased with, he gestured me forward to stand in front of him.

"Fencing is about balance. Not speed. Speed can only come from control and balance, and it will. If you wish to create speed, and therein speed of movement, it cannot be done without balance. Watch, and copy. *En garde.*"

I'd seen the position before, some privileged boys at my school had had fencing lessons at home, and in our silly mock battles we had attempted to emulate it even thought we considered it all looked rather over-formal and stupid. But now, seeing Philip in position, flexible and powerful, it didn't seem stupid at all. I knew that with the slightest lunge towards me he could strike on any part of my body and there was nothing I could do about it. After staying in the position for a moment or two, he straightened up and stood beside me, demonstrated how to place my feet, turning them out and putting my hips on a slight angle away from the opponent.

"Now, bend your knees," he ordered. "Not too much, not yet, you aren't ready for it. Use the left arm for balance, hold it up, like so. Now, take one step forward."

"I can't," I said. "I feel that if I move, I'd fall flat on my face."

He went into position beside me, again, as elastic and springy as some kind of predator. "Like this. Small step – and keep it low to the ground. When you master the balance you can lift your feet more, but the higher you do, the less control you have, and the more you give to your opponent." He slid his right foot forward and nodded at me to do the same which I did, with considerably less grace. "Good." His voice was warm. "Good! You kept in position. Again."

"My legs hurt."

"Of course they do," he said without any sympathy whatsoever. "You are using muscles you've never used before. Riding will be worse."

"I can imagine," I said, sliding forward again. Philip touched the underside of my sword to keep it on the horizontal. "Jude can hardly walk."

He made a strange sound, almost like a gasp, but I couldn't see his expression. "You should all have had this education," he said, sideswiping his sword with sudden violence. "I can't promise any of you will be masters at what you try, but by God I'll make every effort to make you passable."

My heart seemed to swell in my chest at that, and I felt even worse for admiring his body. I could no more have spoken at that point than fenced him to a standstill.

We did nothing more than footwork for an hour, taking a short break for a glass of wine and then straight back to it. An hour was just about all my body could take and by the end of the hour, I was sweating and aching all over. Philip was pleased with me. "You aren't the worst I've taught," he said, peeling off his mask. He was hardly glowing from the exertion. I felt a thrill of pride until he continued. "Nor the best, but I think you have some promise."

I took off the jacket, finding my hands would hardly obey me, and for once was grateful to have someone dress me. "Albert will help with the cramping you'll get," Philip said. "I'll see you after lunch. As to the fencing, I'll expect you to practice what you've learned, so get the others to practice with you. I'll wager you are all as inexperienced."

I couldn't see how I'd be in any fit state to dance after the morning's activities but I staggered off, attempting not to show the pain in my calves and thighs. Myles was at the dining table when I arrived and he raised an eyebrow at my gait; as soon as I was out of Philip's sight I'd stopped pretending I wasn't in pain. "Well, I know you weren't riding," he said.

"Fencing," I said, with a groan, "and it wasn't much better than Latin."

"But no headache."

"Thank the Lord. But I think I'd have rather have faced Jude's horse. Who would have thought that keeping a sword straight would be such hard work? And what," I said, grimacing as I tried to ease my legs in the chair, "is the point of it? In case someone insults me and I can get my nose cut off?"

"Gentlemanly pursuits, dear thing," Jude said from behind me. "I have been pirouetting with a chair for most of the morning, which for the first half an hour was painful in such places I would rather not mention in mixed company." He sat down beside me rather gingerly, then beamed at both of us. "Saddles were invented by eunuchs. It's the only explanation. Or women. It would make a lot more sense if *men* rode sidesaddle, when you come to think of it."

"How did you get on with Heriment?" I said to Myles, ignoring Jude, and leaving him to eat, for he seemed up for mischief by the gleam in his eye.

Myles snorted in disgust. "I've met too many masters like him. Dry sticks, with no conversation and no life outside the ancient world. Strange, though. He certainly doesn't look the type." He paused and looked into space.

"What does he look like? What type is he?" Jude asked. "I don't think I have him until the end of the week. I'm rather dreading it, seeing the devastating effect he had on dear Crispin." I nearly jumped out of my seat as Jude's foot, obviously slipped from its shoe, rubbed against my leg. I wondered at his capacity to eat, continue a conversation and be so very wicked all at the same time.

"Oh, you'll probably find him perfect," Myles said in an undertone, carefully watching our attending footman. "He's tall and dark and handsome. But lacking in personality."

I wanted to take part in the conversation but now Jude had pulled my right leg a little nearer to his and was tangling my ankle with his. It was as much as I could do to pretend to listen to the others, and to eat my beefsteak. My trousers strained as my member pushed against the fabric. Part of me wanted to kick him, but the sensations his feet were causing in me were too nice to give up. By the time he'd finished with me, I knew I was probably pink around the ears, and I gave an excuse when they left the table, so I could recover my equilibrium and let my passion dampen down a little. I swore that if I could get Jude alone that evening, I'd pay him back for every sweet torment.

❦ Chapter Fifteen ❧

As I stood after lunch, my leg (and other parts) still warm from Jude's teasing, the extra watch bumped against my side and I remembered what I had meant to discuss with them. "Wait," I said. I pulled the watch from my pocket, and placed it on the table. "One of you misplaced this. I found it in Philip's study."

Jude patted his waistcoat, and frowned. "Not mine." He looked at Myles.

"Mine's upstairs," Myles said. "I know it is."

"It can't be," I said. "You must have dropped it somewhere. One of the servants brought it into the study while I was there. When did you have it last?"

"I tell you, it's upstairs," Myles said. "I saw it this morning."

"Well, obviously it isn't," Jude said, with an anxious glance at the clock, "or it wouldn't be here on the table. Just admit that you were careless, Myles. It's not a crime. No-one's going to think worse of you if –"

"And I tell you that it's not mine!" Myles strode toward the table, snatched up the watch and shoved it into his pocket without even looking at it. "But if the pair of you don't believe me, I'll take it." He stormed out, slamming the door behind him.

"Well!" Jude began.

"Jude, don't," I warned. "And what did you think you were playing at? Do you think he didn't notice?"

"I didn't, no," Jude said, a little petulantly. "He's so busy being angry with the world, he never seems to notice anything."

I looked at the door, and wondered. I thought Jude was wrong, but I didn't want to upset both of them in one day, and it was time for the afternoon sessions, so there was no time to discuss it. I gave Jude a quick smile and he pinched me on the arse cheekily just as the footman came in to clear the plates. "We have unfinished business," he whispered as we left the servant to it.

My afternoon consisted of learning the niceties of the ball-room, reading incomprehensible dance moves – whoever thought that putting the steps to a dance in a book was in any way a boon to mankind? – and being asked to waltz (the one dance I already knew) pretending to hold a young lady in my arms. This was not at all enjoyable, and a little like torture. Having to slide around the floor to Drummond's over-emphatic *one-two-three, one-two-three* on the poor piano was mortifying and after a while, extremely painful as I held my arms out in my charade. I don't think I impressed Drummond that much. He muttered that it was a mercy that Mr Smallwood had not been there to see. "Such footwork. Saints preserve us!" he growled as he left me.

Doubts began to assail me as to whether I was truly suited to be raised in my station, as so far my sojourns into the gentlemanly pursuits were not covering with me in glory. Dabbing the sweat from my face and neck with a handy cloth set aside for the purpose I felt – and more embarrassingly, heard – my stomach growling. I was looking forward to dinner, not just because my exertions had made me ravenous, but because Philip was to be joining our little party; it would help to lessen the tensions between the three of us caused by Myles' obstinacy at luncheon. Thinking of that, and the way he'd looked as he'd left the dining room sent me up to his room, instead of going to my own. I knocked. Receiving no answer, I tried the handle. The door was locked, so I knocked again.

"Myles?" I waited, but no reply came. I wasn't about to give up. I hated the idea that he was in his room, angry and unhappy because of something I'd done. I should have thought, should have approached them separately, and not put either of them through the embarrassment of being found out. But surely, I reasoned, the important thing was that the watch was returned, safe and sound and no harm had been done.

"Myles? It's Crispin." I waited for a moment, checked along the corridor then said, "I'm sorry if I embarrassed you, Myles. It wasn't something I meant. I handled it badly." I waited. "I just wanted you to know." It was clear that he wasn't going to answer the door, so I went back to my room. Albert was busy being busy, doing something minute to one of my jackets, but as they were all brand new I couldn't imagine what. What a bore it must be to fuss over clothes, I thought as I sat and glared at the fire. Even more so to have to fuss over some chap who has no right to them. I watched Albert's back as he replaced the jacket in the wardrobe and wondered what he really thought of us three. It must be obvious to him, judging by the state of the clothes that we arrived in, that we were nothing, and I wondered what went on behind that impassive, perfect, servant's face.

"Shall I bring you some tea, sir?" he asked me.

I nodded without answering him, and sat there, as he went to fetch it, wondering what I could do to assuage Myles' hurt feelings. It wasn't surprising that we didn't automatically believe each other, I reasoned; he had lied to me, and I had done so too – by omission.

I was still lost in thought when Jude arrived, gliding into the room and collapsing onto the window seat.

"I don't see why we can't all have these dashed lessons together," he said. "There's nothing as boring as learning on one's own." I didn't answer him, and he rattled on, filling the silence with his chatter, to which I half-listened. His afternoon had been taken up with mathematics, followed by an hour of archery with Philip in the knot garden behind the house. He continued to rattle on when the tea arrived and I performed the ceremony dutifully, my mind more on Myles than on what Jude was saying.

I roused from my reverie when he mentioned archery, the first syllable being still close to my heart. "I have tried that," I said. "Perhaps there might be something I can do without anyone rolling their eyes in revulsion."

I had left myself wide open with that remark, and I realised it too late, as Jude grinned lasciviously. "Surely not just one thing?" he asked, impishly.

"I would roll my eyes at you," I said, "if it were not so completely ironic."

Jude slid over to me, and stood behind my chair, running his hands through my hair, then stroking my cheek. I leant towards his hand, then let him return to his seat where he continued to talk of his adventures with archery.

"...and I asked Philip about the letters, Crispin," he said finally.

My attention wavered from the fire and I turned to look at him. "What did he say?"

"He took a while to think about it, but he gave us permission to write to our friends," he said, "with one qualification."

"Which is?" I found my heart thumping at the thought of writing to Arch. It was probable the letter would not get through; his father might circumvent its delivery, but it might, it might.

"That we are discreet, only. It was a...delicate conversation, even though we were out of earshot of anyone around us. The man has an ability to say what he means without actually saying anything of the sort." I processed that for a moment and found that, although I had only seen a little of that part of Philip's personality, it was a fair assessment of the man. "I assured him," continued Jude, "that none of us wished to embarrass him or ourselves in any way and that if he wished to examine our letters he was at liberty –"

"The devil you did!" I exclaimed.

"Crispin," Jude said, with exquisite patience and not a little pomposity, "let me finish, dear boy. It is negotiation. I offer, Philip counteroffers, I offer with new terms, and we revert to his more reasonable terms and all decorum is assured."

"You sound like a solicitor." Arch's father spoke in much the same way.

"Thank you," he said with a smirk. "I was considering my options in that direction. A barrister, though, don't you think? I don't fancy being stuck in a stuffy office. I think I'd rather be in court, using my not inconsiderable eloquence to save the ruffian, the dastard, the sodomi –"

"I rather think that even barristers have to serve an apprenticeship in the Temple, which would rather suggest that there will be stuffy offices involved at some point. I can't imagine they let you loose in court on your first day."

"I'm sure you are right, although I'm sure I'd be a natural," he said.

"Arse," I said affectionately. I was somehow determined to spend some time alone with him after dinner, but I did want to see Myles before hand and Jude seemed not at all concerned that Myles was so annoyed.

He left me after a while, with nothing more than a teasing peck on the lips, and although I went to grab him, he skipped sideways and avoided my attention. I was left alone, thinking chilly thoughts to force my body to lose some of its rigidity. Finally under control, I sought Myles out again, and finding his room still locked I paced around the house in a determined manner one floor at a time in case he wasn't actually in his room at all. I paused at the stair to Philip's tower and wondered, for a moment whether he was there, explaining to Philip how he'd managed to lose the watch, making a clean breast of things. I waited for a good quarter of an hour at the foot of the stairs to the tower, but there was no sign of movement. Eventually, plucking up the courage, for I had not been expressly forbidden to seek out Philip's apartments, I began to move up the corkscrew stairwell into unfamiliar territory but I had not gone more than four steps when a voice behind me fairly made me leap out of my skin.

"What the devil are you up to?" I spun around to find Myles at the bottom of the stair. His voice had been loud enough to frighten the life out of me, but low enough to – I hoped – be unnoticed, were Philip in his rooms.

I felt myself colour at the idiocy of my situation, retraced my steps and led the way into the Long Gallery, with Myles at my heels. Around the corner at last, and sure there was no-one else in sight, I rounded on Myles with as much pent-up nervousness as I felt. "I was looking for you, you oaf. I've been looking for you since luncheon."

He looked completely surprised, all the wind taken out of his sails. "If you were looking for me," he said, "why were you sneaking up the stairs to Philip's room?"

"I wasn't sneaking." I was getting angry now, I wasn't the one in the wrong and somehow he always made me feel so. "I'd looked everywhere else, and that was the only place I hadn't tried."

"Oh really? You looked everywhere? Obviously you didn't because I wasn't up there was I? Have you not considered the design of this house? We could both be walking around it for hours and not find each other." He seemed just as angry as I, and just as annoyed as he had been earlier. "Do you know how old this house is? I'm quite certain you don't know of everywhere, let alone searched everywhere. Did you look downstairs? Or up in our old rooms?"

I didn't answer him, but he guessed my response by my face.

"And the first place you thought to look for was in Philip's rooms?"

"Well, not the first… I did look around for quite a while." I suddenly realised how me ascending the stairs might look, and how Myles might not even believe my explanation. "Oh look, can we forget it? I wanted to apologise to you for embarrassing you in front of Jude."

He frowned. "What?"

"At lunch. I should have asked you individually about the lost watch. I'm sorry."

"The not lost watch, you mean."

Now it was my turn to be puzzled, why was he still insisting on this? "Jude had his –"

"Oh, Crispin," he said heavily. "You'd better come with me."
He pulled me back towards our corridor, letting me go as we exited the Long Gallery, but setting a fast pace until we reached his room. Unlocking the door (which I'd never considered doing, if I wasn't in mine) he led the way in, and moved to his desk where he opened a drawer. Then he turned to me with both hands open. Resting on each of his palms was a silver watch – each one identical to the other.

"There," he said. "It galls me that neither of you had the decency to take a chap's word for it when given. This one," he held out the watch in his right hand, "is mine. This one isn't. And before you start behaving like Doubting Thomas all over again, I'll wager you my dessert for a week that if you were to find Jude right now, he'd have his on him too. I'm not trying to trick you. This is mine." He put his own watch back in the drawer and sat down on the edge of the bed, pulling a book off his bedside table and tossing it at me. "Here. I found this in the library." He then handed me the watch. "The marked page relates to hallmarks for silver. Have a look at your own watch first."

I knew what he meant, for it was often a hobby of boys, in the way some boys collected coach numbers, or stamps. I took out my own watch, searched the outside for a hallmark, and not finding it, opened the case and looked further in. There was nothing inside to the immediate inspection other than the inscription, now dear to my heart, but I dropped the working out of the case and examined the other side. The hallmark was fresh and clear, and large enough to be seen without a glass, but in the oil light I found I still had to turn the case around to read it. "There's a standing lion," I said, "what looks like a lion's head, a letter, another head and a name."

"I'll spare you the study," he said, quietly. "For I've done it for you. The letter is the important one. An ornate 'L'. It means that it was made last year. Now check the other one."

I picked up the other one, and more sure now, opened it in the same way I had mine. It was, to all intents and purposes, identical. The engraving, the inscription, the workings. The watch itself fell into my hand and I peered at the embossed markings, which were, even to my uneducated eyes, obviously different. "Another standing lion, a lion's head," I squinted, for the letter was smaller and harder to make out. "I'm not sure," I said, finally. It's blurred. It could be an 'o', or a 'q'."

"It's a 'q'," he said. "I asked Paul to find me a magnifying glass. It's this 'q', specifically." He shunted up next to me, opened the book at a marked page, and ran his finger down a list of letters. "Here. This one."

"But, that says this was hallmarked in 1831," I said. I went cold. "Oh no, this must be Philip's own watch."

Myles tapped me on the side of the head, "No, woodenhead. You've read the inscription. It's identical. '*A welcome gift for a welcome arrival, Philip.*'" He raised an eyebrow and looked at me. "So, convinced now it's not mine, are you?"

"That's fifteen years ago," I murmured, turning the watch over and over in my hand. "Who –"

"I think it must have been his son," Myles said, his eyes meeting mine. There was a sadness in them that I'd never seen before, a sense of empathy and loss. "It would explain a lot."

I nodded, the confusion in my thoughts clearing. That did make sense. It would explain the odd distraction that Philip revealed at unguarded moments, and it would explain why he'd taken on three young men, to attempt to fill his life.

"Doesn't help us with our immediate problem though," he said and I stopped staring at the watch, which was suddenly an object of intense pity, and looked up at him.

"Which is?"

"How to get the watch back to Philip without him finding out."

Chapter Sixteen

W
e discussed the matter further, and although we both of us came up with various schemes – from slipping the watch onto the post tray when no-one was around, to trying to gain access to Philip's study and secreting it into a drawer, to simply leaving it around for someone to find – none of them seemed desirable, or indeed honest. The thing had been done badly, and for whatever reasons I had done it, I felt it was mine to rectify without drawing the others in further. Myles suggested asking for Jude's advice, but he wasn't in his room, so nothing had been decided when we parted to dress for dinner.

After dressing, I walked along the corridors of the house alone, my mind a little perturbed, and reached, once more, the stairwell to Philip's tower. This time as my feet ascended the stair, there was no voice to call me back, although I admit that I looked back, more than once, as if wishing that my friends were there for support would imagine them there. This was impossible, however, as I had told neither of them what I was planning to do, if indeed I had any sensible plan at all.

I took the stairs slowly, partly wishing to delay the inevitable interview, but also because the stairwell itself was magnificent. Panelled from floor to ceiling in a warm golden wood, each panel portrayed a different scene, or view of the house in different stages of its development. In this way, it was impossible to tell how old the panelling was – or whether it had been a work in progress since the house had first been built. Protected as it was in this part of the house, the wood had not been spoiled by sun or over polish. It seemed to be as fresh as when it was first installed. My prevarication could not last long, as the stairwell itself, being finite, brought me to an imposing door – just one, although I remember one of my friends having told me that there were, in fact, two apartments in the tower. The King's Suite and the Queen's Favour.

I waited a moment on the carpeted landing, then took a deep breath and knocked, knowing I'd feel immensely stupid if Philip was not even here. The door opened, and he himself stood there, breathlessly handsome in evening clothes, a bow tie yet untied around his neck, and his collar unstudded. He looked past me for a second as if expecting, perhaps, to see the other two behind me, but it was only for a moment and he turned his attention to me almost immediately.

"Crispin," he said, with a warm smile. "What a surprise. What can I do for you?"

"May I speak to you for a moment?"

He didn't speak for a few seconds, then seemed to decide something and stood aside to let me pass. "Of course, come in. We can go down together. Make yourself comfortable while I finish dressing." He indicated some chairs by his fireside but after entering his room, I closed the door and stayed just inside. The room was beautiful; the entire room took one whole floor of the tower, large, airy and square with multiple windows on every side, which would, in the daylight, give a panoramic view over the Mere and the rest of the house. The ceiling looked as though it had been made from piecrust, small wooden frames covered the space above my head and in each one, an oil painting resided. It staggered me; without a ladder or some kind of magnification glass it was almost impossible to make out what the details of the paintings were and I wondered what kind of man would commission such a thing, and why, here in his own room where it could not so easily be shown off as if it had been in his more accessible rooms.

Seeing me staring upwards like some bedazzled tourist he walked back towards and joined me in gazing at the ceiling. "Amazing, isn't it? I believe it was inspired by some Italian ceiling. My grandfather had it installed. I don't think even the one in the Long Gallery can compare and yet –"

"No one sees it," I said, echoing my earlier thought.

"Exactly. Let me tie this wretched thing," he said, indicating his rather mussed appearance, "and you'll have my full attention. Sit down, I won't be long."

He left me alone, in an odd parody of our meeting that morning, going through a door which I assumed led up some internal stairwell into his bedroom. I heard his feet on the stairs and on the floorboards above, there was a murmur of voices – his valet I assumed, and then I heard his footsteps descending more hurriedly. Emerging once more into the room, he was finished off to perfection, his tie straight, and his hair tidied into fashionable curls over his forehead. Looking at him, I had to admit that I was glad that he had not succumbed to the obsession of a preponderance of facial hair, and decided that I, too, would not attempt to cover my face with a beard or moustache.

"How are you this evening?"

I stood to face him. "Perfectly recovered, thank you."

"Good. What was it you wanted to speak to me about? You can tell me as we go."

"If…if you don't mind," I said, "I'd like to wait a moment."

"If you insist," he said, looking a little more serious and mildly puzzled.

There was nothing to do but to come out with my admission. I pulled the offending watch – how I wished I'd never seen the damned thing – from my pocket, and my own, attached to its chain – and held them both out for him to see. As I did I knew I'd done something terribly wrong, for his entire countenance darkened, and he took the spare watch immediately, snapped it open and examined the marking. "Where did you get this?" he thundered, sounding just as angry as the first time I'd met him. "Tell me, where did you come by this watch?" It remained open in his palm and I could see his thumb brushing across the silver, stroking it with gentle, tender strokes, a strange juxtaposition to his face.

"In your study," I said, unable to do anything but tell the truth. I was transfixed by the change in him, and the way his eyes came to life. I had hardly noticed it until this moment, but it was as if his eyes had been hiding his true nature. Not angry, but so full of passion that I wondered how ever I could have thought him anything but. Somehow I stammered out my mistake, and as I did, I could see the fire in him subsiding, as if someone was inside him, banking the coals down. By the time I'd finished it was as if someone had replaced the man and he was just Philip again; urbane and sophisticated. All but those eyes, which were the last to fade, the last to regain their friendly composure, but now I'd seen them unleashed, I saw he kept himself in check, for they were clearly shuttered.

"And so I thought the best thing would be to –"

"Come here and admit your mistake." He turned away, running his free hand through his hair, and walked to the fireplace. "And instead of listening to you like a sane person, your guardian flew into a fury and frightened you instead."

"Not at all, sir, you have every right to be angry. I took it without asking."

"You were trying to protect your friends." He looked into the mirror and met my eyes there, and he smiled, a heartbreaking smile that at least now I understood. He thought he'd lost his son's watch. "It's nothing less that I would expect. It's a trait I highly admire, Crispin. Don't ever lose it." He looked at me for a long moment and then, as we heard footsteps over our heads he started a little, as if reminded of the time and place. "Lord, if my valet finds me still littering the place, he'll shoo us out like the mother hen he is," he said with a smile. "Let's go down to dinner, shall we?"

All the way back to the dining room he spoke of other things, the subjects and pursuits we were being set, and how much he was looking forward to taking part as much as possible. "I have other demands on my time, as you can imagine," he said. It was clear he was attempting to put me at my ease and mostly he achieved his aim, but I couldn't help but be intrigued by the man who had revealed himself to me, even if it was only for a moment. How much he had been hurt, losing his son. I wondered how the boy had died, and how old he had been, what had happened to Philip's wife and whether he'd marry again, and if so, what that would mean for the three of us. I dared not ask him anything about the watch, but I noticed that he had not left it behind in his room, but had slipped it into his pocket, and his hand had not left that pocket as we walked.

A nd that's all he said?" Jude said, after dinner. "And you didn't even ask him about it? Honestly, Crispin, one might have thought that once you had had the courage to go up those hallowed, panelled stairs, you might have quizzed him a little. I'm sure Myles would have done." He looked over at Myles, "Well, wouldn't you?"

"You weren't there," I said, a trifle put out at his attitude "It was very clear that I'd annoyed him sufficiently." I hadn't told them just how far Philip had gone and how his mood had switched so fast.

"He seemed entirely sanguine by the time I arrived at dinner," Jude said.

Myles swung his feet down from my windowseat, "But he re-marked on you being late to both of us," he said. "Even if you were spared it. I'd not make a habit of it, if I were you, I get the impression that Philip is not one to tolerate tardiness." He stood up. "I'm off to bed, and you've any *sense* you'll follow my example." Jude gave him a swift brittle smile, but Myles had already turned away and had missed it. "The watch mystery that wasn't a mystery at all." He tapped me on the head with his knuckles as he passed. "Let that be a lesson to you, and don't pinch things from Philip in future."

There was an awkward silence after he'd gone. The double en-tendre in Myles' words hung between us and my bed seemed to take up more space in the room than it normally did. It took all of my willpower not to keep glancing at it. Jude seemed a little lost in thought, his eyes in some middle distance, and not seeing me at all. As the silence stretched to breaking point, I could not bear it, for who knew when we'd get such an opportunity again? But it was difficult, for we sat opposite to each other, and I was not in the habit of pouncing. That delicious activity had generally been left to Arch, who took delight in ambushing me in our rooms, or even in a deserted corridor or classroom. Racking my brains, I decided to lock the door, for that at least gave me an excuse to stand up. My task done, and with Jude still lost in thought, I came back to his chair, and, as he had done to me on the earlier occasion, I stood behind him, running my fingers through his hair and bending down to wrap my arms around him. Excitement rose within me at the scent of him, musky and warm, and I kissed his cheek, surprised at his lack of response.

He twisted up and out of his chair and, assuming he had done so for ease of access, I stepped towards him, attempting to capture him in my arms, but he moved away with that same feline grace I'd always admired, leaving me frowning. "Jude?" I caught hold of his hand and held it, despite his obvious reluctance. "What's wrong?" I replayed the events of the day, of the last few days, to gauge any reason for his evasion but could think of none. After the events in the withdrawing room, I'd assumed that he had been looking forward to an opportunity to continue where we had left off – at the very least I owed him the return of the favour he had done me. I know I had been looking forward to it, of course, but now he stood silent, his jaw tight with some repression that I could not guess of, his cheek twitching as if I had actually offended him.

I let go of his hand, finally, stung and upset. "Jude? If there's something I said, something I did, you must tell me. You must. Unless – unless you were just amusing yourself." I could hear my voice taking on a priggish tone, but there was nothing I could do. "That was it, was it?"

He looked at me then, his eyes dark and shocked as if I'd hurt him, and I took another step towards him, confused, but he moved away from me once more. That was all I needed, I had made passes at boys before, I knew the signs. My pride rose up in an angry wave and I marched to the door and unlocked it, but left it closed.

"Crispin…" he said, but he trailed off, dropping his eyes away from mine, and without another word, he left me alone. It wasn't until I'd closed the door and locked it again, that I realised I was shaking with the all-too familiar trembling that presaged an attack. I couldn't ring for Albert, I just couldn't do it. It was as much as I could do to rip my tie from my neck, shrug myself from my jacket and shoes and collapse onto the bed, familiar nausea and black, numbing pain overcoming me.

❧ Chapter Seventeen ❧

I woke to a pounding like I'd never experienced, and not all of it was in my head. Someone was calling my name: *Albert.*

I'd locked the door. I'd assumed that he'd leave me alone after a while, so I murmured, "Go away," which would have never been heard and tried to sleep, knowing that it was impossible. The pain behind my eye was like a needle, making even the soft, down-filled pillow an instrument of torture, so I dragged myself to my feet, and, supporting myself with the furniture, made my way to the door, where Albert still knocked. I had to pause a moment, collecting my composure, and while I did I could hear other voices, Philip's authoritative tones and others, perhaps servants, in the background.

"Is that the key?" Philip was saying, his voice sounded commanding, but decidedly concerned. "Give it to me."

"Yes, sir," a voice answered.

"If he has the key on the inside, sir –" Albert said.

"Let me see first," I heard a metallic sound and then a muffled curse. "It's no good." Philip said. "Witheridge, send –"

I tugged at the key, unlocking the door, and opened it, dreading the sight on the other side. Philip, in his dressing gown and looking paler than I'd seen him, was nearest to me, with Albert a step or two behind him and Myles leaning on the balustrade.

"Thank God," Philip muttered, taking one look at me, he strode into my room and swept me up in his arms as if I were a child, as light as a feather, and carried me back into the room, all the while muttering instructions to fetch water. "Damn it." A cool hand touched my brow and I grunted in pain. "The boy's on fire. There's no choice." I tried to open my eyes, but couldn't. I felt his breath ghost over my face and then he spoke very softly. "I'm so sorry, Crispin, I wish there was someone else I could get in a hurry. Albert." The bed creaked as he moved away. "Get downstairs and wait for Tom, tell him to get Baynes here as fast as he can."

"Dr Baynes, sir?" I heard a gasp, and Witheridge's voice speak the question, all at the same time. Then Philip's voice faded, speaking to Witheridge as it did, and I breathed out and tried to relax.

The attack was not as bad as the one I'd had previously and within an hour or so I was well enough to be sitting up and having Albert fuss over me. All my lessons had been cancelled for the day, and I was feeling a little guilty as I lay propped up in bed, a tray of eggs before me. I'd just finished what I could of the food, and Albert took the tray out, letting Philip in as he himself disappeared. With him – with whiskers just as terrier-like as ever – was the good doctor from my journey, and I slid up in the bed. I'd seen a doctor once or twice at school for childhood ailments, but had never been in bed when examined. It seemed rather too intimate. Although I knew it was entirely normal, it did not seem so for me, particularly in the recent change of my circumstances.

At my feeble attempts to disengage my legs from the heavy covers, Philip said, "Stay where you are, please. You remember Dr Baynes, of course."

"Of course, how do you do, sir?" I held out my hand, which Baynes shook, with the smallest of smiles as he surveyed me in my throne-like bed.

"Well, sir, quite well. But it seems you are not."

"It is only a headache," I said, looking in mute appeal between Baynes and Philip, "it was not necessary –"

"My ward considers that his health is his own responsibility," Philip said, with a firm, quelling look as if to remind me of our earlier conversation. "But it is not. If I am his guardian, I am that in all matters, is that not so, Baynes?"

"Quite right, quite right," the doctor agreed. "Be guided by your guardian, young man. Your care is no longer just your own concern. Now, let me look at you. Philip, you need not stay, he's in good hands."

As the doctor rummaged in the bag he had brought in with him, I looked up to Philip to say thank you but the words stuck in my throat, for Philip was looking at the doctor's back with such loathing it took my breath away. I don't think that for those few seconds he even remembered I was in the room. It was as if he'd just noticed the doctor's presence and had reacted to something utterly filthy, completely loathsome, an evil that had walked into his house, trailing vileness in its wake. Despite the fact that I had guessed that all between Philip and Dr Baynes was not well, I couldn't have been prepared for the sheer depth of hatred that showed for a few scant seconds on my guardian's face. Then, just as his passion had vanished when we spoke in his bedroom, the expression melted from him. He cast me a quick smile – obviously not having noticed I'd seen him betray his feelings, and left me alone with the doctor.

I was unsurprised when the doctor remarked that my heart was racing, for I could feel it was although I could hardly say why – whether it was the attack or Philip's reaction it was hard to choose which had started it. I answered Dr Baynes' questions regarding my headaches as best as I could. As to the latest attack, I had to lie as to the circumstances immediately preceding it.

"I had dinner," I told him. "The three of us met here, in my room to talk for a while, and then when they left I became ill." It wasn't entirely a lie.

The doctor pulled the nightshirt over my head, then put one end of his hearing tube into his ear, and holding the other on my skin, he listened to whatever it was that doctors listen for, front and back. He looked in my eyes, my ears and even in my mouth, then, unexpectedly he asked me walk across the room a few times and watched me carefully. Ordering me back into bed, he packed up his bag. "Well, you seem recovered," he said.

"They don't generally affect me for long."

"But they can be much more severe?"

I nodded. "But truly, sir, I don't find them more than an inconvenience."

"That's right," he said, examining my eyes again, one by one. "But the army might, eh? Or the Navy? Or even the church? Damn superstitious types there, who might take it as something more than a malady, don't you think?"

I swallowed. It was something I'd considered, but up until recently I didn't think I'd had any hope of a decent profession at all. Now I knew he was right. "Is there any cure?"

"We can try, lad, we can try." He walked to the room and pulled open the door. "Ask your master to come back," he said to whoever was lurking outside. Then he joined me again, sitting on the edge of the bed. "Well, then, you look like you've settled in."

"I'm terribly grateful to Mr Smallwood."

He cast his eyes over my face as if still examining me. "You mentioned 'the three of us.' Whom did you mean?"

"Mr Smallwood's other wards."

"Others?" He looked entirely surprised. "I had not heard that there were more."

"Three of us, sir."

"And what do they –"

"Well, Doctor?" Philip's voice cut through our conversation. Neither of us had noticed him re-entering the room. "How is he?"

"He has made a good recovery this time, but he will need both symptomatic and prophylactic treatment. If we can withdraw and let the lad rest, I'll discuss it with you further."

Philip gave Albert instructions not to leave me alone for a moment, and led the way out. At the door, the Doctor turned back. "Look after yourself, Mr Thorne. I look forward to meeting you again."

Personally I hoped not, but I wished him a safe journey.

I dozed for a while, while Albert stood guard by the door. When I woke I was hungry and bored, eager to meet up with my friends at the very least. A footman that Albert called Samuel brought up my lunch, a hearty soup and fish. I am ashamed to say I dispatched it as though there was nothing wrong with me at all. By now I felt a proper fraud and wanted to continue my lessons that afternoon if allowed. "Albert," I asked, as I handed him the tray, "would you ask Mr Smallwood to attend me?"

"I believe he said he would visit you directly after lunch, sir, once Dr. Baynes had left."

With the memory of Philip's expression still clear in my mind, I was rather surprised that Philip had extended him such hospitality, but did not comment on it. "And Mr Graham and Mr Middleton, are they lunching with Mr Smallwood?"

"I am not certain, sir, but I can ascertain if you wish it."

"No, no. It's all right," I grumbled. "I suppose I'd better stay where I am until I speak to Mr Smallwood."

"I have to agree, sir,"

It seemed an age before Philip joined me. He sat on the edge of the bed. I spoke before he could.

"I'm quite recovered. It was good of you to call the doctor, truly, but I would much rather return to my lessons this afternoon."

"Out of the question," he said. "Baynes assures me that your balance is affected and I'm not having you falling from your horse and breaking your neck. "Am I pushing you too hard, Crispin?"

I shook my head, which hurt, but I wanted to give the impression that it didn't. "Not at all," I said, firmly. "I'm grateful –"

"Thanks are not necessary. I'm simply concerned for your health. I had planned to announce to the three of you today that I'm opening the house up for the first time in years, I plan to have a small party in a day or so. I want my neighbours to meet you, and more importantly, for you to meet them. But I think, with you unwell, I should postpone it. We can easily have it when the weather, and your health, improves.

"No, please!" I said, smiling. "Please don't cancel it. I'm much improved, and Dr Baynes said he can help me, he mentioned treatment. I promise you I'll be fine, Philip. I'll do whatever I'm told, stay in bed all week if you insist. Please don't change your plans."

He seemed to deliberate this, and then smiled back at me. "Well, I'll take your word on it, but you must take care of yourself. And as for the party, you are not to overtire yourself. You must promise me that you will leave the party if you feel at all unwell. Another attack so soon, Baynes says, might be a lot more serious, could cause any kind of brain fever."

"Did he say what it was that was wrong?"

"He suspects that it's megrim, or migraine as he tells me we should call it. Do you know the term?"

"My school…they said it might be."

"It's not certain. And I know that Baynes – quite over my wishes – suggested that your future prospects might be spoiled. You are not to think of that. Can you promise me?"

I gave a self-deprecatory laugh. "If it were not for you I'd have no prospects to spoil."

He stood up, shutting his concern away behind that handsome mask; as if a light had gone out in a distant house. "You are not," he repeated, "to concern yourself with your future. Only promise me that you will take my word for it that it is assured."

"I will." I had a thousand questions and for the moment all thoughts of his behaviour towards Baynes had disappeared from my thoughts. I could only imagine what a 'small party' might mean to Philip. I had no doubt that it was very different from anything I'd attended at Arch's house. *Arch* – I could write and tell him all about my experiences, and now I had the party to look forward to, it would not look as though I were only writing to brag. I doubted he'd mind, for all that, for he knew I'd had nothing to brag about before.

Philip stayed only for a few moments more, gaining my assurance that I would not stir from my room, and I in turn begged that he would let Myles and Jude visit me after dinner, to which he finally acceded after a show of reluctance. As soon as I was sure he'd left, I slid out of bed before Albert came back and, bundled up in a dressing gown (to allay any complaints from my over-zealous valet), I sat at my desk and pulled out some paper and a quill. Philip had provided my desk with one of the new pens, but I had done little more than hold it. I had not dared to use it.

Dipping the quill into the inkstand, I pondered a moment on how to start. It had been more than a year since we'd parted; his life may have changed entirely. Knowing his family, I assumed that they'd have procured a private tutor to see him through his missed months of education, but where he might be now it was impossible to know. However, I wanted to try to find out. To make sure he was all right, if I could. That he didn't think badly of me, or worse, himself. I was sure that his father would have had no mercy on his son – and it wouldn't surprise me if Arch had been sent to India, for all that his father had wanted him to follow in his footsteps into the law.

There was only one was to find out, so I dated the headed notepaper and wrote.

"*Dear George,*"

I paused and looked the words. I'd never called him George, not once in our time together. It looked wrong, and although he was George, in my heart, if I'd had the chance for one long night in his arms, I know I would have whispered his name in his ear, I couldn't start a letter – not this letter – this way.

"*Dear Archeson,*" That was better.

I doubt you've heard, but since we last met I discovered I'd been made a ward of Mr Philip Smallwood, of Horsey, Norfolk, and after coming down I journeyed here. It is as strange and as remote a place as any I could imagine; peculiar dialects, odd birds, windpumps – which are the only thing keeping this marshy land from the sea – and a chill that cuts through to the bone.

After the coach I was taken by boat and deposited on an island on which the house sits. What an adventure! I wish I'd had you

*here to share it, but I'm not alone. I share this house – castle almost
– with two others, and we are fast becoming friends.*

*As to what it all means, and why I've been so favoured with
fortune, I can't say. I know that now, were we to meet again, and
I cannot but hope we might one day (do you not?), we would be at
least equals and you would not be ashamed of*

Your,

Thorne.

Albert had entered as I was writing and sat quietly on his chair
in the corner, wisely making no comment on me being out of bed. I
finished the letter, read it through and frowned. It was hardly even
a letter, and after a year of separation, I was quite sure that Arch
would be as disappointed to read such a short correspondence as
I was to send it, but there was little more I could add without
becoming more intimate than such a letter would allow. I couldn't
reminisce over our time together at school without sounding like
a fool; merely writing of cricket and cross-country running would
sound inane and false to Arch, and to myself.

What I really wanted, I thought, stroking the letter on the underside so Albert could not see, was to write down how I missed
his voice, how I was forgetting the colour of his eyes. How the
curve of his back felt under my hand, and how the sweet violence
of his hurried love-making made me ache with a kind of home-
sickness of a home I had never had. *I miss you*, I wanted to write.
But I need to make a life here, and let you live yours. I longed to ask
him questions – *Where are you? What are you doing, and do you miss
me?*

I wondered as I had many times, if he had bent to his parents' expectations for him, or whether his affections were engaged
with some young sportsman or subaltern and he was resisting the
pressures of marriage. I found it hard to imagine which would be
more difficult for him. I couldn't help but wonder what my future
would hold. At school I hadn't thought that far ahead, for there
was nothing much to see. Now, Philip's concern cocooned us, and
I no longer had the concern of poverty staring me in the face. But

would Philip expect us to marry, knowing our pasts? Would he consider them experiments or aberrations and something best left behind? If what Myles said was true, and the watch had belonged to a son, then it was more than likely (but not absolute) that Philip himself had been married.

Perhaps then, this first party was the first step along the way to finding us wives. It wasn't an appalling thought for me, although I knew clearly what aroused me, but I couldn't help but smirk at anyone suggesting marriage to Jude, and I think I wanted to be there when someone did suggest it.

Suddenly remembering Jude for the first time since the head-ache began I wondered – as I had wondered last night, and had received no reply – what had happened between us, what had caused such an abrupt change. Try as I might, as I played every conversation we'd had again in my mind, I could not find anything I had done. All I could do was try to ask him when I saw him again.

"Shall I take the letter for you, sir?" Albert's voice cut into my reverie and I found I was still staring down at the letter in my hand. He was standing over me, and I hadn't even noticed him move, as I'd been so deep in thought. Pleased that there was nothing in the letter to be misconstrued, I folded it up, and slid it, with no little delight, into one of the new ready-made envelopes, for I had not used one before. With care, I sealed the envelope with the wax and the Bittern's Reach seal, then handed it to Albert.

"Thank you," I said. "The incoming post, does it all go into Mr Smallwood?"

"Yes, sir. Perhaps you should rest again now? Doctor Baynes will be sending over some medication as soon as he can."

It seemed pointless to medicate me after the fact, but he was the doctor, and not I. I could also see that Albert was not going to take no for an answer, and so I gave in, graciously, and climbed back into bed.

I woke once more with my book on my face and Albert dozing in the corner. I lay there, lazy and with thoughts full of Arch and what he'd think of my letter, whether his father would give it to him at all, and whether he'd write back, when the door opened and Myles' head appeared around it. He cast a cautious look at Albert and tiptoed in, came all the way around the bed and sat next to me.

"Well, you don't look like you are at death's door, and by the confusion you've caused this last day, I would have thought you were, at least. How dare you be so deuced well-looking?"

"I'm feeling hugely fraudulent, and there's no way that Albert's going to let me up, and Philip has banished me to bed for the day. It's nonsense, I feel perfectly well."

"A bit pale around the gills, perhaps."

"A little pain, that's all," I lied. "So, tell me, what's been happening? Where's Jude? Will you have dinner with me? Do you think Philip will mind?"

He laughed, and Albert gave a snort and woke up.

"It's all right, Albert, you can go," I said. "Mr Graham is capable of keeping me in bed." I attempted to look dignified as Myles snorted and pretended to look on the floor.

After Albert had gone, Myles said, "Shove over," and he launched himself onto the bed next to me. "I've been out today, although my departure was postponed until after the fright you all gave us this morning. You'll be pleased to hear that my shooting is better than my dancing, but the ducks have nothing to fear from me."

"Is Philip dining with you tonight?"

"Yes." He looked thoughtful. "Not that any of us know him well, but he was like a man possessed this morning. I heard Albert knocking at your door, you see, then he stopped, and I assumed he'd gained entrance. Then I heard the commotion when Philip and Witheridge accompanied him and they all tried to open the damned door. Then after he came out his face was…"

"What?"

"He…well, he looked as though you had died."

"But he knew I –"

"I know, I grabbed Albert. You weren't even aware of what was going on, and Albert reassured me. Us. Me and Jude. But Philip looked like he'd lost you. I wonder…"

"What?"

He was silent for a long moment, then turned to me with a sunny smile. "Oh, nothing, really. Now. Shall I send for Albert to ask Philip if it's all right for us to dine together? I'm sure he won't mind at all."

Chapter Eighteen

Albert reported back that Philip did not think too much company at dinner would be good for me, so I could dine with one of my friends or the other. As Myles was already with me I could hardly ask him to leave. The choice was easy and we had a fine dinner together, swapping stories, exaggerating our importance at school, and speaking of nothing very important. We laughed a lot.

I felt much recovered by the time Myles said goodnight. Jude stopped in to see me after his dinner with Philip downstairs, shortly followed, almost on his heels, by Philip himself. I was happy to see both of them, and Jude, I was pleased to see, behaved perfectly; giving no clues at all to our last encounter.

They did not stay long, but before they left me, Philip stated his concern for my health. "I feel perfectly well, Philip," I answered in response to his enquiry, "I know you feel that I am saying that I am better than I am, but it is not so. This attack was not in any way similar to the severity –"

"Crispin," Philip laughed, causing Jude to laugh with him, "I give in. If you feel recovered I shall bow to your stubborn will. You will grant me one favour however before you ride rough shod over all my concern for you?"

"Of course." His good humour was infectious.

"Two things, actually. One that you take the medicine that the doctor has prescribed for you, and the other is that you will never again lock your door at night."

I couldn't accede to that, I knew I couldn't – and panic washed through me. The luxury of being able to be alone, to be entirely private was one that was new to me but something I was entirely unwilling to give up. "I don't know if…" I faltered, unable to meet his eyes, but glanced at Jude for support. Jude wasn't even looking at me, and I felt my face warming, ashamed of my resistance, and unhappy at Jude's silence. I felt sure I would have supported him in the same situation. "I'd like…"

Philip turned to Jude. "Jude, could you leave us alone?" Jude gave Philip a startled glance, but stood, said goodnight in an overly formal manner and left. Philip put his hand on my arm, bringing my attention back from where I'd watched Jude exit. "Crispin. Look at me." I raised my eyes to his and found nothing but kindness there. "I think I know your concerns, it might surprise you to know that I was a young man myself at one point. But on the nights you are unwell, and most especially on the nights you take your medicine, I must insist that you leave the door unlocked. I don't want another fright like the one we all had this morning."

I nodded, "All right." I had to agree, and it was sensible. "I promise."

"Good boy. Now get some sleep, and as you insist you are fully recovered, I'll see you in the morning. Tomorrow we see what you are like on a horse."

I returned from my first lesson on equitation and carriage driving with a far better respect of the pain that Jude had clearly been in, and a little sorry that we had teased him quite so hard. "You'll be worse tomorrow," Myles said. And when Drummond tells you to straighten your legs you won't be able to."

Albert was rubbing some foul smelling liniment into my calves. My posterior was hurting more than my legs but I couldn't think of any way I would ever ask my valet to massage me in *that* area.

"I'm beginning to think that being a gentleman is overrated," I grumbled, "I seized up entirely during dinner. I don't know how I made it back up the stairs."

Jude wafted in at that point, a box in his hands. "Dr. Baynes had this sent over while we were at dinner. Philip said you'd probably seen enough of him for the time being, or he'd have brought it up himself."

I admit that I did feel rather like that, for Philip's ease and skill with a horse had made me feel like the worst kind of incompetent. He sat his own horse – no matter how much it swung its hind-quarters around (and it did, most alarmingly) – as easily as he sat in his chair at dinner. More so, if anything, for I would wager that if his dinner chair were to swerve at the sight of a sudden footman, Philip would be unseated more easily than he would have been from the beast he rode. He seemed part centaur to me. My own efforts were at least tinged with the success of not falling off (or "cutting a voluntary" as he informed me was the current term), but I found it incomprehensible that anyone could order a horse about with merely a touch of the leg. No matter how I 'touched' my animal with my leg it steadfastly refused to go where I directed it, nor at any speed that suited Philip. He was a good deal less patient when it came to riding than he had been with fencing, his concern for the horse seeming to override his concern for me. I was actually pleased that he wasn't fussing over me the way he had been, and was treating me more like the others.

He was laughing when I dismounted at the end of the lesson, and helped me down himself, supporting me as I slid down the side of the horse, and ensuring I didn't fall. His arms were strong, helping me to my feet and ensuring I was stable before he let me go. "Not bad," he had said, which warmed me. I hadn't realised how eager I was to please him.

Even so, I had been in his company most of the day, and was happy to spend the evening with my friends.

"What's in the box?" Myles asked. He was spread out on the window seat, and hardly raised his head more than an inch.

"Crispin's medicine."

I made a face, "If it's anything like the concoction Albert made, I doubt it's anything pleasant." Albert's face was a picture of indifference.

"When is medicine pleasant?" asked Myles. "Unless your matron in the San. gave sugar treats for good boys who took theirs without a complaint?"

"We didn't have a matron," I said, wishing I had something at hand to throw at him, although I think it would have hurt me to try. "That's fine, Albert, my legs feel much better." I reached out to Jude for the box.

Albert stopped his massage, and dried my legs with a cloth, "Shall I take that, Mr Jude? I will lock it away for you."

I had wanted to look in it, but I feigned a disinterest. "Certainly." I waited until Albert had gone, then turned to Jude who hadn't sat down. "Hopefully I won't need it again in a hurry anyway."

"What about if you can't straighten up for the party?"

Jude snorted from across the room. "Well, he'll just have to greet people bent double. That could cause some interesting comments."

"I'll be fine. You managed, and," I added nastily, "at least I didn't fall off."

He was almost right in his guess, however, as the next morning I was not only stiff but had discovered bones in my posterior that I had not known existed. It was only Albert's massages that kept me moving, and by the morning of the party I was sufficiently supple enough to stop worrying about whether I'd be able to dance at the party that evening, even if Drummond proffered pity for any young lady's toes I would invariably, according to him, be trampling.

After breakfast, I emerged into a house of organised chaos. I leaned over the balustrade for a moment to watch the activity below, where servants, and other people I had not seen before, were busy carrying chairs, buckets of winter greenery and candelabras across the hall towards the ballroom. Philip appeared in the hall and after a few words with Witheridge, who appeared to be directing operations with a quiet competence, he took the stairs, two at a time to where I stood. After enquiring, and having my affirmation that I was quite well, he joined me, leaning over the rail as I was. His face was full of life and he looked to me, almost as if seeking assurance. "I admit to being a little excited myself," he said, "I haven't held a party here for...over five years."

"I think if I had a house like this I'd hold parties and dances all of the time."

"You'd get tired of them, especially in such an insular society as this. Even Yarmouth can provide a more varied social gathering." His eyes shone and he looked almost boyish as he hung over the banister with me, his smile fixed and happy. "You'd soon get bored of the society around here. I'll take you to London in due course, Crispin, then you'll know what parties should be like. You might be dreadfully disappointed about this evening."

"I doubt it, sir," I said.

"I'll remind you of that later," he said, pushing himself upright. He put a hand on my shoulder and squeezed. "Eventually you'll come to consider this quite provincial, I promise you." He set off along the hallway towards his room, then called back over his shoulder, "No lessons today, Crispin. Make the most of it."

I grinned and wished I'd known earlier, I would have stayed in bed, still unused to the utter luxury of being able to do so. Instead I went downstairs, informed George the footman on sentry (I was finally putting names to faces) that I wished to go out, and once thoroughly bundled against the cold, escaped out into the bright winter air.

I walked briskly down to the boathouse, and tried the door once more. It was still locked, and I was not surprised at it, if a little disappointed. I wandered around to the waterside to ascertain if I could see inside at all. I found that, if I lay on the frozen ground and slid forward so my head and shoulders were almost touching the water, I could just see inside the closed gates. It was clear there was a boat in the boathouse after all – so Heriment had lied to me, or he had not known.

The water gates were inaccessible from the house-side. One would have to be in a boat to be able to reach them. For one moment I considered slipping into the brackish water and ducking under the doors, but realised almost immediately how entirely mad I would be to even try it. Dipping one hand into the water proved that it was colder than even I had imagined; do it naked and I'd not have warm clothes once I gained the inside of the boathouse, do it clothed and I risked not only the danger of being dragged under by the weight, but then would probably die of cold anyway.

I pushed myself to my feet, brushing the frost from my clothes, feeling angry and frustrated. The boat was tantalisingly close and it would be immense fun to learn to sail; perhaps one of the others had more of an idea of the art of it than I did, but it would be amusing to try to do, even if we were all as idiotic as each other. It wasn't until I was halfway around the walled garden, walking as fast as I could in order to warm up again, that it struck me that I should ask Philip. He hadn't been around when I'd investigated the boathouse before, after all.

I ducked in through the entrance from the herb garden to the kitchens and trotted though, casting hungry glances at the profusion of game and pastry that the staff were working on, and found Witheridge just outside the kitchen, concentrating on a sheaf of papers in his hand.

"Witheridge, is Mr Smallwood in his study, do you know?"

"He asked not to be disturbed, Mr Crispin. Is there anything I can assist you with?"

I knew that if I asked Witheridge he'd tell Philip, and although we hadn't been specifically banned from sailing, I had my suspicions that if Philip had wanted us to sail, he would have included it in our lessons or he would have left the boathouse open, so I shrugged it off. "No, it's nothing important. It can wait until this evening."

"Very well, sir." He lost interest in me almost as soon as I'd moved away. I went to seek out Myles, waving away George, who wanted to take my coat and hat. I should have felt wicked but I didn't, I felt adventurous, and Myles was probably just who I needed in my adventure. I finally tracked him down in a small room on the first floor, an unfurnished one, the last room before the stair for the staff bedrooms. He was kneeling on the floor with his one hand on the wall – it looked as if he'd lost something, but he leapt to his feet when I opened the door, guilt flashing across his face before he wiped it away.

"What are you looking for in here? It's freezing!" There was no fire in the abandoned room, and my breath gusted in front of me almost as much as it did while I had been outside.

Myles jumped to his feet, dusting off his knees. "Nothing." It was obvious he was lying.

"The fact that you didn't invent something," I said, "makes me suspect you. But while you are obviously up to mischief, come with me and perhaps we can put your talents to work." He followed me, quietly, but clearly curious. I put my finger to my lips when he asked me what I was up to, and I felt master of intrigue as I led him outside. "I want to get inside there," I said as we rounded the bank and came upon the boathouse.

"Hmm." I loved the way he didn't ask for explanations but fell in with my idea as easily as Arch had always done whenever I came up with some nefarious scheme for sneaking out of Hall early or disguising ourselves as older boys and going into town for a day. He walked around the boathouse, testing the door with rather more vigour than I had, then walked down to the water to examine the water doors. "Without freezing to death, preferably," I called out.

"I don't think there's any major problem," he said. "When were you thinking of breaking in?"

"Breaking in sounds so criminal," I said. I took him by the arm, grinning. "Myles, you are my kind of reprobate."

To my enormous surprise he blushed, but I could have been mistaken, it might have been his cheeks being pink due to the cold. "Perhaps when Philip is away next?" he suggested.

I gave him a conspiratorial grin, and arm in arm we marched back inside to enjoy our unexpected day off in more warmth and comfort.

❦ Chapter Nineteen ❦

Primped, preened and tidied, the three of us descended the stairs together. Our valets had obviously conferred, for we each wore a different evening jacket, even if the differences were so slight as to be almost unnoticeable. Jude looked tall and slender, one hand casually in a pocket, the other resting lightly on the banister, and Myles filled his jacket beautifully, his shoulders deliciously wide, showing off his athletic figure.

No-one had commented on my appearance, so all I could do was hope that I looked half as good as my companions, although I wouldn't have minded a compliment to still my nerves. I might have attended parties before, but only as a very minor participant, never as the focus of attention.

Philip stood at the bottom of the stairs, watching us descend, and the light of pride in his eyes made my insecurities melt away, I hardly needed voiced compliments when my guardian looked so entirely sure of us. I had a small quiver of guilt at what Myles and I were planning. We had yet to bring Jude in on our plans – other than at lunch we hadn't seen him, but I wanted to try and breach the gap between us, whatever had caused it.

"Witheridge," Philip said, "we will be in the withdrawing room to receive."

"Yes, sir," Witheridge said.

Philip led the way down the corridor. Once ensconced in the withdrawing room, and we were furnished with a glass of Madeira we had just enough time to join Philip as he raised a toast to the success of the evening, before we heard muffled voices – our guests had arrived, and my nerves started up again.

It wasn't a large party – and in fact I had expected much larger – but for all that I had difficulty remembering everyone's names. The women, elaborate and colourful, were easier to identify, but the men, all dressed alike and many looking alike, dour faces and sandy colouring, a remnant of the Viking invasion I had no doubt, were harder to tell apart. It amazed me that these people, dressed as elegantly as any of the Archesons' guests have ever been, had travelled across the choppy water of the Mere in pitch darkness to attend. Obviously they thought no more of it than did the Venetians in their maze of watery streets. There was a Colonel Lewson and his wife and daughter, Doctor Baynes, gruff and alone, and a group of other notables, some with their wives, some without. I am ashamed to say that without Myles' help I would have been struggling with their names all night.

Philip dealt with the introductions, and we all shook hands dutifully. Jude, in his own inimitable style, even had the cheek to kiss the hands of several of the married ladies, but it was not something Myles and I attempted. We couldn't help but notice the smallest of smiles on the corner of Philip's mouth, gone as swiftly as it appeared, as he watched Jude's outrageous flirting.

I had time for a quick word with Doctor Baynes and he looked me over with an appraising eye.

"How are you feeling, young man?" he asked. "Still bossing Philip around?"

"Quite well, thank you, sir," I said. "It is good to see you." This was true, it was good to see someone I knew. He felt like my first friend in this place.

"Surprised to be asked," he said. "My wife would have liked to have attended, for it is many years since she last visited Philip but she wasn't up to the journey."

I wished her well, and was struggling for something else to say when I was literally saved by the dinner bell and we went in.

I was paired with the wife of a local squire, a Mrs Dady. I was soon to find that she was quite effortless company. That is to say, I only had to ask her the simplest of questions such as "And where do you live?" for her to chatter on in an attractive, voluble and unstoppable manner, totally oblivious that I was not able to interject any further comments until she ran out of information to impart. It was then up to me to provide her with another question – and I'd had plenty of time during her soliloquy – and then I could relax again, until the next time she wound down.

In the lacunae between questions I was given the opportunity to look around at my friends. Myles seemed to paying more attention to his food than to the lady beside him, and to be honest I couldn't blame him, for the woman was talking almost entirely to Philip, who sat to her right. Philip was paying as much courtesy to her as he could, but his focus was divided for Mrs Lewson, the good Colonel's wife, was on *his* right.

As for Jude, it didn't seem to matter to him where his speech should be directed. As I had expected, he was the centre of attention at his end of the table. Whether he was inventing the anecdotes he was sharing with the people around him or whether each tale was really something he had experienced, I had no idea, much of it was spoken so quietly I could not hear him, with details whispered into his neighbours' ears to shock and amuse. I envied him. I knew, of course, of his ability to spin stories and to divert, but I'd not seen him quite like this, entertaining as he was. It was his element and he swam in it perfectly. It struck me then, as never before, of his similarity to Arch – not his physical appearance, for Myles was more like Arch in that, but for his ability to blend into his surroundings, and not disappear as I often wished to do. At Barton Hall, I had learned of a lizard which some said could change its colour dependent on its surroundings. Brown for earth, green for leaves and so on – as unlikely an animal as it seemed to me, it struck me that evening that Jude was such a creature and there was no surrounding he could not blend with.

All torments finish eventually and as there was no hostess, we all left the table together, a novelty to me. After the brief and necessary pauses while relief was sought by all, we gathered in the withdrawing room.

Philip, who had toasted his guests more than once already, and whose face was faintly flushed with wine, began to speak. "As you know," he said, standing with a glass in his hand, "I have not been much of a neighbour to you all over the last five years." The gentlemen particularly uttered cries of denial, but Philip waved them back to silence. I looked around the room and noticed that Baynes was leaning back in his seat, had not joined in with the slightly inebriated rebuttal, but was watching Philip intently.

Philip continued, "You are kind, but I cannot accept your forgiveness." The assemblage continued to try to deny that he was anything but a good neighbour, with the exception of Baynes. Jude and Myles, like me, were simply sitting and watching Philip. "However," Philip said, as the noise abated, "I intend – with the exception of the time I need to spend in London – and I'm sure I will see some if not most of you there during the season – to return to the duties I owe you all, and Bittern's Reach will be once more be hosting parties." General cheers were raised and even several of the ladies applauded. Philip gestured at one of the footmen and yet another magnum of champagne was taken around the table, filling each person's glass. "And to usher in the new spirit of neighbourliness, I offer you a toast to a new beginning. To my wards, who have brought life back to Bittern's Reach after all this time. Jude, Myles and Crispin."

I was too inebriated to blush, but I still felt hugely embarrassed as everyone stood, every eye turned to the three of us, sitting together like birds on a fence, and every glass was raised in our honour. I was only grateful that no-one expected us to make any speeches. Once our toast was over conversation began and we were left alone, although curious glances were directed towards us from time to time. Jude left Myles and I to continue his socialising, but I sat where I was and didn't follow his example. The room was beginning to spin; I was regretting the champagne. It wasn't a drink I'd ever had much of, and two large glasses were more than my head and my stomach, groaning with game and fish, could cope with.

I had that cold, gut-churning sensation which threatened my equilibrium. I felt the room twist again and quietly put my hand on the seat to steady myself. Myles, who had not chosen to circulate yet, was quick to turn his attention to me. "Aside from your red nose," he said, "you've gone quite pale."

"I feel rather unsteady," I said quietly. "I'm going to have to excuse myself for a little while."

"I'll come with you, you might get worse."

"No, it's all right," I said. "I think some air will help. No, please, I can manage. Just let Philip know I need to clear my head." Myles nodded and I pushed myself to my feet and made for the door.

Evans let me out, and I escaped from the fug of cigar smoke and drone of conversation to make my way to my room. I was pleased not to find Albert in attendance, but then he wouldn't have expected me back this early. I relieved myself, then held a damp cloth against my forehead until the room stopped spinning, which took a while. I was anxious to get back, for I knew that Philip would note my absence and we were supposed to be the point of the evening's gathering, after all. At last the nausea dissipated sufficiently for me to feel well enough to return, but as I walked back along the quiet corridor past Philip's study, I was surprised to hear voices, and voices raised in argument too.

I shouldn't have stopped. Half of me warred with the other for I knew the right thing to do. I actually made as to walk by when I recognised Dr. Baynes' voice. It surprised me so much that I paused; Philip had so deliberately avoided him in the ballroom I couldn't help but be shocked that he had chosen to converse with him in private.

"...must see, Philip, how it looks."

"The hell with how it looks, I've never cared before and I don't care now."

"They are young men, for God's sake. Not dolls! You can't... You can't do this! Perhaps no-one else noticed the clothes, the hair – it's been five years, but they will if you continue in this way. The staff... People talk..."

"That's enough!" Philip's voice roared so loudly I was surprised the whole house wasn't set in action. Then his next words were vicious whispers I could hardly hear. "I won't be lectured – not by you. Not by you of all people! What did you care? What did you do? Other than the worst? You're a butcher!"

"Philip." Baynes voice went soft, as though he were talking to a child. "Philip, lad. I cared, I did what I could –"

"You did nothing! Worse than nothing! Get out! Get out, get out! I was a fool to invite you here tonight – just for appearances. A fool."

"Philip –"

"*Get out!*"

I heard footsteps and I fled down the corridor, making the library just in time as Philip's study door opened. I paused, controlling the very sound of my breath, until it was clear that Baynes had gone straight for the front door. I hated to have heard their conversation, and wished there were some way I could unhear it. The bitterness, the desperation in Philip's voice had torn me apart. I'd never heard anyone so full of pain and anger – and it was all aimed towards Baynes, and why? It sounded as if they knew each other well, Baynes even sounded fatherly if anything, and Philip had continued to attack him.

They are young men, for God's sake. Not dolls!

I checked the corridor. The door was closed and no sound from within the room. It seemed as though Philip had no intention of leaving. I fairly ran to the front door. I ignored the footman on duty as he stepped toward me with an expression of concern, and I pulled open the front door, stepping out in the chill wind. Philip had provided torches either side of the path for his visitors and the dock itself was ablaze with light. I could spy the doctor making his way down the gravel towards his boat so I hurried after him, catching up with him before he was halfway there.

"Doctor," I said, a little out of breath. "Doctor Baynes, please, wait."

The man stopped, turned and peered at me in the gloom. "Who's that?" he barked.

"It's me, sir, Crispin. Crispin Thorne."

He moved his face closer and brandy fumes hit me like a mallet. "Crispin? Get in out of this wind, boy."

"I…I wanted to speak to you, sir."

He took me by the arm and propelled me toward the dock. The light from the torches lit many small and medium-sized boats tied up to the jetty and along the bank; Baynes led me to a slender rowboat with a covered section sat squarely against the wooden walkway. He gestured to a man standing by. "Simms, help Mr Thorne into the boat and pour him a brandy. He must be frozen."

I stepped stepped gingerly into the craft. It was a lot smaller than Tom's wherry and wobbled alarmingly as each person boarded. Baynes directed me under the canopy which was almost a small cabin by itself, and passed me a rug which I wrapped around me.

"Now, what's this? Why didn't you speak to me in the house, where we both could be warm and comfortable?"

I realised that I'd have to admit my fault and spoke before I changed my mind. "I couldn't help…you were both rather loud…I overheard Philip and yourself."

"Overheard, eh?" Baynes said. He appeared to be bristling with indignation, but under all that hair, and even wrapped in scarves as he was, I discerned a definite gleam in his eye. "Well, you young men are curious creatures. Get yourselves into more trouble than cats, I always say. So, out with it. What d'you think you heard?"

"I heard you arguing," I said.

"Well, I'm afraid that Philip and I haven't seen eye to eye for a long while. You mustn't worry about what he said to me, you know. We used to be quite good friends. The boy has a hot temper, but it fades as fast as it flares."

I remembered the look of sheer hatred I'd seen when Baynes had attended me, and wondered if the Doctor was fooling himself. But he was right about Philip's mercurial moods. I balled the blanket in my fist. "You said something about dolls. You were talking about us – the three of us – I think."

"Ah." Baynes leant back. "I really shouldn't let your guardian get my goat the way he does. I shouldn't have said that to him."

"But you did mean us?"

He nodded and was silent for a moment. "Philip is a man very set in his ways, always has been. The house, the servants – it's all the same. Perhaps we are all a little like that, out here in this tideless waste. Maybe it takes a tide to make a change."

"I'm not sure what you mean, sir."

"There's something very unchanging about the Reach," he continued. "Oh, yes, the house has been changed over time, you can see that by the additions and modernisations, but since I've known it – and I remember it from Philip's grandfather's time – it's been the same. Always the same. So I shouldn't have been surprised that he was dressing you like Dominic, it was just a bit of a shock. Myles, particularly, looks very much like him, you know, with his hair like that."

Something, a shiver of wrongness, slid over my skin. *Dominic.* "That's my name," I said, "Dominic. My middle name. It was added to mine when Philip became my guardian." I had a sudden vision of Jude, that first morning *"Jude Dominic Middleton, to be utterly precise,"* he'd said. I'd known even then that we all must have taken the name, but I'd never brought it up with either of them.

Baynes looked at me hard, almost the same way he had on the day he'd first met me. "Is that so?" he said. "And you don't know of anyone of that name, is that what you're saying?"

I hadn't said that, hadn't thought that, but I nodded. "No, I don't."

"Well Philip did," he said, and each word was said with such emphasis that I sat dumbstruck. "Dominic Rowe. Son of a schoolfriend. The boy came here when he was fifteen. His parents died while travelling and they always wanted Philip to be his guardian should anything happen to them." He peered at me in the torch-light. "You'd not heard of this? Not from anyone?"

"No," I said, "no, not a word. I thought," I fumbled for my watch, "I thought he'd lost someone. I found a watch, identical to this but it wasn't mine. I thought it was his son."

"In all but name," Baynes said. "From the day Dominic came here something woke in Philip. He'd always been such a serious young man, the only time I'd seen him laugh was with his sister, and she…well, he lost her when he lost his parents. He took over the responsibilities of the Reach when he was very young and he took it very seriously. Philip's very thorough; you must have al-ready realised that. He does nothing lightly. Well, he was not even thirty when Dominic came here, but Dominic seemed to let him have a new life. When Dominic died – well, I think part of Philip died too. Well, it's too damned cold to tell you the whole story now, you are shivering already, lad."

"But, what happened –"

"I am your doctor." Baynes continued. "Even if Philip says he won't have me on the premises, he has little choice, unless he wants to risk sending to Yarmouth each time one of you get a fever. You get in now or you'll have one yourself. I'll come and see Philip to-morrow, smooth things over. He's let me in now, he'll not keep me out for another five years." He motioned to his man to help me out of the boat, and despite the cold, I stood and watched the boat as it pulled away and vanished into the inky blackness of the Mere.

Chapter Twenty

Deep in thought, I went back to my room and rang for Albert. A swift glance in the looking glass confirmed that his attentions were needed, for my hair was a mess, blown about by the buffeting wind, my clothes a trifle damp, my collar entirely ruined. Assessing me with the least amount of fuss, Albert set to repairing the damage, and in minutes I was restored to my former perfection, or very nearly. My hair was still wet, but after a fresh application of macassar it was at least held in place.

Then I returned to the party. I was claimed almost immediately by Philip, who broke away from his guests, his face a study in concern. "Are you all right?" he asked, with that sharp, perceptive glance he had, but on being reassured that I was fine, and he was please, not to worry, he returned to his guests and left me to sink back onto the couch I had so recently left. My mind whirling with what Baynes had said. I scoured the room for my friends, but only managed to attract the attention of my dining companion Mrs Dady who probably thought I was alone and in need of her loquacity. However, my mind being stirred by the events outside, I was unable to even formulate the simple questions her narration required, and after a while we sat in awkward silence. She made an excuse eventually, and I stood as she joined her husband, but at that moment Myles reappeared, much to my relief, took my arm and led me over to the group he had left, where Jude was in full entertaining flow. Myles seemed to sense that my thoughts were disturbed, for he squeezed my arm in reassurance, pressed a very large glass of wine upon me and whispered, "Tell me later," before pulling me down on the settle next to him.

Later, as we waited in the hall to bid farewell to the last of the guests, Philip, revealing no indication of his disagreement with Baynes, pronounced the evening a resounding success. "You need not be concerned," he said to us, "that you will be forced to tolerate such provincial types terribly often. They are good people in their way, and most of them have known me all my life." He pulled his tie undone as he led the way upstairs. "But their minds and mine – and I hope, yours – run in different ways. They see the world turn, and I prefer things to stay much as they are."

"Dr Baynes said as much earlier," I said, without thinking. I was tired and my thoughts were slowed by alcohol.

Philip stopped at the top of the stairs and looked down at me. "Did he? When was this?"

"Oh, at some point, can't remember exactly." I knew I hadn't spoken to the man at dinner, as he'd been closer to Jude than I, but I hoped Philip hadn't noticed that we had not spoken once dinner was over. I decided to continue, for it might have seemed more suspicious had I changed my mind. "It wasn't you he referred to, sir, it was more the Reach he meant. Unchanging, he called it. I don't know that I caught his meaning, he said it was probably because of the lack of tides."

Philip seemed placated, and continued along the corridor towards his tower. "Exactly," I heard him say, "Baynes would blame nature. For that's something he can do nothing about."

Jude was nowhere to be seen. Myles took me by the arm again and steered me into the nearest room, which was his.

He let Michael take his jacket and pour us a small port each before dismissing him. I held back a wry smile that Albert would probably have objected, insisted on taking all of my clothes for cleaning, but Myles seemed far more the master of his small domain than I. "Come on, Crispin," he said, falling onto his window seat with a sigh as he kicked off his shoes. "Tell me."

"What?"

"Oh, come on. You went out to recover your wits, and came back looking worse than when you left. Didn't you wonder why Philip jumped on you like a protective tiger?"

I was still a little reluctant, there was much I wanted to mull over – things I wanted to decide whether I'd ask Philip about. "It was nothing, really, I went for some air. I suppose it didn't help. I told Philip."

I concentrated on my glass, and Myles was silent for a moment, then he stood up, and came and sat opposite me. "Now tell *me.*" His gaze was gentle, far more so than ever I'd seen before, even when I'd been ill.

Defeated, I told him; about the overheard argument and the swift, cold and shocking revelations in Baynes' boat. Throughout the entire story Myles kept quiet, but kept his eyes on mine, only nodding from time to time as if in encouragement. When I finished he sat back, "Well, it's no more than we suspected," he said. "And yes, it's strange that we've never mentioned it to each other but, like you, part of my arrangement to come here was taking the name of Dominic as one of my own. I thought little of it at the time, as did you, I am sure. A whim of my new guardian, a family name, one of his own."

I nodded. "I did think that. But now… I can't explain it…"

"Instead, it's a memorial –"

"And there's nothing wrong with that!" I said, hurriedly. "I can understand, I do understand…"

"You understand a man who calls not one, but three of his wards after the dead son of a dead friend?"

I drank my drink in one draught. "No. Actually, no. Not when you put it like that."

He poured me another glass. "You shouldn't worry about it, you know that. It's likely to –"

Suddenly I was sick of everyone hovering, making allowances – being over zealous. "For God's sake!" I erupted, "not you too!

Myles, you are the one person who's treated me as though there's nothing wrong with me. Just keep on doing that, will you?"

He scowled and the consideration disappeared from his face. I was pleased, it suited him more, was more like the Myles I knew. "What I meant, you arse," he said, "was that Baynes said he'd explain more of it, so there's no bloody point working yourself up."

"You think we should tell Jude?"

Myles looked at me as if I was simple. "Now? Hardly." There was an acerbic undertone to his voice I'd heard before more than once.

I glanced at the clock, and pushed myself to my feet, "No, you're right of course. I'll tell him tomorrow, somehow."

"Unless he knows already," Myles said, darkly, as he accompanied me to the door.

"He can't do," I said, wearily, leaving without looking back. I found myself repeating myself even after the door had closed behind me.

We were granted a day of rest the next day, which meant that we had no lessons until the Monday. I woke with a clear head, which at first surprised me, until the clock chimed and I realised that it was gone midday. I rang for Albert immediately and ate whatever was put in front of me. It was not until I was stretching back down into bed again, feeling deliciously sybaritic for being in so lazy so late in the day, that I remembered Myles and the boathouse and in moments I was wrapped in a gown and knocking on his door. I found him reading, and at my appearance he put down his book and scowled at me. "Well, for God's sake, Crispin, you took your time. Go and get dressed and we'll go and see what mischief we can do." I spared him a swift grin, glad to see his was his normal cantankerous self and not enquiring over my health, before flying back to my room to dress.

I was pulling on my boots when a knock came at the door. Albert opened it to admit Jude. It was the first time we'd really been alone together since our disagreement and as he closed the door and leaned against it I felt odd, as if suddenly he was a stranger, and the little steps we'd taken – that I felt he'd made me take – towards a more intimate relationship had been almost entirely wiped away, putting us almost as far back as the day I arrived.

"Philip's just asked me to tell you both that he'll be away for a while," he said.

"All right," I replied, shortly; more shortly than I had meant to, but I hadn't really forgiven him for his flirting and sudden change, and anyway, I was bent over lacing my boots, so perhaps he didn't notice. "What are you planning to do today?" I knew I was being a little brutal, but I wasn't in a mood to play his games, and selfishly I decided I wasn't going to share the information I had. Let us keep it to ourselves, and let him be put out when he realised we'd been keeping it from him.

"I was going to ask you the same question, actually."

I finished with my laces and sat up to find him still leaning against the door. He looked strangely brittle, and looking at his face, flickering with emotion, his mouth working, I recognised the signs for I often felt like that myself. I just hoped I wasn't so damned obvious about it. I almost gave in, but I was still angry. He should have left me alone, that would have been better – just because we shared certain tastes didn't mean that he should think he could just *taste* me because on a whim and then put me aside.

"Myles and I are going out."

"It's bloody freezing, Crispin."

"Well, thank you. We know that."

"You and Myles."

I glared at him and pulled the bellrope viciously, feeling the anger flow into me. I wanted to hit him – or kiss him – and I hated I couldn't decide which. "Yes, Jude. Myles and I. I hope that's all right with you?"

I saw a flicker of something cross his face, and his eyelids fluttered. "Well, it's hardly up to me, is it?" Something of his previous haughty sensuality, the aloof and sexual Jude returned, but I could see it was a shield he wore, and that he hadn't come in to mock. It didn't help me be any kinder to him.

"That's right," I said. "It's not." We sat in awkward silence for a long while until Albert arrived with a basket of provisions, making Jude move at last. "Thank you, Albert. Well, we'll see you at dinner, Jude."

Wrapped up well, and out in the cold courtyard, I waited for Myles and he joined me by the steps. As we walked across to the gate, I told him about Philip. "Jude told me," was all he said.

"Jude and I," I said, finally, after a long silence. We were nearly at the boathouse. "I'd like to tell you. I –"

"You don't need to," Myles said. "With the three of us – the way we are – well, it's likely that something would have –" He marched ahead, his hands plunged firmly into his pockets. "Let's leave it, Crispin."

It didn't settle things as well as I wanted, but at least I had said something.

Cold as it was, the sun was out, and any frost on the reeds had melted, leaving a light mist on the water. Even though it was early afternoon, the sun was already low in the sky, giving a lemon tinge to everything it touched; the thatch on Philip's boathouse glowed almost gold under the winter light.

"Stand behind me," Myles said. "Keep a look out; we don't want anyone seeing." I did what he asked, casting glances up the path. We were only in view from one corner of the house, that which held Philip's bedroom, as trees blocked the view from everywhere else. Philip might be away, but it was perfectly possible that Witheridge or any of the other staff might be in Philip's tower and see us lurking where we shouldn't be. I peered over my shoulder at Myles to see he was struggling with the padlock. "No good," he muttered, finally. "Damned thing is rusted solid."

"You were going to pick it?"

"If it wasn't stuck fast, yes, why?" He'd already moved around to the side of the boathouse and I trotted after him.

"No reason," I said, grinning, wondering what other nefarious skills he was going to show. If word of that talent had become common knowledge at his school, it was no wonder that any thefts from behind locked doors would be blamed on him.

"Don't believe I can?"

For answer I simply punched him in the arm, and he turned to smile at me. "There's another way in," he said, nodding at the water doors."

"Well, you aren't going in, Myles. You'll freeze."

"It won't take more than a minute." He was already peeling off his coat and scarf. "The water doors don't actually go all the way down to the water line, I can see that from here, I'll only need to duck under and I'll be in."

A shudder went through me, and not from the cold. "No, don't. It's not worth it, just for my curiosity."

He stopped for a second, his fingers on the buttons of his waist-coat. "Oh come now, you aren't backing out on the idea now. This was your idea, and now I want to see what's in there as well as you do. You do, don't you? Admit it!"

I couldn't help it, he was right, but it was cold. "And I promised Philip that I wouldn't go swimming."

He continued undressing, shivering already as the layers dropped onto the ground. "Well, *I* didn't. What did you do a stupid thing like that for?"

"He asked me," I said, stung, watching him slide down the bank, dressed only in his boots and drawers. "I could hardly refuse – you refused him?"

"Ahhh – Oh shut up, Crispin…" he shouted, his voice shooting up half an octave, betraying the icy feel of the water against his skin. "Of course not. I said I wouldn't swim, and I kept my word. I *can't* bloody swim, remember? Just watch out no-one comes."

He waded forward towards the water doors. I could hear him breathing, gasping with the cold, and his arms flailed above the surface of the water as he propelled himself forward. I was worried now, imagining him caught by something beneath the murky surface and dragged down into the depths – and he couldn't swim. Why hadn't I remembered that? Why did he volunteer? I put down the basket, and went to the edge, for what reason I have no idea – he was out of my reach. He made it to the doors, turned and said, "Wish me luck," and ducked under the water, under the doors, and vanished from my sight.

It went very quiet, the noise of his progression through the water, the sound of his breathing, cut off, and I began to worry, and then, my stomach churning with worry, I started to panic.

"Myles!" My voice sounded lost and alone, swallowed up by the expanse of water, deadened by the brooding hulk of the wooden shed. I ran back up the path to where the walls of the shed were, and pounded on the side. "Myles, Myles! Say something, damn you! Answer me!" I raced back to where he'd entered the water but could see nothing but the brown-grey water lapping against the doors. "Oh, God… Myles!"

"For God's sake, Crispin, I thought this was supposed to be a secret?" Myles pushed open the padlocked door. "You are making enough noise to let the whole house know. Get in here quick, and bring my bloody clothes and the basket, and if Albert has not packed port or brandy he's not the man I thought he was. Damned padlock was a dummy. The stupid thing unlocks from the inside."

Chapter Twenty-one

Almost laughing in relief, I followed him in, wrapping his coat around him and cursing myself for not being fore-sighted enough to realise he'd launch himself into the Mere in the middle of winter. I should have brought a blanket, for it wouldn't have been too difficult to smuggle one out.

It was dim inside the boathouse, but I turned my attention to him, pushed him down on a bench which ran along the short side of the boathouse, and wrapped his scarf around his neck and damp hair. His teeth were chattering and I kept up a stream of invective against his idiocy as I attempted to warm him. I did the only thing I could think of, sat beside him, as Arch had once done to me when I had come in frozen after a cross-country run; wrapped my arms around him, rubbing his skin all over, while he rum-maged through the basket for a small stone bottle and drank from it gratefully, giving out a sigh which I felt could only mean that Albert had not let us down.

Draping his coat back over him, I knelt before him and unlaced his boots, which were sodden. It was no easy task as the laces were soaked, but I managed it eventually, pulling them and his socks from him and chafing his icy feet in my hands. "You should take these off too," I said, slapping his wet underthings. He had my scarf wrapped around his head and looked ridiculous, his hair pok-ing out like a baby bird peering from its nest, but his cheeks were flushed with a little colour and he had stopped shuddering.

"You seem to have a penchant for wanting to remove young men's drawers," he said, in a passable impression of Jude. "Not that I blame you in the slightest. I'm fine," he said, returning to himself. "They're warming on me. Just lend me your socks, will you?" He pulled on his clothes and I set about transferring my socks to his feet, drying his boots as well as I could before putting them back on. Eventually he declared himself as good as he was going to be and we stood up to take stock of our surroundings.

Our eyes had adjusted to the dim light, and watery sunlight poured in through knotholes and cracks in the wood, making dust-bright lances of sunshine. The boathouse had a wooden platform which extended all the way around, liked a squared off horseshoe, the walls lined with paraphernalia that obvious had some relation to boats – I admit the only things I recognised were oars. What all the ropes and rusted metal implements were for I had no idea, and we paid them scant attention, for tied to the dock, and covered to the waterline with a sail or some such material, was a large shape which could only be a boat. We turned to each other with grins a mile wide.

"I knew he had to have one." I said. "Baynes said everyone does here. So why does he rely on Old Tom?"

Myles was busy working at the sheeting from one side of the boat. "I don't know. God, I should have brought a knife. See if you can find something to cut these ropes with, Crispy, will you?"

Rummaging around in a heap of stuff piled in a corner I found a couple of knives but they were too rusted to be of much use. In a drawer on the far side, I unearthed something like a short saw; the blade was wrapped in oiled silk and seemed serviceable. Gingerly I carried it back to Myles and handed it to him, handle first.

"That'll do," he said, and started to cut. I thought for a moment to deter him, for we were causing damage to something that did not belong to us, but as we were only compounding a crime already committed, there seemed little point. The ropes came away from the sheeting easily enough and together, and with rising excitement on my part at least, we heaved the heavy, stiff material away from the boat and looked at what we'd uncovered. I could only stare in shock and disappointment; the boat was – or had been – beautiful, of that there was no doubt. It – or I suppose 'she' was more correct – probably had a special name as boats did, but I had no idea what it was. She was about thirty feet in length, with one mast lying along the deck, but she was a wreck – not just from neglect, and that was rampant enough, the varnish faded and cracked, mould growing everywhere. But she had been deliberately hacked to pieces.

Now she was uncovered, we could see she lay awkwardly in the water as if she was still in the throes of sinking, but it was clear that someone had set upon her with what could only have been an axe. The tiny cabin was broken open, the wood splintered and ravaged. Even the windows were knocked out, not one of them entire. The mast was smashed into several pieces, and although we couldn't see it from the dock, it was obvious from the way she listed that she was damaged below the water line. Even the piece of wood that stuck out from the front of the boat, like a narwhal's unicorn-like horn had been hacked off, leaving only a foot or so as a stub.

"I don't understand," I said, as we stood staring down at her. "Philip's a rich man, isn't he?"

"He certainly gives that impression," Myles said, in typical fashion.

"So if someone did this – for whatever reason – spite, revenge, hate…"

"Why didn't Philip buy another? Yes, that's rather the point, isn't it?"

"Not only that, he uses Old Tom to get around –"

"And others," Myles added.

"I didn't know that."

"Yes," he said. "It's part of your charm."

"And why smash it to pieces? If you wanted to destroy a boat, wouldn't it be easier to burn it?"

"Not without taking the boathouse, and maybe even the house with it."

The name, painted in flowing letters on the back, was old, cracked, difficult to read.

Myles rubbed at the dirt crusted on the boat's name. "What's it say, do you think? *Nag...lfar*? What the devil is that?"

"It's the end of the world... Hang on..." I said, leaning forward and rubbing at the paint. "There's another name here, too. Underneath. Give me that blade." I chipped away at the paint as carefully as I could – not really knowing why I was doing it, what did it matter what the boat was called? But something pushed at me, here was something else we didn't understand, and, like a metaphor, it was painted over, concealed with another mystery. "*Zephyrus.*"

"Well, that's a wind, that's a sensible name for a boat, at least. What did you mean, the end of the world?" For a moment, my sensible Myles looked a little disconcerted.

"She was the death ship of Norse legend. Made of fingernails and toenails she was built to carry the enemies of the gods to wage war against them at Ragnarök. What the Norse believed was the apocalypse."

"Toenails? Well that's just revolting. You know the oddest facts." Myles said, jumping across the gap onto the deck of the yacht.

"Myles, for God's sake –"

"I'm all right," he said. Pushing back the sheeting further, he revealed the rest of the boat. Myles ducked under the last bit of sheeting. "There's a lot of water, she's sitting on the bottom, or her keel is, I think. I'm afraid your socks are wet now, too."

"Idiot, you should have let me go."

"There's a dinghy here, though. Looks undamaged."

There was a silence and after I called his name his name a couple of times he emerged from the sheeting, his hair all standing on end. "Shut up and get in here and give me a hand."

"Why?" I didn't much fancy the idea of jumping aboard a sinking, or rather, sunken, ship.

"Because I want to push the dinghy into the water and I can't do it on my own, that's why. There's a mast, a sail and even some oars. You wanted to sail, didn't you, or was this only about finding out what was in here? The good ship Toenail is entirely useless, in case you *hadn't* noticed."

I clambered onto the deck and joined him at the front; together we freed the dinghy from the sail and the mast, part of which was trapping it in place, and managed to heave it overboard. After that, we lost interest in the wrecked yacht as we blundered about together, working out what was missing and what went where.

"Should we put the sail up?" I asked. "Do you even know how?"

"Not really." He looked at me and we started to laugh like madmen. He pushed against the yacht's hull and propelled us towards the water doors. Both of us were still grinning like fools, and once we'd opened the doors and pushed out into the Mere I for one was feeling marvellous. The landscape opened up, giving an entirely different vista on the Mere and we just floated for a while, letting the wind take us gradually out into open water. Myles wrestled with the oars, got them into the rowlocks while I shunted back and took hold of the rudder.

"Do you know how to row?"

With a defiant expression he dug his oars in the water – then landed on his back after one stroke, giving me not only my answer but a filthy look as he picked himself up, so I decided to say nothing more, trying to keep the smirk off my face. Somehow it seemed warmer on the water, or perhaps it was just the activity that had warmed us through. Myles battled for a while, with me keeping a very straight expression, until he seemed to get the hang of it and we moved away more smoothly. The banks of the Mere seemed much as I remembered them from my trip in, edged with pale, bleached reeds, and once out on the water, a fine mist shrouded the banks with a grey blur. Myles was just getting into his stride, and I was just starting to enjoy myself when I looked down, feeling my feet cooling, only to see that the bottom of the boat was dark with water, and that, judging by the bubbles rising from the centre of the base-board, more water was entering through holes we had not seen.

"Myles…" I called out. "There appears to be water coming in."

"All boats leak," he bellowed back. His face was pink with exertion, and he was smiling at his own success.

"No, seriously, it's not just leaking…it's pretty much pouring in."

He stopped, sat up straight and looked down. With one anxious glance at me, he pulled desperately on one oar, turning the dinghy around in a clumsy circle, rowing as best as he could for the shore. With every moment that passed, more water poured in, and I had nothing with which to bail. I tried using my cap, but it did little more than soak up water rather than hold it. "Myles…"

"I'm trying."

"Try harder!"

The wind had picked up, perversely against us, so if we had had any notion of how to sail, and thank God we didn't, we would have been blown speedily away from the Reach. As it was, it seemed whilst every stroke of Myles' rowing took us forward, the wind blew us back half as much as we had progressed. The bank was tantalisingly near, less than forty feet – if we had managed to aim for the boathouse, we'd have been safe under cover, but the wind had blown us further into the Mere, where the shore curved away.

"Try shouting," Myles said, puffing from his work. He seemed, at least to have learned to row, in extremis.

"They'll never hear me, it's –"

"Just *try!* You damned well told me to."

I hallooed and shouted for all I was worth, but the wind either snatched my voice away and blew it to Hickling or there was no-one in the house to hear, for no-one came. The bank came a little closer in the time I spent shouting so, with a worried look back at Myles, I leapt into the water, hoping against hope that I would not plunge below the surface and never return. The chill was astounding, but I shocked myself more that I landed only knee deep, and staggered as the boat hit the back of my legs. Myles turned around, took one look at me, standing there with the rope in my hands – which I had over-dramatically thought would be my only lifeline when I heroically launched myself into the Mere – and burst into raucous laughter.

"Shut up," I said, glaring. I turned around and pulled the boat to shore, feeling stupid, clambering up onto the bank and helping Myles get out, which he did without getting so much as a toe wet.

We dragged the damnable dinghy up onto the bank and dumped it unceremoniously back in the boathouse. Then we ran for the house. Witheridge materialised as the footman took our coats, and I'll never know how he managed to appear without being summoned. He instructed the footman to fetch our valets, despite our assurances that we could manage. I realised then, it would be impossible to keep our wretched state from Philip, but that was something we'd have to deal with when he returned. We parted in the upstairs hall with a conspiratorial look and submitted to the ministrations of our valets. After which, warm, clean and dry, I joined him in his room and we sat around the fire, sipping hot chocolate laced with a little rum, until Jude joined us, sliding easily to the floor, sitting cross-legged and leaning against my chair, but not quite against my legs. He sat quietly, running elegant fingers around the rim of his chocolate bowl with a small smirk on his face.

Myles was the first to break the silence. "Come on, Jude, I can see you're bursting to say something. What is it that you know?"

"Oh, nothing," he said.

"We aren't convinced, are we, Crispin?"

I wasn't too much concerned, truth be told, but it was just like Myles to worry at something with his teeth until it came loose. I decided to back him up, just to get at Jude, if nothing else. "No. Come clean, Jude."

"It's just that I was sure that Philip asked us not to go on the river, that's all."

Myles gave me a swift glance, then looked down at Jude again. "Out with it."

"I couldn't help but notice you and Crispin learning to row a boat. You were lucky, from what I could see."

"He didn't say anything about boating, only swimming," I said hurriedly, because Myles looked like he was ready to tell Jude what he'd told me.

"Perhaps," Jude said, looking sideways at me. "That's because he didn't think anyone would break into the boathouse. I don't think he would be at all pleased about that."

"Well, he's not going to find out, is he?" Myles growled. "Not about the damned boat, anyway. Because if he does, we'll know where it came from."

"We?" Jude looked from one of us to the other. He stood up, as gracefully as he'd sat down, unfolding from the floor. and put the chocolate bowl on the table. "I didn't realise, I apologise. Goodnight. And your *secret* is safe with me."

I strode after him, caught up with him as he reached the door. "Jude, Myles didn't mean that, you misunderstood, what he meant –"

"It's all right, Crispin," he whispered. "Neither of you is really my taste. So… provincial." Then he went with a blown kiss and a wave.

I stood there, watching the closed door, feeling my face flush with heat and not wanting to turn back around. I wished that Myles hadn't seen that, hadn't heard what Jude had said. I'd known he was highly strung, but I couldn't work out what was wrong with him, why he fluctuated from amiable and flirtatious to uncaring – pushing us – pushing me away.

"Don't worry about it, Crispin." Myles' voice was surprisingly soft. I had expected he'd be mocking.

"I should be going, it'll be back to normal tomorrow, and it's been a long day."

"Crispin –"

"Oh it's all right, Myles. Forgive me for causing a scene in front of you. I'm sure you found it highly amusing."

Suddenly he was there, by my arm. "Crispin." He sounded angry now and he pulled me around to face him. "It doesn't suit you. He doesn't –"

"He doesn't suit me? Oh, you know so much, don't you?" My temper flared, taking it out on Myles. "Just like that first morning, at breakfast. You knew so much about me, even then. You got some satisfaction from making me angry then, too, if I remember."

"All I'm saying is that Jude isn't –"

"I think it's quite obvious, thank you. I may be dear stupid Crispin who can't see his hand in front of his face, but I don't need it spelled out in ten foot letters that Jude isn't interested." I stormed towards the door.

"You are a bloody idiot! Yes, that's exactly what you are!" Myles shouted at me, but the expression in his anger made me stop and turn around. "You're too damned young for him, that's the trouble – don't you see? Haven't you seen, almost from the beginning?"

I turned around slowly, and it was like a wall rocking, badly made, as his words sliced through my own denial. Jude's absences, his words here and there…

"Yes, Crispin, yes." Myles was up close, pinning me against the door, angry and yet, not altogether angry. His face an inch from mine, his eyes flickering over my face. "He's been with Philip, from the earliest moment he could manage it." I breathed in to answer, but he kissed me hard, taking my breath, and any answer I might have given. There was no tenderness in the kiss, no preamble and no teasing, but it was hard, penetrating, claiming, and just what I needed to convert my anger into lust. While he reached behind me to lock the door, I clawed at his clothes, finding them not the delicious and teasing wrappings that I had with Jude, but in the way – too many buttons, far too many layers. His hand rubbed furiously against my groin, his tongue found its way into my mouth, but like an invader, searching for something hidden while his hands clutched my head as if he'd never let go. It wasn't comfortable, it wasn't sensuous and languid, but it was hard, and more than that, it was *real*.

I got his clothes open to the waist, plunging my hands into the gap, wrenching his shirt tails out from his trousers and scoring his skin with my nails. At that, he turned, still kissing me, and awkwardly we marched backwards to the bed where he pushed me over, only letting me get in the centre of the covers before continuing his assault. With Jude there had always been talk, teasing, encouragement, wicked things whispered in the heat of the moment, but with Myles it seemed that actions spoke louder, much louder. He had my braces undone and my trousers off before I'd even managed to finish stripping him to the waist, and with a swift flick of the wrist he bared enough of me to give him access to my prick, which had been paying attention at least and was ready for him. With a sigh, not unlike the one he'd given finding brandy in Albert's flask, he sank down the bed and his mouth closed over the head, and the sensation was so much, so entirely raw, that I almost spent immediately. I shoved my fist to my mouth and bit hard, while my hips arched towards him.

Intense, rapid strokes, heat and an edge of pain as he scored his teeth gently against my most sensitive areas were enough to make me concentrate almost entirely on biting my own hand, but he must have seen what I was doing, for he grabbed me by the wrist, pulled my hand down and all I could do after that was to feel his hair, still damp, and let my body explode with shuddering pleasure. Three, four spasms, each one sweeter and slower than the last, and I was nothing but a limp doll, strings cut and only half undressed.

Myles crawled up next to me after a moment or so away, entirely naked. He kissed my neck, just under my ear. "I've waited too long for that, and waited in line for you to come to your senses. When you've taken off the rest of your clothes, perhaps we can continue."

I reached for him and pulled him on top of me. Questions I had – although I felt I knew the answers now – but as I took his prick into my hand, I knew they could wait.

As a lover he was entirely Myles; a touch aggressive, impatient, but then surprising when I least expected it. I found that he loved his skin touched, just about everywhere, anywhere I could give him the attention. That afternoon, as we learned each others' bodies, I don't think there was a piece of his skin I didn't explore with tongue or lips. He tried to repay the compliment more than once, but his impatience would take over and he'd want to suck, be sucked or finally to fuck me until the bed rocked so much I was sure someone would come running to see if he was being murdered.

Y ou really had no idea, did you?" I lay on my side, with Myles curled behind me, his arms and legs tangled in mine. I could feel his breath on the damp curls at the back of my neck, and his heart, thudding as we recovered, against my back. "About Jude."

"No. You must think me very –"

Myles arms tightened around me, "If you are going to say 'stupid' then please don't waste your breath. If I thought you stupid, I wouldn't have…waited, wanted. I never wanted Jude, even if you were swept away by his desperate charm."

I couldn't answer straightaway for the varying emotions flowing through me at that moment. I pulled his legs in closer so we could hardly have been nearer to each other and kissed his hands. I could feel his prick, lodged comfortably between my arse cheeks, twitch in a half-hopeful manner. "You'd call him that? Desperate?"

He kissed the back of my neck. "I like him, please understand that, but right from the first day I could see what he was like. He…well…"

"I think I can guess. He called you persistent. I thought it meant that you were asking him to… I see now what he meant."

"And what he meant you to think."

"And Philip? When did that start?" I could hardly believe it even now.

"Quite soon after you arrived, I think. I'm not entirely sure, but I noticed a change in him almost immediately. Remember what he said about his friend at school? How we teased him for boasting it was a master? I think that our Jude likes an older man." He gave a small laugh. "Anyway, Crispy –"

"I really wish you wouldn't call me that."

"But it suits you so much; all brittle around the edges, but with a soft interior." His fingers were wandering over my chest as if he'd forgotten where my nipples were, which was very unlikely seeing as he'd given them so much attention quite recently.

"Anyway what?"

"Oh. What I was going to say, we should be grateful." He bit my neck. "No-one is going to care what we get up to, are they?"

As his questing fingers found my left nipple and teased it into life, I was grateful for many things.

ᠵ Chapter Twenty-two ᠵ

The next few days were some of the happiest that I had ever known. Although I was worried about Philip finding out my secret, and although Heriment was as strict as ever, and all the lessons continued, I glided through them with a smile on my face. Two weeks passed and Philip showed no sign of returning; Myles and I tried to conceal our new entanglement, but I often found myself staring across the table at him, and wondering why I had not considered him so handsome before. It seemed impossible to me now, looking at Myles in quite a different manner – previously, he had spent so much time scowling it had been easy to miss. But with the curls that fell over his forehead when not under control with hair dressing, and with his wide capable mouth and hands, just looking at him was enough to make my stomach flutter and my all too fashionable – and therefore tight – trousers to feel even tighter at inconvenient times.

With our shared sin between us, Myles, contrary creature as ever, found the whole thing amusing. A far more daring proposition than Arch, he took risks with our lovemaking. Even though Philip was absent, and we had no one else to dodge other than Albert, Michael and Witheridge, I shied from taking the risks that he seemed to enjoy – to kiss in a room that might be invaded by staff at any moment, to fuck in haste, forgetting to lock the door – all these we did, foolhardy at least, and we were lucky indeed we were never caught *in flagrante*.

I don't think we fooled Jude, although he never said anything to me, and Myles said that it was the same with him. I found Jude's silence on the matter – something I thought he would have taken delight in teasing apart with that delicate sarcasm of his – slightly disquieting, but since Philip's departure he had been almost a different person. He lost much of his sheen, became a little less "Jude" in some indefinable way.

"He's missing Philip," I said to Myles one evening, when, once again, Jude had retired to bed after a brief discussion with the two of us on nothing much. "And he's worried about something."

Myles stopped pouring the coffee and looked up at me, suddenly intent. "What?"

"He's worried."

"Yes, I heard what you said, but what is he worried about? Other than…"

"What?"

"You tell me." He leaned back and stared at me in a challenging fashion.

"I don't know," I said, eventually, admitting defeat.

"Perhaps you should ask him. You, after all, have been closer to him than I."

I flicked some of my coffee at him to shut him up.

Later, leaving Myles happy and more than slightly mussed, I called into Jude's room with the intention of seeing if I could help him with his troubles but to my surprise, although the door was unlocked, the room was dark and empty, the fire unlit. So I didn't ask Jude what was troubling him, and now I know that Myles – damn him for always being so – was right. I should have.

Philip returned eventually in early February, and in a particularly ebullient mood. He had been to London, he said, and had decided to bring us back each something we would enjoy. Like most young men who have been deprived of treats and presents of any value, we were still dazzled and excited to receive anything, especially affection. We were instructed to be patient, and only to wait until just before dinner, and by the look on Philip's face, he was just as excited as the three of us.

It was worth the wait. Jude received a small wooden crate filled to the brim with oranges, a fruit none of us had seen more than a handful of times in our lives. Myles's gift was a box of sweets: Pontefract cakes, humbugs, toffee, butterscotch and delicate sugar mice. As for myself, I was more than thrilled to receive a full set of everything that the good Mr. Dickens had so far published; each book inscribed *'to Crispin from Philip with very good wishes.'*

"They are beautiful, Philip. Thank you."

"I saw you were always reading," he said. "Although I had to guess at your taste. I hope you have not read them all?"

"Only *Pickwick*, to be honest. And *Dombey and Son* – and only some of that – I was dependent on the issues of serial making it to Hall, and they often did not," I said. "Thank you so much."

Myles' cheeks were already bulging, and Jude, aesthete that he was, or liked to be seen as, had an orange in each hand, savouring their smell and feel as no doubt I would do too in his place. Philip ordered our gifts to be taken away and dinner began in fine spirits. We were into the mutton, and deep in discussion about the Irish and why those poor people found it so difficult to grow potatoes when it seemed the simplest of pursuits, when Witheridge entered, his hands empty of any dishes, and spoke quietly and urgently to Philip. Philip pushed his plate away, almost untouched I noticed, although he usually had a good appetite, and made for the door. Jude followed his action almost simultaneously – indeed he'd hardly had eyes for anyone except Philip since his return – and Myles and I trailed out in their wake.

In the entrance hall stood a group of men wrapped up against the cold. I recognised all of them as neighbours and men who had attended Philip's party, all except the tallest man there – dressed impeccably in black wool – who peeled away from the main group when he saw us approach.

"Ah, Smallwood," the man said, holding out a hand for Philip to shake. "Bad business, this."

"Townsend." Philip shook the man's hand but didn't refer him to us. I recognised the name; Edward Townsend, local MP and magistrate. He had been in London at the time of Philip's party. I remembered Jude telling me that Philip was disappointed the man could not attend.

We three standing a small way back exchanged hurried glances, but kept quiet.

"How long has he been missing?" Philip said, "I was with him only yesterday."

"Ah, yes. Mrs Baynes told us you'd been there."

I felt the hairs on the back of my neck rise, and I listened intently, dreading what I might hear.

"Come through to the drawing room," Philip said.

We all marched through; no-one told us we three weren't to accompany them, so we did.

Once seated, Townsend spoke. "What happened while you were with him?"

Philip looked visibly shocked, as well he might, I supposed. If Dr. Baynes was missing it must strike him hard – they'd known each other a very long time. "I'd been in London, and on my way back I'd been thinking about Baynes, and how bridges needed to be re-built. I changed my plans – I'd meant to get back for dinner with my wards, but I stayed on the coach to Waxham and walked across the fields to his house from there."

"It's not a secret you and Baynes have no love lost," one of Townsend's companions growled. I heard Jude give a small gasp and I for one expected Philip to explode.

"If you have something to say to me, Byrne," Philip said, turning his head slowly to meet the eyes of the man who had spoken, "then say it. Am I being accused of something here? Is this what this delegation is about?"

"Don't be ridiculous, Smallwood. The man's missing, that's all." Townsend glared at Byrne who murmured an apology which Philip did not acknowledge, still bristling with pent up anger. "I'd like to hear your version of events once you arrived at Baynes' house."

"My version? My *version*? It seems that it's not just Byrne who has something on his mind."

"Smallwood. You've been a magistrate yourself, man. You know as well as I do that I have to ask these questions. You were, by your own admission, probably the last person to see Baynes last night, so please, indulge me, and stop being a stiff-necked fool."

Philip took a breath. "I arrived just after dark. Baynes was surprised to see me, of course, as I had – as you *know* – not been in his house since…well, for quite a while. However, he welcomed me in and we had a congenial dinner. Mrs Baynes was there, of course."

Townsend nodded. "Go on."

"I was planning to go on, to walk back to Horsey and hire a man to row me to the Reach, but neither he nor his wife would countenance the idea. He insisted that I stay the night and I would have done had he not received an urgent call."

"Where was this call?"

"It was Mrs Bilney, from the other side of the Mere. She sent word of her son. He had been ill for some time, and had taken a turn for the worse. Baynes had mentioned it at dinner, in fact, and was quite concerned."

"And Baynes decided to go that late at night without his manservant?"

"How did you know…? Oh, you've spoken to Laetitia Baynes," Philip said. "Yes. His servant was away from home, and Baynes wanted to hurry. Didn't want to leave the child overnight." He paused, his mouth twitching a little, obviously fraught with emotion. "He was concerned for the child's safety."

"And nothing happened? It must have been a difficult journey in the dark and cold. Surely he could have made the journey with the man that summonsed him?"

"I suggested that, as a matter of fact, but he said that as I was there, he could bring me home, and it would save the messenger making four trips. It seemed a sensible solution. Baynes is well used to the Broads at night and alone. His little yacht is well equipped with lanterns fore and aft."

"Did you go all the way to Bilney's with him?"

"No. I offered, but he said he could find his way with his eyes closed. He dropped me off at the Reach and went on alone."

"And that was the last you saw of him?"

"Yes. I offered him hospitality on his way home, but I didn't think he'd take me up on it. I assumed he'd be with the Bilneys overnight."

"He never returned home, and he never arrived at the Bilneys'. The boy died."

I expected Philip to answer, but he didn't. Instead he continued to look at Townsend, his expression not changing one whit as he did. Eventually Townsend's eyes dropped to the floor and the silence grew longer and longer until I found I was almost trembling, hoping that someone would say something.

Myles, unintroduced and unbidden, finally broke the silence. "We should look for him, then, surely."

"It would be impossible tonight," Townsend said, with a warm, penetrating glance at Myles. "The wind is positively dangerous."

"You'll stay the night, then," Philip said, immediately. "And begin the search in the morning? I can offer rooms for all, and of course, as much manpower as you'll need."

"Excellent suggestion," Townsend said. "Although…"

"Yes?" Philip nodded at Witheridge, who faded from the room to prepare the accommodation.

"Another man I might have suspected of running off – we've seen that sorry tale often enough – but not Baynes. I don't like it. If you and your boys are coming in the morning, they might want to be pre-warned about what we might find."

₹ Chapter Twenty-three ₹

D inner was postponed, and then reconvened in an hour, where we did justice to a second soup (for some), turbot, chops, beetroot and potatoes. I chose my favourite chocolate cream from the dessert and felt uncomfortably full, having started my dinner once already. During dinner, at Philip's request, we discussed everything but Baynes' disappearance, and afterwards we decamped to the library with our coffee and port and, with the use of the large table there, and maps, Townsend marked out the area to be searched, assigning various people to set areas.

"Smallwood, since you've no yacht, you and Carteret will sail the edges of the Mere on Carteret's *Ascension*. Woodforde, you and Morley will take my *Grebe* and check the Staithe then sail up Waxham Cut to Baynes' house. You can drop Philip's wards and myself on either side of the Cut, and pick us back up when we reach Baynes'."

"Or if you find something," Morley added.

"I'd rather go on the Grebe, if you don't mind, Townsend," Philip said, his eyes scanning the map.

"I understand, of course. Morley, you go with Carteret."

"And what happens if we do find something?" The man indicated as Woodforde spoke for the first time. "Voices won't carry well in this wind. Should we fire guns?"

"Did you bring a shotgun? Do we look like we are carrying guns?" Townsend said, testily. "I'll not have guns on my boat in this breeze." He paused to think and Philip cut in.

"The church. If anyone finds anything, make for Horsey church and tell the vicar to ring the bell. We are all sure to hear that."

"Good idea," Townsend said. "Come back to the Reach after that, if that's convenient, Philip?"

"I'd rather not," Philip said, shooting a sharp glance at us.

"We can hardly descend on Laetitia Baynes en masse," Townsend said, firmly. "I'm sorry, but you are the only option, this side of Hickling."

"Excuse me, sir," Myles said, leaning forward and examining the map. "I don't know this area at all, of course –"

"That's all right," Townsend said. "The Waxham cut is as straight as a ruler, you can't get lost."

"It's not that," Myles continued. "I can't help but note the riverbanks around here are nothing more than reeds."

"There's a footpath of sorts, on both sides of the Cut. Bound to be a little marshy, so wear your Wellingtons if you have them."

"They do," said Philip. His face was grim. For all his concern, I wished he would not fuss, although I was at least grateful he didn't say anything.

We certainly did own Wellingtons. They were part of the clothes we'd been treated to, and they'd had little enough use. The next morning we were all suitably booted and were – thanks to the diligence of our valets – sweating under the myriad layers of clothing we had been bundled into. When I commented on this, saying that I *might as well put the entire wardrobe on, and heavens, Albert, you've missed off one of the waistcoats*. Albert did his usual dignified demurral and almost entirely ignored me.

"It's a brisk east wind, sir. I'm sure Mr Smallwood will be thankful that you are walking the bank, and not on one of the boats in this weather."

We followed Townsend and the others out to the boats moored at the jetty. Both elegant little yachts, although there wasn't much room for all six of us in the *Grebe*, and three of us were entirely useless in the matter of sailing. It was a different proposition indeed from Tom's wherry, and once the sails were up, and we turned into the wind, it lurched alarmingly from side to side, causing Jude to go quite green. Not much of his face was visible between scarf and hat, and his eyes were closed more often than not, but what could be seen was an odd colour. Myles's arm was through mine and he squeezed against me reassuringly, his leg pressed warmly against my own.

Instead of sailing back towards the Staithe, where I had, so long ago it seemed to me now, first set foot on the wherry that would take me to the Reach, we swung around the island, the wind blowing us fast across the water, causing Townsend to change the position of the sails more than once, and sailed north. It was Myles who pointed this out, as I had lost all sense of direction the second time we tacked, the position of the banks seemed to change with dizzying speed and I was tempted, like Jude to simply close my eyes.

The other yacht had moved away in the opposite direction and I have to say I didn't envy either captain, battling against the fresh breeze. As our yacht neared the north bank, Townsend dropped the sail and we bumped so hard against the bank I was dislodged from the wooden seat, ending up on the wet slatted floor.

Philip assisted us as we disembarked, and we splashed calf deep into the cold water, then he waved as the craft left us, making its careful way up the Cut. Jude and I clambered up the slippery bank to the east path while Townsend and Myles took the other side. Townsend shouted out to us from the other side. "Stay away from the banks, and if you do find anything don't try and pull it out, you'll end up joining it. Bodies are hellish heavy things." It had been the first time anyone had admitted out loud that we were looking for a corpse.

"Come on," I said to Jude, feeling slightly sick as my imagination took over. "We may as well make ourselves useful." I marched ahead of him, not really knowing what I should be doing, and not particularly wanting to engage in conversation. We were friends again of sorts, but we'd never regained that happy casual intimacy we'd once had. More like polite brothers who aren't particularly close, rather than people who had ever been intimate. He seemed as unwilling to converse as I, thankfully, and we made our way up the squelching track, looking to the left and right. In the best novels, I dare say there would be a scrap of cloth found snagged on a branch, or macabre animals attracted by the presence of dead flesh in the water, but we found nothing at all. We took Townsend's advice and didn't get too close the bank, concentrating more on the bank to the right of the path and the ditch on the other side of it. At one point Jude clutched my arm and moved towards the water, his eyes dark and concerned.

"What is it?" It was the first time we'd spoken since leaving the boat.

"Movement. There. Just to your right." He stepped forward and it was my turn to clutch him by the arm to prevent him going too close. "Hold onto my hand," he said. He knelt down, and leaned over the water.

"Can you see anything?"

He didn't reply at first, but gave a sudden laugh. Something in water splashed, causing Jude to start back, still laughing. "Look," he said, pointing. No corpse; nothing more than a disturbed, wet water vole, pushing its furry body out into the water, its beady eyes fixed firmly on the far bank.

That was all we found, and finally, after about an hour's careful searching we came to a house, set squarely against the water but obscured slightly by trees, its boathouse low in the water beside it. Townsend and Myles were standing outside by the *Grebe*, while Woodforde stood in the boat.

"Your guardian is inside," Townsend said. "He won't be long."

"Should we – ?"

"I wouldn't. Time enough to pay your respects if we –" Before he finished, the sound began, so quietly at first that all of us turned our heads as one, as if we did not trust the evidence of our ears.

"Was that – ?" Townsend said, looking across at Woodforde, and pulling the scarf from around his ears.

"*Quiet*. Wait."

A second later another toll cut through the cold air and we all knew there was no mistaking it. The church bell was ringing, and for better or for worse, Baynes had been found.

Mrs Baynes came out of the house, her face as white as the bleached reeds. Philip was with her and although I couldn't catch what he was saying to her, I could tell he was attempting to reassure her, and as he held her, he was trying to prevent her from going towards the boat.

"No, Philip," she said, loudly, but sounding composed, not frantic as I thought she might, "I need to know, not wait here for another hour, another day. I have done enough waiting." Philip exchanged a glance with Townsend, who paused for a moment, then nodded. As the church bell continued to sound its sombre tidings, we boarded the yacht once more and made our way to the Reach.

The journey back was cold and miserable; the rain had set in, solid and heavy, and while it wasn't as bone-chillingly cold as the morning ice-winds, we huddled together like three damp and depressed birds, the rain dripping off the brims of our hats, all deep in thought as we neared the house. Mrs Baynes stood with Philip, having refused Jude's offer of a seat, her arm through Philip's for support, her face toward the island.

The lights of the Reach should have raised our spirits, with promises of hot drinks and dry clothes, but now, with the memory of the mournful tolling still in my ears, I dreaded landing on the jetty again.

None of us, with the presence of Mrs Baynes onboard, had dared to speculate out loud as to what might have happened, but I was sure that the other two were as convinced as I was that there was no good news waiting for us.

Philip handed Mrs Baynes down onto the jetty, and waited while the three of us disembarked. There were other boats tied there now, mostly small rowboats, but one or two yachts, together with Tom's wherry, others come to help, or seeking news, I was sure. I dodged away before anyone could waylay me because as much as warmth and comfort beckoned, more than anything else I wanted to be alone. The stress of the day had touched me at last, and one of the reasons that I was trying to deflect any solicitude for my health was that I thought if I could be quiet and alone, I might avoid the headache that I was fairly sure was coming.

In the house, Witheridge reigned in the midst of the activity. Servants were taking coats and carrying steaming warm water here and there. Witheridge was in his element, organising the staff and directing the searchers as we straggled in. As I shrugged myself out of my soaking wet outer things, Philip and Mrs Baynes entered and all attention was directed towards them, giving me the opportunity I needed to get away from everything.

Ahead of me, just ascending the stairs, I could see Albert, carrying a tray of something that steamed, and my stomach gave a small growl, reminding me it had had nothing since breakfast. I couldn't face my room. I wanted solitude to think things through, darkness so I would not be found, and there were few enough rooms I could find that, not with so many guests in the house, and the staff bustling around from hall to kitchen to drawing room. The murmur of voices grew fainter as I moved along the dim hall; I thought I heard Philip speak my name, but it wasn't a summons – probably just asking where I was. I would join them later, I told myself. But just for now, I needed to just stop. To let myself think.

I opened the door to the library; it was dark in there, nothing but the banked fire to give a dim ruddy glow. I let an enormous sigh of relief flow from me as I slid inside and closed the door, then slid down the door to sit on the floor. My head throbbed, but I told myself that if only I could stay here, stay quiet, I wouldn't let Philip down. I couldn't bear to be seen as an invalid with so many people around, on a day when he needed us to be quietly by his side in a local crisis. Once or twice I heard swift, light footsteps hurry past the library door, which caused my pulse to race a little faster, thinking that perhaps I was being sought out, but after I while I reasoned that it was probably servants taking the swiftest route from kitchen to drawing room.

I don't know exactly how long I sat there. I heard the grandfather clock in the hall chime the half hour, but what time I had hidden myself away I could not recall, so what hour it was I couldn't tell. However, the dark seemed to do me some good, for by the time the chimes announced the three-quarter, I felt strong enough to stand and seek out a change of clothes and company. I knew that staying away for much longer would eventually cause Philip to have me found.

With a grunt, I pulled myself up, not realising how chilled and stiff I was, and pulled open the door. The light from the hall seemed glaring, spilling golden tones into the dim seclusion, and I turned away for a second to shield my eyes from the light, as it seemed to send sparks of pain behind my eyes. As I turned into the room, I spotted the table, the one we had – not yet one day before – spread the maps on to facilitate our search, but it was in the middle of the room, not under the window, which was its normal position. The shape was wrong. There was something lying on it, covered with a sheet. Although I knew what it was, immediately, my brain rebelled from the truth and something perverse, something not in control of myself, made me step into the hall's light and pull the sheet away.

Baynes' face, lit from the side, was warmed by the honey oil-light, giving him a cruelly healthy glow, but where the moonlight hit his cheek from the window it revealed the truth; a blank pallid horror. His face was slack; mouth open, dark coins on his eyes, and his hair dripped the murderous Mere onto the parquet.

Chapter Twenty-four

The next thing I remember clearly was looking down and seeing my hand, still clutched tightly around part of the sheet. My knuckles were showing white even in the dim illumination, and my whole arm and hand was shaking, almost independently of my body, which was rigid. The only things I seemed able to move were my eyes, and the only thing that they were able to look at was the horrible apparition beneath the sheet, the sheet I was now incapable of placing back over Baynes' drowned face.

I wanted to move so badly, but that same lack of control I felt earlier swept over me and I found I couldn't, not even to stop my hand from shaking like some palsied old man. I made an incoherent noise, and felt wetness on my cheeks; I was frightened, not just of the corpse and the terror of its proximity, but of my inability to move. How long had I been standing there, staring at the husk of a man who only a few hours before had been so full of vitality?

The murmur of voices from the hallway became louder and Philip's voice, unmistakable and clear, cut through the fog of my distress. "Oh God," I heard him say, and his voice was filled with the horror that I felt. "Witheridge, get him out of there, *now*. How the devil did he…?"

I felt the sheet pulled from my hand, and I was turned away from the table. I had closed my eyes, not wanting to stare at that slack face for a second longer, and I kept them shut as I was led away, my body at last responding to Witheridge's lead. "Take him upstairs, for God's sake, go the back way, I can't have Townsend or the others seeing him like this. Crispin," he said, gently, and soft fingers touched my cheek. "Open your eyes."

"I can't." I started to shudder uncontrollably and the pain behind my eyes seemed to slice my mind in half. "I can't. Baynes. The Mere…"

"*Stop it*, Crispin. Open your eyes, I tell you. The door is closed. I promise you."

I did as I was ordered to find Philip's face close to my own, his eyes dark and concerned, but his voice harsh. "Take him; I'll come up as soon as I can. Tell Albert not to leave his side and get the medicine into him immediately."

"Let me go with him." Myles' voice sounded from somewhere, and at that I looked around but couldn't see him, couldn't find him. There was too many others crowded around.

"Not now," Philip said. "Leave him be."

Witheridge and a footman supported me as we made our way away from the main hall and up the service stairs towards the far side of the house. By the time we reached my room I was good for nothing. I tried to order Albert away from me, but he would not go. Instead of leaving me to my shame in my incapacity, he held my head while I vomited nothing but bile and he bathed my forehead. He fetched the box that Baynes had left me, and sitting by the side of the bed, I could hear him mixing some concoction, the crystal tones of the glass boring like bullets into my tortured mind. If I opened my eyes, the light, however dim, hurt me; if I closed them, I could see nothing but Baynes. Swollen, cold and very dead – water pouring from mouth and ears, water pouring endlessly onto the wooden floor, splashing over my feet and soaking them.

I remonstrated as Albert lifted me, for my head seemed too heavy to lift. I could hardly sit up as Albert held the glass to my mouth; some of the liquid spilled from my mouth and slid thickly down my chin. Albert was patience itself, letting me swallow as slowly as I needed, but was insistent that I take it all.

It tasted vile, although the headache stopped the worst of it registering; it wasn't until I was lying flat once more and the pounding had lessened, that the cloying bitter aftertaste struck me. It was clearly full of sugar, no doubt in an attempt to disguise the revolting taste, but it hardly helped. If I were to swallow that again, I vowed to myself, I'd be sure to hold my nose.

"It should work fast, sir," Albert said. "Or so the note promises. Lie still."

The relief came as promised, although it couldn't be swift enough. And with it, as the headache receded, came a lightness in the limbs, so much so that I felt I was hardly anchored to the bed – and could, if only I pushed gently with my fingers lift myself away and float upwards. It was a peculiar sensation, indeed. The pain did not dissipate entirely, but it did lessen, and for that I was grateful, although I found it hard to tell how much time had passed. I could hear the clock in the hall chiming, and I lay there, waiting to see what the next chime would mean, but try as I might I found it increasingly hard to discern the quarter or even the hour. Counting the chimes became difficult – I lost count every time I tried, and once found myself counting the beats of the half hour and being sure it was two in the afternoon when I knew – or thought I did – that I had returned to the house around four. I remember being given more of the mixture, but by that time I could taste nothing, and swallowed obediently in concurrence with the silent command.

The room darkened, but whether it was Albert dousing the lights or my eyes closing, I was unable to tell. I thought my eyes were open, in fact, thought that I could make out the delicate patterns on the cornice, but how could that be, if the room was dark? It wasn't logical. I thought sweat broke out on my forehead, but when I went to feel – my hands clumsy and heavy, smacking myself hard on the brow – there was no moisture to be felt. And yet, I could feel it, I could; trickling down from my temple, colder than any sweat could be, bright cool beads of ice.

I was hot, that was it. I was sweating because I was hot. That made sense. With the pain at bay I sat up and found I was already out of my jacket and waistcoat. I giggled at that, how could I forget taking them off? My shirt was already half undone and my cravat lay by my hand – how could I see it with the lights off? There must be a lamp still lit, I thought, taking the cravat and throwing it senselessly into the space beyond the bed, but as I drew my hand back I met with resistance, as if something was pulling at my elbow. It seemed baffling, and for a moment I moved my arm, or tried to, back and forth – the way you would if you were suddenly stuck on a fence you were trying to cross, as if brute force would set you free instead of delicate untangling – but whatever held my arm stayed firm. I twisted, thinking I'd caught myself in the covers or that my arm was still enmeshed in my jacket in some way, but I couldn't turn, the gentle pressure holding my arm. Then like a breath of cool air, a voice said "Gently, Crispin," although the voice seemed far, far away, even though I could feel the force of the words gust against the cold beads on my strangely dry forehead.

I caught a whiff of cigar smoke. Was someone smoking? Why could I not see?

"Jude? Is that you?" My tongue felt thick and the words were hardly recognisable even to my own, ragged hearing. It sounded not at all like a name, but a guttural cry of relief. "Jude? I can't move my arm." And I laughed, for no reason.

"Yes." Jude's voice – it *was* Jude's voice – but so far away. "I'm here, Crispin."

There was a shift, the bed moved, like Tom's wherry moving across the Mere, and I was cut loose as the pressure on my arm stopped. Then I floated, drifted up, smiling. I could still feel breath against my cheek and cool air on my legs, although I didn't remember undressing. "I'm flying," I said.

When he answered, it was strange. He said: "Say yes." The scent of cigars gusted past me again – I had a vision of them flying around me.

"Yes." I said, obediently, but wondering why.

"Yes, Crispin," Jude said, from far away. Then, "Keep talking," he said, right up close again. Perhaps he was flying too. Hands, beautiful cool hands touched my legs, and I smiled, imagining Jude's pale fingers sliding up my thighs. He must have been kneeling between my legs although I couldn't see him. He touched me, cupping my balls, kneading them gently. I could not help but groan with pleasure. I could feel his breath on my prick. "Jude, reassure him," he said. Why he said that, I don't know. But the reassurance came again, from far away. "Crispin, it's all right."

"I'm Crispin, you idiot, why...why?" I said, then let my mind melt away as he swallowed my prick and my thoughts melted into his mouth. I had something to ask him, something wasn't right, but I was damned if I could recall what it was.

All the while he sucked me I could hear him saying my name, over and over. He sounded like the clock, out of rhythm, and hard to keep track of, for he didn't stay in the same place. Sometimes he sounded as though he was crying. I cried for him as I peaked, arching back on the bed, laughing as he sucked me in, and kissed me, and bit me, and all I could think how clever that was until I lost sight of everything and gave myself to the night.

It was still dark when I woke next but my sight was normal at last and the dark was a reality. My mind was clear. I lay naked and chill on the outside of the covers. Rolling sideways, I vomited violently onto the wooden floor, only just managing to miss the bed. Finding myself shuddering, all I could do was hang there on the edge of the bed for what seemed like hours.

Eventually I recovered enough to roll myself back, and I wrapped myself into a cocoon in the covers and let the nausea pass. Whatever Albert had given me had taken the headache away but the dreams – the loss of control – was that any better? And I had still been nauseated, and still was, so that was no improvement at all. I thought back, trying to grasp the memory of what had happened after the drug had taken hold of me, but it was like trying to hold a nightmare in the sunshine. Had Jude been there, or had I just dreamed him? If he was here, why did he sound so strange, say such strange things? And why would he have come? He'd made it clear he wouldn't come to me again. No, of course not. It must have been the drug, combined with wishful thinking, nothing but a boyish shameful dream, something I thought I had outgrown.

But what wishful thinking. For all the nausea, I'd never had a dream as vivid as that. The floating, rising high above the mattress while Jude sucked my prick, his fingers between my arse cheeks, why, I could almost feel the heat of his hands now. He'd gone further in my nightmare than ever he'd gone in life, I remembered now, for his fingers had penetrated me and I remember crying out for more and being denied. "Not yet," he'd said, in a voice unlike any he'd used before, quite unlike his own. "Not yet. Soon. My sweet Crispin." But I'd wanted it all, wanted him to fuck me. I would have turned over and begged him, but I couldn't twist around.

Guilt came in waves then. It had been Jude I had dreamed about; Jude and not Myles. It was something I could never admit to Myles, for I was certain he was quietly jealous of our former relationship, however brief it had been. And yet, Jude had appeared in the most erotic dream I'd ever had in my life, and the most vivid, for all the disjointed and confusing perceptions. It was, after all, just a dream, although I wondered what could have been in the concoction to have produced such lasciviousness, and wondered if the drug normally had that effect. Doctor Baynes, perhaps could have…

Then it hit me. *Baynes.* That was how I'd ended up in such a bad way. I lay quietly for long while as the memories flooded back, but they came back clearly with no recurrence of my shameful incapacity. My thoughts, whilst dark, gradually became more lucid. What had happened to the poor man? Philip himself had said that he was a good sailor, that he knew the Broads as well as any man. What misfortune could have happened to have capsized the boat, and where had his body been found? None of this I knew, and I was anxious to find out if anything new had been discovered.

I was ravenous, too, despite having been violently ill. And so thirsty. I listened for the clock, and was rewarded with it being only four, far too early to ring for Albert. The clock rang two more quarters before I realised that there was no possible way I was going to sleep further and I couldn't last for several more hours without something to eat. I dragged myself out of bed, fumbled around for a candle, then pulled my robe from the wardrobe and set off slowly. I was still more than a little dizzy, but I needed food.

The house, in the small hours, and with me alone and still carrying the remnants of my dreams, seemed like a cavernous and empty place. Although I knew that in reality all around me were my friends, my guardian, and many servants, all asleep, as I made my way down that staircase, leaning heavily on the handrail, it seemed that I was an interloper into a hidden and forgotten castle. The weight of the years and the history of the house seemed to pull at me, every portrait had eyes that followed my progress, sneering at my common blood, and every suit of armour waited for me to pass before raising the weapon it bore as if to challenge my right to walk in the Moinsbois halls. I knew I was being fanciful, but by the time I reached the ground floor and stood clinging to the newel post, it took all my courage to continue and not to flee back up to my room. Even the shadows seemed to laugh at me and mock my weakness. Holding the candle aloft, I made my way down the corridor and towards the green baize door, unexplored territory for me so far. *You are Crispin Thorne*, I said over and over to myself. *You are Philip Smallwood's ward. You are not an intruder, you are entitled to help yourself to food – and anyway, you'd feel worse if you had to ring for someone.*

I hardly convinced myself. In my heart of hearts I knew that Philip would have rung, no matter what the hour, and that in creeping down here like a thief in the night, I was letting him down in some way I still didn't really understand. But I couldn't have rung. Not only would it have roused Albert, but no doubt several other staff as well, and by the time all this activity had been set into motion, I could be down, and back, before anyone noticed.

On the other side of the servants' door, the stairway was cold stone, and I regretted not putting on my slippers as my feet registered the icy stairs, but it had the effect of making me hurry. I was soon down in the servant's hall, which led off a cavernous kitchen. Suddenly weary, I sank into one of the chairs around the table for a moment, letting myself recover. Cold, clammy sweat still hung around my forehead and my arms and legs felt heavy as lead, but hunger, ravenous hunger, drove me on, and I dragged myself up.

After a little investigation, I found one of the larders, a large alcove off the kitchen, open to the outside to keep it cool, but the windows covered with a thick wire mesh. On the shelves I found enough to satisfy me, and grabbed a small basket with two rolls in it, added a piece of steak pie I found under a cover and a jug of milk, half empty. The food seemed essentially tempting, in a way I'd never experienced before; I had one of the rolls in my mouth before I thought about it, washing it down with all of the milk in the jug. Never in my life had I felt so hungry, felt such urgent compulsion to eat, so I sat down at the kitchen table to eat the pie, not caring that I stuffed it into my mouth with my fingers, eating like some kind of ravening animal.

Sated at last, I took a handful of soft ripe apples and shoved them in my robe pocket, refilled the jug from a larger ewer of milk, and left the pantry for my journey back to my room. The food, while filling that strange desire to eat no matter what, seemed to weary me at the same time, and it was as much as I could do to clamber back up the stairs. Halfway up, I paused, leaning heavily on one of the suits of armour to recover. The candlelight caught my reflection, yellow and unattractively warped in the shining metal; with my sunken eyes and unkempt hair, standing on its ends. I looked as bad as I felt. But then…I peered harder, tipping up my chin to examine what I'd thought I'd seen. It was difficult to discern, but I could have sworn that, showing reflected in the difficult reflection, were bruises on my neck I was certain I had not had when I'd set off on the hunt for Baynes – when was it? Only the morning before? I pressed my fingers to the marks. I could feel nothing, but there was a better looking glass in my room.

Pulling myself to the top of the stairway, I rested, clinging hard to the banister and feeling my heart race. It jumped even further as a light appeared around the corner from the direction of the Long Gallery and I froze. I was less than ten steps from my room, but I knew that by the time I reached it, I'd be seen if I hadn't been already, and as my legs felt like one of cook's jellied puddings I couldn't move anyway.

I leant hard against the banister, wanting desperately to sit down, and as the light approached I felt a blackness encroaching, and was prevented from falling by a strong arm under mine. "Crispin, you idiot, you look like death." Myles' voice, unmistakable in its concern. "Hang on, let me put the candle down, or we'll be on fire." He left me for a moment, then was back, supporting me around the waist and divesting me of my burdens.

Once we were safely in my room he helped me into a chair, then lit one or two of the lamps. I sat, feeling ashamed and stupid as I watched him. Stupid for being sick enough to be supported, and ashamed of my nightly fantasy that should have included this best of lovers, the best of friends. He sat down, poured me out some of the milk and watched me drink it, which I did as if I'd not drunk anything before in my life.

"Philip told us you'd be asleep until at least the middle of the day, after what Dr. Baynes had prescribed for you. What the devil were you doing? Sleepwalking down to the kitchen?"

Shaking my head, I took another drink. "I woke and was hungry."

"Well, obviously," he said. "I think that even I've worked that much out. You've a stronger constitution than many of us considered." He sat back, and his lips tightened as if he wanted to say something else, but was holding himself back.

"What about you?" I said. "You were wandering around too. And you're fully dressed. Considering you are right down the hall, and it's not even five, don't say you were coming to see me, because you came from around the corner."

He gave a wry smile. "I was actually coming to see how you were, even if it meant sitting and watching you drool in your sleep for an hour or two until breakfast, but you are right. I had been… exploring."

"Is this really the right time for that? I mean, I know you seem to be addicted to it —"

"What?"

"Oh, Myles — I've found you at least twice in areas I would never have expected you to be. I'm getting a little tired of being treated as if I'm mentally deficient. I get headaches, that's all." Whether it was the day before — being whisked out of sight by Philip, not wanting his guests to see his useless ward — or whether it was the nightmare and my guilt about it, but I found myself getting angry. "So, you were — inexplicably — exploring. With a dead man mouldering in the library. I repeat, do you really think —"

"Shut up, Crispin," he said quietly. "Don't speak of it." He slid out of his chair and knelt at my feet, took my hands as if to warm them and stopped suddenly as his glance landed on my neck. "What are those marks?"

"What — ? I don't know…" I said, intending to deny all knowledge but my body gave itself away as my hand flew to the place I knew they were and touched the skin there.

"Move your hand," he ordered, and when I wasn't quick enough he pulled it away. "*These* marks, and don't say you were hit by some tree when we were out, because you damn well weren't." His fingers probed the marks quite ungently.

"I spotted them for the first time on the stairs, I don't know — or rather, I thought I didn't know…I swear… It was a dream, or I thought…" The confusion of the night before crowded back, and I frowned in concentration, trying to pull the memories back, pin them down, keep them *still*.

"Calm down," he said. He leaned forward and kissed me on the forehead. "Calm yourself." It wasn't until he said that that I realised I'd been getting upset again. "What happened? What dream? God, I *knew* I shouldn't have let them just drug you and leave you alone."

"If it wasn't…Oh God, Myles, if it wasn't…"

"Shhh. Stop it. Take a deep breath and tell me."

"I can't, it doesn't… I can't remember. You know what dreams are like."

"Then tell me what you *do* remember."

Slowly, with his hand in mine and prompted when I faltered, I told him what little I recalled. The way I thought I was flying, then tethered, as if I'd float through the windows and be lost. The way Jude moved, nearer and closer. When it came to the more intimate details I could hardly bear to speak of them. They weren't words I had said aloud before, but he held my hand, tighter and tighter, and didn't let me stop until I really could remember nothing else. His expression was as dark as anything I'd seen before. I'd seen him angry, angry at me more than once, but had never seen him look the way he did that morning, as if I'd told him that someone precious to him had been murdered.

With the completion of my story, he lost eye contact, dropped his head and kissed my cold fingers. He seemed, for once in his life to be struggling for words. "Wait here. Drink some more of that milk." His matter of factness hidden behind that angry expression almost made me laugh. But I watched him as he strode the bed, and he pulled aside the sheets as if looking for something.

"Myles, what.?"

He turned around, his face pale and still just as angry but his voice was hushed. "Just shut up and listen to me. Have you had any reply to your letters?"

I found myself blinking at him in confusion at the sudden change in subject. "My letters? Well, no, but…"

"How many have you sent?"

"Just two. I didn't think it was worth it if Arch's father wasn't passing them on. Look I don't understand what that has to do with anything."

"I've sent a damned sight more than two," he said, and his voice dropped even further. "Crispin, this is probably entirely the wrong time to let you know this, but you need to know."

I put the glass down, as I was getting angry myself, frightened and angry and felt an insane need to smack him over the head with it. "Will you just bloody explain? What is it that I need to know?"

"Wait here," he said.

"Why?"

"Just...look. Trust me. Just wait here. I'll be one minute." He gave me the briefest of warm kisses, and ducked out of the door leaving me bewildered and wondering if I was still in my nightmare, for being awake felt hardly any less confusing. In less than a minute he was back, and he locked the door behind him. In his hand he had a bundle of letters tied up with string and he scattered them onto the carpet in front of me. "Look. Here. All these are mine. To Southerton, Thomas, Pennington Minor – all of these are mine. And these... I'm sorry, Crispin... These two are yours to G Archeson, Esq."

Chapter Twenty-five

I sat and stared at the letters, feeling blank, and lost. *He sent them back. He didn't even care enough to open them.* The seals were still intact on the backs of the envelopes. I remembered sealing them. Feeling so proud, knowing how impressed Arch's father would be at the address, knowing he'd ask around about Philip, and his avaricious little heart would beat all the faster. I'd hoped, when I'd handed Albert the letters, that perhaps one day Arch would be allowed to visit. But there the letters were, unopened. Maybe it wasn't Arch who had received them. Perhaps that's why they were unopened. Maybe he'd never got them, his father must have stopped them reaching him after all. Yes, that must be it –

"Crispin." Myles' worried voice brought me out of my reverie. "You've gone uncharacteristically quiet. What's wrong?"

I didn't want to tell him, especially after the nightmare. That, together with memories of Arch, seemed doubly disloyal. "Nothing. It's nothing." I went to take the letters from the floor but he caught me by the hand.

"No. I don't think you understand," he said, his grip so tight around my wrist that it hurt.

Attempting to shake free, and failing, I got angry, and the action forced me to my feet, dragging him with me. "Oh, I understand all right. Arch... Jude... It's more than bloody obvious to me. Our friends want nothing to do with us. Even...even those we thought were more than – look, just *let go*, will you?"

He held on fiercely, his face contorted in concentration. "If you'd let me explain," he said, grunting as we started to wrestle with each other. "Bloody hell, Crispin." He grabbed me around the waist with his free hand and manhandled me to the bed. Being heavier and stronger, he had little trouble subduing me, although I like to think that if I had been in sound mind without the residue of my medicine washing through me I could have lasted a little longer. He waited, pinning me to the bed, his face pink with exertion, but wearing more of a bemused expression than anything. "Listen…to…me. It wasn't a nightmare. Last night. Do you understand me? And the letters weren't sent back. They were never sent. Do you understand, you idiot? Your precious Archeson didn't reject you – so you can stop sulking. They were *never sent*. We've more important things to worry about than letters."

I felt something sink within me and I felt as cold as Baynes, dripping water onto the parquet. Myles let me go, and rolled sideways across the bed, gathering up his letters. "Look. No stamps. I thought the same as you when I found them –"

"Where did you find them?"

"I'll tell you that, if you'll let me talk. I thought the same, but noticed that none of them have stamps on."

"But, why?"

"Which question do you want me to answer first?"

I lay there, feeling almost too exhausted to answer. Too much had happened, it was all too broken and confused, like a jigsaw; it was as if I was still in that dream, hearing Jude but smelling cigars. Nothing fitted. "Just tell me. I promise I'll shut up."

"I found them in Philip's room."

"How –"

"You promised you'd let me speak. After I realised what Jude was up to, I'd been watching him, following him when he didn't think I was, and seeing him go up to Philip's rooms. Eventually I noticed that he went to up to the King's chamber even when Philip wasn't here, and that meant he had a key. So I took it." He had the grace to look a little abashed as I glared at him. "I know; you disapprove, but then you aren't me."

I struggled up to my elbows. "I…" I couldn't say anything that wouldn't have annoyed him, so I decided to err on the side of cowardice rather than bothering to preach at him, but I wondered how many more shocks I could take and whether they would get any easier or harder to hear.

He gave a patient look, the kind you give a child, and continued. "I was just interested in what he was up to – no, not that," he added, grimacing as I gave him a sharp look. "It didn't seem any reason to keep going to Philip's room while he was away, made no sense to me – it's not like the house isn't big enough, after all; there are plenty of places he could go to escape us or the staff, if that's what he wanted. All he'd have to do is lock his door."

I nodded. "And what was he doing?"

"I don't know. Nothing that I could see. Seems all he is doing is enjoying the feeling of being in Philip's room. Perhaps he feels it makes him better than us."

"That's uncharitable of you."

"How well do we really know each other? We hardly know anything – other than what we've chosen to tell each other. In this…place. It's like a theatre. Exits and entrances and all played out in front of a painted backdrop. Don't you feel that? No, of course you don't. But I'm getting off the point. Crispin, there's something wrong here, very wrong. You've got to believe me."

"What is it?"

He stared at me for a moment, then raised his hands to his head and all but tore at his hair. I'd never seen anyone make such a gesture before. It was unsettling. Myles was calm. Cynical. Myles didn't panic, but that's what how it appeared. "I don't *know*," he said, desperation in every word. "I don't know. But we've got to find out. Last night. Look… You're not *listening* to me. I think you know as well as I do that it wasn't a dream."

"I… Myles…" The words stumbled out, not wanting to make sense. Since finding the marks it had seemed pretty damning.

I'd made bites like that on Arch once, and they'd caused no end of problems. "I didn't... Jude and I – we haven't, and I didn't ask him..."

"I didn't think that." He was frighteningly silent for a long moment, and he sat on the bed next to me. Then he exploded. "How dare he. How *dare he!* What sort of cad takes advantage of a man when he's drunk, or drugged?" His face screwed up in sheer incomprehension.

"Perhaps he thought I..."

"No, he bloody didn't, and you know it. Stop standing up for him." Somehow he seemed to be shouting in a low voice. "I heard what he said the other night. He'd moved up to Philip and you weren't enough for him anymore. I thought he was a bloody fool, but I didn't think... I should have – after school – people just take what they want. God! I'll kill him."

"We don't know for sure."

"Come on, Crispin! The proof is there, and I certainly wouldn't have been reckless enough to mark you, you know that."

I had to agree with him. He'd been careful; he did bite in passion, but had always stopped short of making anything that would show, would embarrass me when dealing with Albert.

"I've a good mind to go up to Philip's room and have it out with Jude right now."

"You can't! Philip will be there."

"Good. He deserves to know what Jude's bloody capable of. *God.* The –"

"Please. Don't, Myles. We'll talk to him. I'll talk to him. Give him some chance to explain. It doesn't need to go further – Don't you see?"

His eyes blazed with fury. He looked as though he could have hit me, hit anyone, just to relieve his anger. I stumbled on, knowing I could placate him. "If we cause problems, we might all suffer from it. Philip might think we're more trouble than we're worth – It's not like Jude, I can't believe it, even now, why *would* he –"

"I won't let you alone with him. Did you think I would?" He pulled me up, wrapped his arms tightly around me. His hands clutched onto the fabric of my night attire and I felt it riding up around my legs. "He'll never touch you again, not if I have anything to say about it."

He kissed me brutally at first, his mouth bruising in its zeal, then again more gently, as if wanting to heal an imagined hurt. Parts of my anatomy could not help but be excited by his attentions, but his timing was less than propitious. I heard a warning rattle of tea-cups just in time, and pushed myself away from him, just as Albert entered carrying my breakfast. We sat there, the pair of us, feeling caught out and probably looking as guilty as each other while Albert pulled back the curtains to the pink-grey dawn and roused the fire. It took me a moment to control my voice enough to speak as normally as I could manage. "Is Mr Smallwood breakfasting in his room, Albert?"

"No, sir. A number of the gentlemen stayed overnight and they will be eating together."

"Just leave the tray."

"Very good, sir. Should I fetch Mr Graham's breakfast from his room?"

Myles cut in before I could answer. "No. Tell Michael I'll be through presently."

Albert nodded, his sang-froid not shaken by Myles' brusque reply, and left us alone again. The interruption had calmed Myles considerably, although I didn't doubt he was simmering on the edge, as easy to reignite as the banked fire now burning in the grate. He turned to look at me. "Now. We need to go and see him now. Get dressed."

There was no point in arguing, he was obviously not going to be put off, and if I didn't go with him I feared that he'd not hold back with Jude, I knew how strong he was and how angry. I dressed hurriedly, while Myles paced. Suddenly he stopped and turned to me. "What did you say?"

"Nothing." I tied my shoes and stood up.

"Not now, just before, before Albert came in…" He frowned. "You said something…"

"I can't remember."

"It doesn't matter. Ready?"

I wasn't. I didn't want to see Jude, not really. If I had to talk to him about what had happened – and I still found it unbelievable, for all the evidence – then I'd rather do it in my own time, not following Myles in what was sure to be a violent confrontation. But with Philip occupied, this might be the only chance we'd have for a while. He led the way through the house to Philip's stairway. At the doorway, I stopped. "No," I said. "I don't want to see him, I just don't."

"Nor do I, but we must. And now." He tried the door, but it didn't open. Quickly he produced a key from his trouser pocket and tried the door again. It still didn't open.

We exchanged glances. "He couldn't have changed the lock," I said, "surely?"

Myles tried the door again. "No. The bastard's trying to keep the door shut. Help me push." Together we put all our weight against the door, and gradually prevailed, as the door slid open, letting us pass. In fact we all but fell into the room at the last, as the pressure released. Jude had jumped back and was backing away from the door, an expression of alarm on his face.

"How dare you steal that key!" he said. He looked haunted, dishevelled, not at all the self-assured veneer he normally maintained. "I'll tell Philip –"

Myles was on him, like a terrier on a rat, faster than I could have believed possible. He grabbed Jude by the jacket and shook him, and took no notice of me as I tried to separate them. "You tell us what you did last night, and you tell us now. Or we'll be the ones going to Philip to and we'll be the ones to tell. We'll tell him what kind of person he's harbouring, the sort of person who would rape a drugged friend."

Jude was hitting out at Myles, but Myles was so angry he didn't seem to feel the blows – he tightened his grip on Jude, twisting his hand in his cravat, cutting off his breath. By the time I managed to get Myles to drop him, Jude had gone bright red, and after Myles had flung him away in disgust, he lay choking on the floor.

"How could you stand up for him!" Myles moved towards Jude as if to kick him while he was down.

"No." I stepped in front of him, held him back. "Whatever he did, it doesn't merit you strangling him."

"It's what he deserves. He deserves locking up. A court should see to him – see what they give a man for rape."

"Stop it. They'd take me too, you idiot." I knelt down by Jude, helped him into a chair while he recovered his breath. "We came here to ask him about it, not kill him." I was rather amazed at my own calmness but it seemed that I'd had so many shocks that I was looking at the world through a glass and hadn't thought twice about facing Myles down – and was surprised that he had backed down as quickly as he had.

"Ask him, then," Myles growled. "Or I will."

I knelt down in front of him. "Where's Philip?"

"He's talking to Townsend – they are arranging for Baynes to be moved to the undertakers in Yarmouth." His voice was sulky, but he kept looking from me to Myles as if he were a good deal more nervous than he felt. "He'll be back soon."

"So what?" Myles said. "We are allowed to speak to you, aren't we? Even if you are fucking your guardian."

"You're only jealous."

"Not I," Myles said. "I think it's revolting."

"Myles, please," I said. "Jude. Last night. I need to know about last night." I decided not to tell him I doubted the reality of it, not to give him the chance to lie. "Why did you do it? That's all I want to know – why?"

He glared once at Myles then looked down at me, still defiant, but only for a moment, then his face crumpled. "I didn't –"

"Liar!" shouted Myles, stepping forward. "Just let me –"

"I swear it! I didn't!" Jude said. "It wasn't me. It wasn't. It was… it was Philip."

I dropped from my haunches onto my knees. "I knew it," Myles said from behind me. "I just didn't want to –" He still sounded furious but not so that he was going to attack. "When you said about the voices…and the cigar smell…You filthy…You were there, weren't you? *Weren't you!*"

"It's not what you think. He promised –"

"You didn't try to stop him? And you didn't say anything?" I said. The earth seemed to move beneath my feet, as if the drug was taking hold again.

"You'd never have believed me, I couldn't really believe it myself. Crispin…, Crispin, are you all right?"

"I'm fine," I lied. But I let him help me up. "I just need…"

"Jude, get him a drink," Myles said.

Jude went over to Philip's sideboard and returned with a glass half full of brandy, which I could hardly stand the smell of, but I sipped it, at Myles' direction. "Now, tell us – what the hell were you thinking of? I thought you liked Crispin – how could you do something like that to him?"

Jude sat on the edge of the bed. All of his poise seemed to have rubbed off, but he seemed sulky still, almost angry. "I told you, I didn't."

"But you were there," Myles said, "from what I heard from Crispin, you were helping."

"He promised me –"

"What the hell could he promise you that would be worth doing that to someone I thought you counted as a friend? I should beat some sense into you? What the hell did he promise you?"

Jude's eyes slid from Myles to me. He didn't seem at all cowed, now. Rather, exulting. "Everything," he said, quietly. "I'm surprised you haven't worked it out, Myles, seeing as how clever you think you are."

"I don't understand," I said. "What are you talking about?"

"Come with me," he said, "and I'll show you."

Chapter Twenty-six

He stood up, picked up a candlestick from the side, lit it from the fire and moved to a door at the back of the room.

He opened it and I let out a small gasp. "The Queen's Favour," I said. "You've been up there? Philip's let you in there? Oh…wait…Was it Dominic's room?"

He led the way up the spiral stairway. "Yes, clever Sphinx. It was Dominic's room. You are beginning to see the truth." He opened the door at the top and led the way in. Where Philip's room was fully glazed, affording an almost panoramic view of the Mere and the house roof, the Queen's Favour had no windows and was entirely dark. "Let me light the lamps and you can see." The room around us gradually came to life, picking up the colours and fabrics as each lamp was lit. "It's a little cold," he said. "No fire. No-one lives here yet, you see."

"It looks as though someone does," Myles said. "It looks as if —"

"As if someone's just stepped out," Jude finished. "Yes. And that's exactly what it is."

I looked about me as the light filled the dark spaces. It was, like Philip's room below, perfectly round, but decorated in much lighter colours. The panelling was floor to ceiling, but of a paler type of wood. The dressing table was laid with care, as if the valet had just left it for his master, brushes and combs, hair preparations and colognes, all the bottles full. By the side of the bed, a book lay face down on a cabinet, and two glasses, each one half-filled with red wine stood side-by-side. On the bed, a set of evening clothes, which looked very similar to one of the sets I owned, was laid out. I felt an unholy shiver run through me.

"It's not a bedroom," Myles said in a quiet voice. "It's a shrine."

"Not…exactly," Jude said. Now he wasn't being threatened he had recovered a little of his elegance. "It's simply waiting for a return."

"Waiting for what?" I said, although I was beginning to see. I moved towards the wardrobe, dreading what I'd find in there, but knowing in my heart I knew I was right. I pulled open the door, a scent hit me as I did; rosemary. I pulled open a drawer to find beautifully folded waistcoats; it took mere seconds to confirm, checking the rail for the jackets too, that my guess had been true.

"For Dominic," I said. "The room is waiting for Dominic to return, isn't it? Philip wasn't just his guardian, was he, Jude? Has Philip told you it all? The watch…the clothes…the –"

"Everything. I suppose Baynes poisoned you about it."

"I don't think even he knew…" I pulled item after item out of the wardrobe and threw them on the bed. Every single thing had been remade in triplicate. For us. My mind went back to the night of the party and the conversation I'd overheard – Baynes' words which had sounded odd at the time – *they're not dolls.* "I really don't think he guessed the whole thing."

"Neither did we," Myles said. "God, how stupid."

Jude moved to section of wall between two lamps and pulled on a string. "Here," he said. "This is what it's all been about." A section of the panelling slid back, revealing a head-and-shoulders portrait of a young man, perhaps in his early twenties. Dark brown hair in a fashion from a few years before, cut exactly as our valets had cut and arranged ours. Clear, dark brown eyes and a mocking smile shone out of the picture, but he had a look that, once seen, would never be forgotten.

A small plaque was set beneath the portrait. Myles stepped up to read it. "*Dominic. 1842. Never lost.*"

I turned to Jude. "How long have you known about this? What did you mean, he promised you? Promised you what?"

He sat on the bed, almost proprietarily, hugging one of the posts. "That I'd be his choice, of course. That I'd be Dominic. He already calls me that, in private. As soon as you've gone he'll change my name entirely. Dominic Rowe. That was his name."

I think Myles was as stunned as I, for neither of us could find anything to say; whatever mystery we'd thought Philip had, it wasn't this.

Jude took our silence as invitation to continue. "He came here when he was fifteen. Parents killed – oh, I don't remember how exactly. Philip hadn't meant to fall in love, but he said it was impossible not to, and Dominic returned it. They lived here – ostensibly as guardian and ward – for ten years. Respectable to the world. But up here, in the dark, where no one could see, they were everything to each other."

I found my voice at last. "How did he die?"

"He went sailing alone. It took him a while to tell me, and I've never seen a man look so broken to tell a tale. Philip and Dominic always went sailing together, they adored the Mere, and the Broads, would sail for days and days, but one Sunday Philip had a cold and although Dominic teased him about it, he could not be persuaded to go with him, so Dominic went alone. Philip says he doesn't know what really happened; the yacht was near the jetty and simply turned over. Dominic made it to the shore, Philip carried him back to the house himself, and Baynes was sent for. Dominic was half drowned but alive – Baynes came, told Philip not to worry…and an hour later he came back down the stairs to tell Philip that Dominic was dead."

"And he never forgave Baynes," I said. "He never stopped hating him."

"He killed Dominic, Philip said," Jude replied. "He was alive, there was no reason why a healthy young man should die like that. No, he never forgave him. He told me that Baynes' death was natural justice, to share even a part of what Dominic went through."

Myles seemed to come to himself at last. "Choice. You said 'his choice.' What do you mean?"

The door shut behind us, and the three of us turned as one. Myles rushed to the door and pulled. "It's locked! Philip? Philip! Open this door!"

"You have no right to be in there, not yet." Philip's voice sounded strange, tight, as if he'd been crying. "Jude should not have let you in there. It's not ready."

Myles continued to try and force the door, but Philip said nothing more. It seemed he'd left us alone.

"I don't like this," I said.

"He's bloody mad." Myles moved from the door to the panelling and started pulling furniture away from the walls. "I'm not staying here like a rat in a trap waiting for him to come back."

"What are you doing?" Jude said, "Don't touch anything! He'll be so angry – don't move anything! He's right, I shouldn't have let you in here. I came in once before and he was so furious I thought he'd gone mad. He shut himself up in here alone all night."

"He *is* mad, didn't you hear what I said? What he's doing isn't normal! He's been planning this for years – he must have!" Myles pulled a tapestry down from the wall with a savage tug, to the obvious distress of Jude, looking on in horror. "He doesn't just 'find' three young men all of the same age, all of whom have the same inversion. That sort of thing isn't a coincidence. God." He knocked on the panelling as he moved around the room. "I think I know what he meant by choice now. He might be dressing us all up as Dominic, cutting our hair like him, making us learn the same things as he did…"

"Except sailing," I added.

"He's not taking the risk of losing a second one, is he? He's too bloody clever for that. But he's not going to want to bed three Dominics, is he? Can't you see that Jude? What did you mean by 'when you leave'?"

"Nothing – nothing!" Jude looked frightened now, as if he was thinking the same dark thoughts as Myles and I. "But when I take…become – well, you know – you'll be sent off somewhere. London, wherever you want to go. That's all. He can afford it."

Myles looked at Jude for a long time without saying anything, then shot a quick look at me, as if assuring himself I was still there, then turned back to tapping the panelling. "There are passages in this house," he said. "I've found two. One leads from the servant's quarters into the library, and one leads from a disused pantry downstairs to a tunnel which comes out by the old ice-house. I don't believe for one minute someone really built a prison here."

His optimism helped me calm down. "What can I do?"

"Just tap the panelling. If there is a gap, I found it like that before."

The two of us worked our way around the room, checking every section of the wood, but finding nothing. "There has to be," he said. "There has to be. Crispin, help me move the bed."

I looked up at the monstrosity, doubting that we'd be able to move it, but I tugged at the posts with him. "It's not going to move," I said. "I think the damn thing must have been built in the room, there's no way they'd have got it through the door."

Myles stopped, scowling in concentration. Then his face cleared. "Get under the bed," he said.

I took his meaning immediately and got down on the floor and slithered beneath it, inching my way to the wall. Tapping what wood I could reach, I found a section that sounded hollow. "That's it!" Myles said. "Stay there."

I wanted to say, in my nervousness, that hiding under the bed wasn't going to keep me safe, but I bit my tongue. Above me I could hear Jude telling Myles he 'couldn't do that,' and Myles telling him to shut up. Then Myles' face appeared by the side of the bed. "Move over," he said. He slid under with me, and pulled a metal pole under with him. "From the tapestry," he said. "If it doesn't work, I'll kick a hole in it."

"Can you?"

"I'll pretend it's Philip's head." He leaned over and kissed me swiftly and unexpectedly. "I'm getting us out of here," he said. "All of us. No-one's being a replacement for that bastard's gratification."

The sound of the pole against the woodwork was so loud I was sure that it would bring Philip in the room, but it didn't. The panelling splintered, then cracked. Myles pulled the rest from the wall with his hands, revealing a small passage, hardly big enough to crawl into, and dark as Hades. "Don't worry," he said. "If it's anything like the other two, you crawl only for a few feet – then there's enough space to walk. "I'll go first with the candle, then you."

"Jude…" I said. "He won't come easily. I don't like to leave him here."

"Let me worry about him," he said. "Get the candle for me, will you?"

I watched him crawl into the hole, then I heard him call out. "All right, it's just the same. Come on through, and I'll come back and get Jude."

It was horrible climbing into that hole. Dirty and awkward. There didn't seem to be enough room, for one thing, and I had to suppress a feeling of panic as I found myself entirely surrounded by stone, with nothing but a small yellow glow to guide me. Myles was at the end to pull me out; he handed me the candle as he ducked back to fetch Jude. The passage I found myself in was very narrow, there was hardly enough room to inch sideways. No-one of Baynes' build could have made his way around, that was for sure. If it was made for the lady of the house to escape when necessary, or for her servants to enter, which was more likely, they were obviously lithe slim people.

After an endless wait, during which I considered going back, Jude's head appeared and I helped him up. As he stood up I could see he had a large red mark on his cheek, and knew that Myles had meted out a little natural justice of his own. I tried to feel sorry for him, but knowing what he and Philip had done to me made me less than generous. I wanted to ask him much more about that, but now was not the time. Myles joined us and we shuffled forward into the unknown.

We turned a sharp corner, and suddenly the passage widened out and a narrow stairway led up. We had no choice but to follow it, and when we reached the top, the ceiling had dropped down to meet us so we were crawling forward on our hands and knees.

"There's a wooden board ahead," I said. "Do you still have that pole?"

Myles handed it forward and I attacked the panel with a will. It gave way a lot easier than the one from Dominic's room, showing natural light ahead.

"It's one of the tower rooms!" I said as I crawled through.

We scrambled out, all of us covered in brick dust and cobwebs. "Someone may have heard that crash," I said, looking around the bare room. It seemed an age since I'd spent my first night here, not a few short months.

"Unlikely," Myles said, attempting to put the damaged panelling back in place. "Not from the bottom of the tower, what with all those tapestries. With luck the servants will all be behind the baize door and into the servants' quarters, and Philip will still be in his room, probably working out how to dispose of two of us." He glared briefly at Jude, before returning to his attempt, but Jude seemed still too traumatised to fight back, either verbally or physically. "Damn it," he said as the wood refused to stay put.

"Leave it, Myles," I said. "Why worry about it? I'm not going to bother about breaking a piece of wood. Leave it and let's go." Heart in mouth, I opened the door just a little and strained to hear anything from below. All seemed quiet, as far as I could tell, but I crept down the spiral trying to prevent my shoes from making any sound against the stone. At the exit to the upper floor I paused. "Wait here," I whispered. "I'll have a look over the banister and see if there's anyone in the hall."

Myles caught hold of my arm. "No. Let me."

"No. You stay here and stop Jude from doing anything stupid. He's coming with us whether he wants to or not." I was more than a little concerned for Jude, for he hadn't recovered his colour and was so changed in demeanour I wondered if he were biding his time to make a bolt back to Philip's rooms and give the alarm, or whether he'd lost his wits entirely.

The hall seemed deserted. I had to trust that Philip either didn't know about the passage, or would never think that we had found it. There was no recourse but to go on. I told the others the way was clear, and we descended the stairway as fast as we dared and fled out into the cold.

We ran towards the boathouse. Myles had Jude by one arm and literally dragged him along. None of us were dressed for the cold and the rain, fine as it was, soon soaked my hair and stood in silvery drops on the wool of my jacket. The lock was back on the boathouse door, but I wasn't fooled by that device twice and pulled at it optimistically, dreading that one of us might have to enter that water again to unlock it. However, it seemed no one had been in since our misadventure and the door opened with a sharp tug.

"Get in," I said, looking anxiously up at Philip's window. With luck he'd not be looking out of the window; he might still even be soliloquising to an empty room. I resolved not to think of him and his madness, and followed the other two into the dim space.

"Myles…" I said, staring at the water. "Look."

Myles pushed Jude down onto the bench. "Don't move," he ordered, and turned to stand beside me. The dinghy had moved from where we'd left her. Now she sat in the water pushed up right against the jetty where we stood. She had been moved to make room for another yacht, one I'd seen before. "It's Baynes' *Elizabeth*," I said. I didn't even need to see the name painted on the side. I recognised the distinctive lamps.

Myles gave a low whistle. "And that's the last piece in place" he said. "He did kill Baynes."

"You suspected that? You didn't say anything."

"You had enough to deal with. I had no proof or I would have gone to Townsend. I think he killed Baynes to stop him talking to you. Now we can go to Townsend. You said he was going to tell you more, didn't you? More about Dominic? Philip must have heard about it —"

"Oh I heard about it, all right," Myles was quicker than I; he spun around while I was still reacting in shock. When I turned, I saw Philip by the boathouse door, his hunting rifle pointed at the pair of us, and Jude beside him, an unpleasant smile on his face. "Heard the interfering butcher. Out." He stood to one side and indicated the door briefly with the rifle. "You thought you could take him away, did you?" He seemed nothing at all like the Philip we'd known. All trace of kindness and softness had gone, replaced by a stern, granite expression, much more like the portraits of his ancestors than the living, caring man he'd shown himself to be. I remembered briefly, as I followed Myles out, fear cascading through me, how I'd felt when I first saw his portrait, a man used to command. And we obeyed him.

We walked out into the rain. The wind had picked up and blew ice-cold needles of water into our faces. "Myles, Jude, go stand over there," he ordered.

Myles just glared at him, anger radiating off him. "I'm not leaving Crispin alone with you," he shouted. "Not after last night. You filthy –"

The gun went off so casually, that it seemed impossible that Philip had pulled the trigger, he hadn't even moved. Jude cried out, and backed away to the place Philip had indicated. I felt frozen, watching him reload, knowing I was dead. Next time he'd hit one of us for sure. I knew now he had no intention of sending us to London. Oh, he'd tell the neighbours that, and who would know any difference?

Myles clutched at my arm, and even though I was terrified of taking my eyes from Philip, I turned to glance at Myles, and my heart dropped out of my chest. His face had lost the anger, he looked more surprised than scared.

"No!" I fell down on my knees, half catching Myles as he fell. He still had that surprised expression in his eyes, but his mouth was twisted in pain. "Oh, God," I said. "Oh, God." Blood appeared, hardly visible on the soaked grey of his coat, but when I raised my hand my palm was covered in red; the rain washed it clean. I could hardly focus. Philip was standing by the boathouse, the gun loose in his hand. He looked almost as scared as I did, but it didn't seem to be because of what he'd done; he had no time for Myles at all, couldn't take his eyes from me.

"Get help!" I screamed at Jude, who was frozen in place by the side of the Mere. "Jude!" The wind seemed to tear the words from my throat, and Jude took as much notice of me as of the reeds on the bank. Someone must have heard the shot, someone would come…but if they were loyal to Philip…

I went to touch Myles' cheek, for his eyes had closed, although he breathed, just, laboured and harsh.

Philip's voice sounded close and quiet in my ear. "Dominic, come away from him."

I looked over my shoulder, ready to shout at him, but the gun was steady now, and aimed squarely at Myles. "Dominic," he repeated. "Come with me. Back to the house. We'll send someone down to see to him. Dr Baynes will see to him." He took hold of my arm and pulled me to my feet.

"I'm not… I'm not leaving him here." I struggled but it was like fighting oak. "I'm Crispin. You know that. I'm *not* becoming part of your madness."

He pulled me close, wrapping his gun hand around me, I could feel it digging into my back and I froze. "You've always been part of me," he said. "I've missed you so much."

He started to kiss me, and I fought him, I tried my hardest. They say the mad are strong, and it's true. He tried to reach my mouth with his, but at least I kept him from doing that – the very idea sickened me. He satisfied himself with kissing my neck, and I could not deny him access to that, for there was nothing I could do, try as I might. "Come in," he said, holding me tighter. "We must celebrate. You're home. At last. My love. My sweet boy. My Dominic."

"No!" A violent weight hit us both, pushing Philip off balance and sending me sprawling onto the wet ground. Jude had come out of nowhere and flung himself into Philip's arms, grabbing Philip around the neck in desperation. "No! You promised me! You said I was Dominic – you can't…not him – I'm Dominic!" Philip seemed confused for a moment, stepping backwards as he tried to focus on Jude, as if he didn't even know who he was. "I did it all for you," Jude screamed at him. "I told you I'd be everything for you – not him!" Jude's voice was broken, ragged. "You can't choose him."

The gun was gone from Philip's hand. I looked around but couldn't see it in the ragged undergrowth, so I crawled around in the soaking grass looking for it. Jude continued to claw at Philip's clothes. Philip still seemed to be like a man in the midst of a waking dream.

He backed away, trying to shake Jude away from him, then caught my eye. "Dominic!" he shouted. "Come." His face was lit up, as if he'd seen someone much loved, much missed. But it lasted a second only; Jude had driven them both to the edge of the water and the violence of Jude's jealousy tipped them into the water.

I had to make the worst choice of my life, and it broke my heart to do it, but it was all I could do. Leaving Myles lying there, pale and bleeding, I scrabbled up, slipping on the slimy bank, and launched myself into the mere, gasping as the water hit me. Of Jude and Philip there was no sign, nothing except the wind disturbing the surface. I remember screaming Jude's name, wading out into freezing water, feeling the mud suck at my boots, and treacherous, clinging plants tangling around my calves like the dead hands of mermaids. The wind whipped my words away. When I reached waist deep all I could do was duck under the water, uncaring now – with Myles unconscious and Jude missing – about my safety and whether I could swim or not, but the mere showed me nothing. Even with my eyes open the water was grey and so murky I could not see more than a few inches in front of me.

Blindly then, I stumbled forwards into the murk, getting deeper and deeper, knowing that unless I found him soon there would be four of us lost, to be found by God knows who, only to wonder how such a tragedy had occurred, and no-one to tell the world of Philip's madness. Surely it was hours since they had fallen in;

surely they must both be swept away? I should go back, save myself and do what I could for poor Myles. As I decided at last, my lungs bursting, to turn around, something brushed against my fingers and I clutched at it. Fabric. A sleeve – an arm and I stood up, dragging precious air into my lungs, and pulled for all I was worth.

He was so heavy I thought I'd never get him to the air but he broke the surface. Jude's face was so white, so still. I stumbled towards the bank, dragging him with me, while the mere seemed to want to suck me back under. I reached the bank and fell backwards, sitting down abruptly, and still I tugged at him, only to find the reason for his dragging weight – Philip, as drowned as Jude – was still wrapped around him, his arms around his waist, his fingers locked with Jude's.

Weeping in fear and misery, I tore at Philip's hands, uncaring whether the man was truly dead, but wanting the taint of him off my friend, whatever he'd done. I broke fingers and I didn't care about it, he was nothing but meat to me, and deserved no better treatment. Finally I disengaged his arms, freeing Jude, and kicked out, viciously, sending the limp body of my guardian back into the icy water. Summoning the last of my strength from God knows where, I pulled Jude onto the bank, next to Myles, and looked for any sign of life in either of them. Why had no-one come? Surely they must have heard the shot? Or was the wind too violent? For whatever good it would do, I pulled off my soaking jacket and laid it over Myles. In fear and frustration, I shook Jude violently by the shoulders, shouting his name, demanding he not be dead, sobs wracking through me.

"Crispin!" A rough hand shook my shoulder and pulled me out of the way. Heriment flung himself between me and Myles, checked the wound, and without a word, picked him up and carried him off, leaving me with Jude. I was still staring after Heriment, as if he were some kind of dream that had softened the worst nightmare of my life, when I heard the smallest of gasps and looked down. Water poured from Jude's mouth and nose and he started to retch violently. All I could do was watch. I had no idea how best to help him, and as for carrying him out of the rain, I doubted I could get myself up, let alone Jude.

Jude's eyes opened. His eyes were glazed, and bloodshot. I lost control then, what little I'd had, great sobs of released fear breaking from me, like a child in the aftermath of a tantrum. "Jude," I said, stroking his face. "Jude. They'll be here soon, you're safe. It's all right. He's gone."

He focussed on me for a moment, as if he didn't know who I was, and I doubt I looked any better than he, for I was smothered in Myles' blood, and drenched to the skin; then his face changed, as he recognised me.

"No." The loathing came back into his face, the same hate he'd shown before he'd thrown himself at Philip. "No. He would have wanted me." He coughed, and blood mixed with the water poured over my hand. I touched his face again, as if my touch alone would restore his mind. "He should have wanted me," he whispered. "I… loved him. I was –"

"Jude," I said, helplessly. "Please…"

"I was Dominic. I could have been everything…" He coughed again, and I heard shouts from the house, but couldn't drag my eyes from my dying friend. "He promised…"

"He was mad, Jude," I whispered. "He would have killed us all."

"No," he whispered. "He'd never have killed Dominic. Never…" Heriment had returned. I looked numbly up to see he was accompanied by others. Heriment knelt down beside me and tried to move my hands from Jude's face but I elbowed him away. "Leave him alone!" I shouted, desperately. "Jude!"

"Don't call me that," Jude said, bubbles forming at his mouth. "My name is Dominic."

"Dominic?" Heriment said sharply, looking between me and Jude.

"Yes…That's me." Jude said, gasping for breath. "That's what he wanted…That's all he want –"

He said nothing more.

I sat in the rain-soaked grass, and watched my poor friend die, while my other friend – my lover – was dying in the house, and I cried harder than I'd ever cried in my life. I don't remember when they took him away, and I don't remember who lifted me to my feet and helped me back to the house. I wished for an attack of migraine for the first time in my life, but it never came. I couldn't lose myself in my illness, but after I was washed and dried – presumably by Albert – and sat, wrapped in blankets like some huge caterpillar, I was as numb as I had been, when neck deep in Horsey Mere. I sat on the window seat and stared out at the water, wondering what the mere had done with the last of the Smallwoods. I wondered if he would ever be found, or would he stay buried in the one place he hated so much. Killed by the mere, just as it had killed Dominic. The same death as his lover – but now separated for eternity. I hoped that was so, at least. I was glad of that.

I felt nothing for him. I was as cold as the water that had taken him. I felt no hate, no fear, not even pity. He deserved nothing from me; he had taken from me the two people I cared about most in the world.

Some time later Albert must have put me to bed for I woke to a new day, and sun spilled into my bedroom, painting golden leaves upon the ceiling. The events of the day before flashed in front of my eyes over and over – Philip's story, the choice, the gun – even when I closed my eyes, the images were still there. Myles' stupidity and Jude's hostile jealousy.

I heard my clock strike eight, and the door opened; surely, I thought, life can't ever return to normal that simply? Breakfast at eight, and then what? I rolled over, curled up in a miserable ball, still feeling the sensation of Myles' warm blood mixed with mere water, spilling over my hands. still seeing the blur of Jude as he threw himself at Philip.

"Mr Crispin," Albert said.

I didn't answer him. I couldn't look at him. Did he know about it all? Did Witheridge? How could I go on – in this place?

"Mr Crispin, I think you should try to eat something."

"No," I said, pulling the covers over me as a hurt child would.

"Well, I don't fancy eating alone," a voice said, "and the doctor said that I have to. So you do too."

Unbelieving, I spun around, tangling myself hopelessly in the quilt, sobs breaking out anew. "Myles! You... I was sure..."

He didn't quite smile, for his eyes were too full of pain to do that, but the edges of his mouth quirked a little. He was leaning heavily on his valet's arm, and Albert was holding a tray with enough food for both of us. Myles' arm was bound tightly to his chest. Michael placed Myles carefully at my little table, and I clambered out to join him. "I'm too tough to kill it seems." He grimaced. "Bullet went straight through my arm, but Heriment got the bleeding to stop. It hurts like... I won't say it hurts like the Devil, because I think we both know that's not true."

We were left alone, to talk, and be silent. To hold hands like long-lost lovers, to kiss and whisper things to each other that were meant for no one else. We were left alone that day to eat, to rest and to love, as gently as we dared. To come to terms with how close we'd come to losing each other.

We didn't speak of Philip, and all these years later – now Myles is a banker with a good future and a spreading waistline, and I'm a struggling architect letting Myles support me – we never have. We never will. We are cured of Horsey Mere, and there are many things of which we'll never speak.

But we talk of Jude, often, and with real affection, our poor misguided friend.

ERASTES is the penname of a female author who lives in the area where this book is based. Author of seven books and twenty short stories, this is her third full-length novel. A Lambda award finalist and keen lover of history, she began writing full-time after leaving the legal profession finding it stranger than any fiction.

CPSIA information can be obtained at www.ICGtesting.com
Printed in the USA
LVOW091725280911

248288LV00002B/75/P